Twice Nightly

– TONY GARETH SMITH –

An environmentally friendly book printed and bound in England by
www.printondemand-worldwide.com

Mixed Sources
Product group from well-managed
forests, and other controlled sources
www.fsc.org Cert no. TT-COC-002641
© 1996 Forest Stewardship Council

FSC

PEFC Certified

This product is
from sustainably
managed forests
and controlled
sources

PEFC
PEFC/16-33-415

www.pefc.org

This book is made entirely of chain-of-custody materials

www.fast-print.net/store.php

Twice Nightly

ISBN 978-178035-348-7

First published 2012 by
FASTPRINT PUBLISHING
Peterborough, England.
Printed by Printondemand-Worldwide

Dedication

For my sisters: Gloria, Deardree, Dianne and Jane.
For Eleno
and all my Maltese Brothers and Sisters
and Shane

With my thanks and love always, Tony
And in special memory of Mum and Ma –
Always with me

The Golden Sands Theatre

South Pier Marine Parade Great Yarmouth Norfolk
Don Stevens proudly presents for a limited engagement

Opening Monday 5th May 1969 at 8pm

Thereafter: Twice Nightly at 6.10 & 8.45 (exc. Sundays)

JUNE ASHBY
The Golden Voiced West End Musical Star

CHOREOGRAPHY: Jenny Benjamin
MUSICAL DIRECTOR: Maurice Beeney

TED RICER	THE DEAN SISTERS
A laugh a Minute	Rolling along in
By Popular Demand	a mind blowing balancing act!

Man of Magic
MYSTIC BRIAN
with his turtle doves

THE JENNY BENJAMIN DANCERS

MAURICE BEENEY and his ALL ROUNDERS ORCHESTRA

Prices: 10/6 8/6 & 6/-
BOOKABLE IN ADVANCE

2

Chapter One   *"Overture And Beginners"*

"Are you sure everything is in place?"

"I think so." There was hesitancy in the reply.

"You think so?" The voice took a firmer tone. "That isn't the positive response I was hoping for. I suggest you have a long hard think and make sure everything is in place, there is a lot riding on this." And with that the phone went dead.

***

The Golden Sands Theatre stood proudly at the end of the South Pier in Great Yarmouth. It was the beacon of family entertainment and during the summer months it played host to many of the variety artistes of the era and the year of 1969 was no different, or was it?

The sea air was bracing as Jim Donnell walked along the pier. The sound of the sea splashing beneath the wooden supports was like music to his ears. Other music could be heard coming from the small funfair, they were always pumping out the latest chart hits and this one held a particular fondness in Jim's heart. Where do you go to my Lovely had been played at his daughter's wedding just three months ago. If only Karen had been alive to see their only daughter wed, but the cancer had taken her a year ago and Jim was left to carry on as best he could. Debbie and husband Peter had moved away from Great Yarmouth to be nearer to Peter's job in Huddersfield and although he had hoped his little girl would make her life in the town, Jim had waved a cheery goodbye and wished them all the luck in the world with the promise of a visit once the season was over.

Jim loved his job, he met so many interesting people and he liked to be able to exchange stories with his best mate Dave who worked the other pier further along the promenade. They always argued over who was going to have the best summer season bill and which one would attract more of the 'visitors'. Once the summer was over, Jim and Dave teamed up and worked together in a nightclub which was owned by Dave's cousin. The money was good, but the hours were often long and Jim longed for the return of the summer when he could go back to The Golden Sands Theatre where he was happiest. Dave, on the other hand, had often said he wouldn't mind working for his cousin all year round if he wasn't so moody. Besides, the people he employed in the summer season were too wet behind the ears, always down from up north hoping to make a fast buck and Dave couldn't be bothered with the drifters.

Jim stood and gazed up at the front of the theatre. The hoardings were already in place advertising this season's big attraction, but before that there was the pre-season show to attract the visitors to the resort who came in groups from various UK locations to enjoy an early summer break. The only problem with May was that the weather could be so changeable and Jim's heart went out to anyone who had to make their way down the wooden slats while the wind howled and the sea lashed over the top of the pier. The weather in May had been known to be sunny, but visitors were advised to keep some warm clothing handy just in case.

June Ashby, the poster read, with the Jenny Benjamin Dancers, Ted Ricer, The Dean Sisters and Mystic Brian. Opens Monday 5th May at 8pm and thereafter twice nightly 6.10 & 8.45 (exc. Sun) until Saturday 21st June.

Jim lit a cigarette and took a long drag. He had seen Mystic Brian before, he had done several seasons at the Sands, and his mystique was how he ever performed his magic while supposedly under the influence. Ted Ricer, the comedian, had

4

played the town before, a good clean comedian, but with an eye for the ladies, which often got him into trouble with his wife Rita, who paid the odd surprise visit. The Dean Sisters had been discovered on Opportunity Knocks, Hughie Green loved them, but the audience it seemed didn't as they only scored five on the 'clapometer'. Jim was convinced they weren't sisters at all. Sure enough they were all blonde on stage, but off stage told a different story. Their novelty was they sang while rolling around the stage on large beach balls which they then rolled up a specially erected ramp. Jim couldn't wait to see them in action. The Jenny Benjamin Dancers were from a local dance school; usually six of them and year in, year out Jenny would put them through some of the same routines in different costumes. Jenny was nice enough but she was getting on in years and someone really should tell her to retire.

June Ashby, who by all accounts had been a big West End musical star, had caused quite a stir when the billing was announced. Why would Miss Ashby who had been absent from the theatre world for five years choose a pier show in Great Yarmouth as her comeback?

The music would be supplied by Maurice Beeney and his All Rounders, a group of six pensioners who relied on tea dances during the winter months and were booked only because they were cheap. Well, Jim thought, the old folks will love them, but not so much the local landladies who came on their complimentary tickets to help fill the theatre on quieter nights. They would be moaning from sunrise to sundown, but be all smiles when they met the company at the usual party that took place at the end of the opening night's performance. Wrapped in faux fur stoles knocking back the free sherry and nibbles while exclaiming to the 'company members' what a great little show it was and how it was the best the Sands had ever seen. Jim would be there with the stage crew and watch in a state of bewilderment and amusement. He didn't say much, but thought all the more.

He stubbed out his cigarette, put his hands in his pockets and walked to the left of the theatre. The stage door was open; Jack the caretaker was already in residence.

"Noises off young Jim," said Jack, as he put his mug of tea down. "The so-called star has arrived and from all accounts she isn't very happy."

***

Further along the promenade and visible from the Sands stood The Wellington Pier, home to a theatre and amusements, and just off the inside of the entrance there was an open-air roller skating rink. David Grant, Dave to his mates, was doing a check of the overhead bulbs that would light up the pier in the evenings. At the beginning of every season this was one of his first jobs. He would record his findings and then give it to the supervisor of pier maintenance for him and his lads to do the necessary. He also recorded any missing items of pier furniture, it was amazing how many waste bins went missing during the winter months. He had always been of the opinion that anything that wasn't nailed down should be removed to storage until the summer season began. However, unlike the privately owned Sands Theatre, the Wellington was owned by the council and everything had to be reported in triplicate.

During the winter months the piers attracted the local fisherman who liked nothing better than dangling their rods into the North Sea in the hope of a bite. None of the facilities were open on the piers during these cold months and the kiosks, cafés and gift shops stood empty. Some years before, the council had discussed the possibility of covering in part of the Wellington Pier to entice winter trade, but like so many discussions, including the heating of the theatre and providing better dressing room facilities, these discussions had never made any headway when money was tight.

Dave finished counting the dead bulbs and totalled up. He saw Mrs Jenner who ran the gift shop at the entrance to the pier unloading some stock ready for the summer season and gave her a friendly wave. He noticed that the lady was struggling with the boxes and wondered why one of her family hadn't come along to give her a hand. He made a mental note to go and see her when his shift was finished.

After some fifteen minutes he walked towards the pier entrance and unlocked the box office door, checking that the required number of chairs were in place with the ever important kettle, teapot and cups and saucers, checking for any chips in the crockery. He knew the box office staff wouldn't put up with just any old thing. He checked the lights were in good working order and apart from needing a fresh lick of paint things looked reasonably okay. He locked the door behind him and headed back up the pier to report his findings to old Ken who would, as usual, make the obligatory huffing and puffing noise and add Dave's findings to his ever-growing list.

"Where's all the extra staff they promised?" he would rant as he did every year, and every year there was just the regular band of brothers, but Ken liked to put his mark on things, much to Dave's amusement. When Ken got on his soapbox there was little anyone could do to stop him, unless the magic words 'tea and biscuits' were uttered and then everything in Ken's world would be all right again.

***

As Mrs Jenner unloaded her stock, she gazed at the poster for the forthcoming summer show, Charlie Drake in Slapstick and Old Lace with Henry McGee, Vince Hill, the New Faces and full supporting company. It promised to be a good attraction for the Wellington and Mrs Jenner hoped that this year she would be able to put aside a nice nest egg for her not-too-far-off retirement. She felt she was getting too old and tired for this annual ritual which had become her inheritance when her mother had died many years earlier. She had made many sacrifices; not employing any other staff over the last two seasons had kept costs down to a minimum, but this meant manning the shop seven days a week and relying on the goodwill of one of the box office staff to keep an eye on it if she needed to spend a penny. If she was lucky her husband would drop her off something to eat if she hadn't had time to make herself some sandwiches before leaving in the morning. The small fridge in the shop was hardly suitable for keeping food any length of time.

Pleased that she had had the foresight to spring clean the tiny shop over the Easter weekend, she would be able to begin unpacking, pricing and displaying the goods the following day. With any luck, her daughter Sara would come and give her a hand. That was provided she hadn't taken on extra shifts at the rock factory. Her daughter's wish to save up as much as she could and move away from the seaside town had often caused her sleepless nights. With one failed marriage to a teenage sweetheart behind her, Sara was determined not to spend the rest of her life surrounded by memories. It was no good asking Alf for help; since he had retired he had become a stop-at-home and had told his wife that if she wanted to run her gift shop she could do it without any help from him. What interest had he in things made of shells with the inscription: A gift from Great Yarmouth. That was woman's work! And so for Marie Jenner and others like her with small seasonal businesses to run this was how life had been mapped out.

***

Within a few weeks the flow of holidaymakers to the resort would soon increase and the special trains laid on from various parts of the country would arrive every Saturday at Vauxhall throughout the summer season where journeys would be completed by local buses or, if funds allowed, by taxis.

Coaches would be chugging down the Acle Straight and heading towards the disused Beach railway station, now home to a coach park, where the weary traveller would either be met by boarding house proprietors or make their own way to the guest house of their choice. Some would be booked into the various caravan parks, where shared wash facilities were the norm, whilst others with more money to spare would head towards the Chalets for what promised to be a home-from-home experience.

The holiday camps in Hopton and Caister would be the mainstays for many families wanting a Butlin type holiday and business at these places would bring more revenue to the surrounding areas of Lowestoft and Gorleston-on-Sea. Oulton Broad, a short distance from the town centre of Lowestoft, would find the river thoroughfare abounding with holiday cruise boats with their own family captains at the helm, most having never steered a boat in their lives. Some would end up on the mud flats and be rescued by the in-shore rescue boats as they strayed into the danger area clearly marked by high white poles, but which the inexperienced sailor chose to ignore.

With the influx of many 'stars' to Great Yarmouth, some locals vacated their homes and let them for the season. Cottages and small houses in the areas of Belton, Bradwell and Omesby were often homes to the likes of Frank Ifield, Harry Worth, Arthur Askey and the like. Many a local was oft to bang baskets with well-known television and theatre stars in the village stores and this all added to the ambience of what was the height of the season when money was to be made.

The Old Time Music Hall was a traditional show that took over the Pavilion Theatre in Gorleston every season. Consisting of nine professional performers, the show was always a popular attraction with its waiter table service throughout the once nightly show with the offer of food, beverages and alcohol. Audiences were encouraged to dress up for the evening and could hire costumes from the amateur drama group The

Masquers, all adding to the fun of the evening. These seasoned performers would pitch up their mobile homes at a park in Burgh Castle along with the many circus performers who came to be part of the annual Billy Russell's seasonal circus at the Great Yarmouth Hippodrome, which performed twice daily expect Sundays. A parade of horses and elephants could often be seen in the rising hours of the morning along the Great Yarmouth beach by the early holidaymaker out for their morning constitutional. Locals embraced the busy summer season and many a discussion could be heard over a lunchtime pint about the pros and cons of the tourist trap that they encapsulated.

The men who ran the riverboats and Broads cruisers were always keen to see the town swelling with visitors. It meant that on warm seafaring days their boats would be full and the revenue would help them through the winter months when such services were not on offer. It gladdened their hearts to see the queues forming on the Great Yarmouth quay. For some it was a trip out of the River Yare to the North Sea to see the seals on Scroby Sands. For others it would be a two-hour Broads cruise, and for the more adventurous an all-day cruise stopping off at various village hamlets allowing them to explore the beautiful countryside and purchase local wares. The named Eastern Princess, The Golden Galleon and the riverboats were newly-painted every season and their jolly bunting and white canopies could be seen from many a bedroom window as they set off along the river.

***

"You are telling me that this is the STAR dressing room?"

"Yes Miss Ashby it always has been and I have to say that many well-known stars like you have been very happy here."

June Ashby looked Jim firmly in the eye. "Some artistes might well be used to small dressing rooms. I am accustomed to West End facilities."

Jim, who had done his homework, knew for a fact that Dora Bryan was coming from the West End after a successful run as Dolly Levi in Hello Dolly and had been secured by Bernard Delfont. June Ashby, on the other hand, had last made a West End appearance over five years ago and had mysteriously vanished from her showcase after only four performances. Ever the diplomat, Jim declined to mention these facts and tactfully addressed the situation as best he could under the circumstances.

"I could ask Lilly to come and spruce the place up a bit. Perhaps I could find you another chair from out the back."

"My dear man, it would take this Lilly person and several others like her to 'spruce' this place up as you put it. What are the other dressing rooms like?"

"Well, this is the biggest we have. The one next door is slightly smaller. The ones on the other side of the stage are much the same and the ones beneath the stage are what we call 'sea view'."

"You mean windows looking on to the North Sea? That sounds rather nice."

"No!" exclaimed Jim, trying not to allow a grin to break across his face. "You can see the sea through the floorboards," he joked, but June failed to see the funny side and her expression went from grim to even more grim.

***

"So the little lady isn't happy." Don Stevens snapped shut his cigarette case as he looked out from his London office window. "She is lucky to get this engagement after the fiasco following her musical flop of the decade."

"She was very rude on the telephone Mr Stevens. She said the dressing room was no more than a broom cupboard with a sink. She wasn't too thrilled to be working with an act that was intent on singing while balancing on beach balls. And she added that whoever had booked Mystic Brian needed shooting."

"That will be me then! Brian may be a funny character but he knows how to please an audience." He paused. "Gwen, take no notice. I shall be going down to Great Yarmouth tomorrow to see for myself what exactly is going on. Never had to do that before, normally these acts are brought together as seen, they have a couple of run-throughs on the stage and then bingo – job done. According to my source, Miss Ashby is finding it difficult to hold a tune. It is just as well that some click-tracks were prepared. Thank goodness it's only a short run. It is only on your recommendation she is there at all."

"Did you want me to come along with you Don? Perhaps I can have a word with her."

"No Gwen, I will handle this my way, thanks all the same."

***

Maud Bennett opened the box office window. "Yes dear, can I help you?"

"We would like two tickets for the show on Friday."

Maud laid down her knitting. She was hoping to finish her latest creation by that evening.

"Which show, which Friday?"

"I don't understand," said the woman in the headscarf.

Maud sat upright and leaned forward a little and with her usual swagger of the head said, "We have the pre-season attraction with June Whitby, sorry Ashby, opening Monday fifth of May. Then we have Dora Bryan with her company for the summer season proper."

The lady looked puzzled. "Oh, I see. Harry, what do you want to see?"

Harry, who was taking a bite from a hotdog, looked at his wife in disbelief. "What do you mean, what do I want to see? You're the one that wanted to go to a show."

"Well we're only here until the end of next week," said the woman, turning back to face Maud.

"What house do you want on Friday?"

"Oh I don't want a house; we've got a nice one in Keighley thanks."

Maud sighed heavily. She liked her sighs. She had worked on them for years. They said something, her sighs, and right then her sigh was saying, "Make your mind up madam, I've got some serious knitting to finish."

"By house I mean the time of the performance; the show is twice nightly at 6.10 and 8.45."

The woman pulled her headscarf tighter, the wind was beginning to get up and she knew it would play havoc with her wash and set. "Well we don't have our meal until half-past-five so we better go to the later one."

"What price would you like?"

"What are the prices?"

Pointing at the information on the front of the box office window, Maud gave another sigh. "Front stalls are ten and six, middle stalls are eight and six and the rear stalls are six shillings."

"Are stalls upstairs? Harry likes to sit upstairs."

"The Sands Theatre does not have an 'upstairs' madam and if you'll take my advice you'll sit front centre about seven rows back and that way you won't be too near the orchestra. They tend to play a bit loud sometimes. So that's Friday 9th May at 8.45, two seats, Row G 15 and 16 and that will be one pound and a shilling, or if you like, one guinea, please."

Maud heaved another sigh as she watched the couple walk away. She picked up her knitting and continued to tackle the final sleeve.

***

"Not much of a bill at the Sands this year is it?" said Freda Boggis, folding her arms in her usual fashion.

Her neighbour put down her shopping bag. "Dora Bryan will be good and I always liked Mark Wynter. I was forever playing Venus in Blue Jeans on the old juke."

"No, I meant the one that starts next Monday with June what's-her-name; I clocked it in the Mercury. Dick came home from the Legion with two compulsory tickets."

"Complimentary Freda," replied Muriel, taking her door key from her handbag. "Barry was given some at the factory. What night are you going?"

Freda rubbed her arm and looked thoughtful for a moment. "I'll have to check with Dick, but I suspect it will have to be an early show so he can go to the Legion. You know what he's like when there's a match on."

Muriel thanked the Lord that her Barry had never wanted to join the Legion, he was much happier with his feet up in front of the telly after a long day at Birds Eye.

"Perhaps we could all go together Freda, be a change from the box. Besides, once the season kicks off I shan't be able to leave this place morning, noon or night. We might be able to cadge an invite to the opening night party."

"That's a thought; we can ask Lilly to have a word. Are you doing full board again?"

"Well, my regulars expect it. Besides, Barry gets some discounts on fish fingers at the factory and they go down a treat."

"I am only doing bed and breakfast this year. I can't stand too long over a hot stove; it brings on my hot flushes something chronic."

"Well, now Dick isn't working he could give you a hand surely."

Freda rolled her eyes and folded her arms even tighter. "My Dick won't lift a finger in that department, says it's woman's work, besides he does a couple of shifts down the Legion, cash in hand, no questions asked."

All right for some, Muriel thought. "Well, let me know about the Sands Freda when you've decided, I must get on," and with that she opened her front door and went inside.

***

"So what do you intend to do about this dressing room, apart from pulling it down and starting again?"

Jim studied June Ashby. Early fifties perhaps, average height, long dark hair. There were visible lines around her tired eyes and her mouth had a slightly crooked appearance. She waved her hands about in theatrical gestures when she spoke and her polished nails looked like the talons of a bird of prey and right at that moment Jim felt he was the prey. She was smartly dressed in a two-piece suit, obviously purchased from some London fashion house, and her silky-stockinged legs were completed by black stiletto heels, not the most sensible footwear for walking a wooden pier. All in all she was a fine looking woman and despite her somewhat offhand manner, Jim quite liked her. There was something vulnerable about her and he couldn't help feeling a little sorry for her.

"Miss Ashby, I am sure we can find some things to brighten up the space. I'll have a word with Maud Bennett at the box office, when she isn't selling tickets she runs a shop in Market Row with her sister and they sell all manner of things. Pictures, ornaments, that kind of thing. Some artistes bring their own things from home. Last year I remember Frank Ifield had a lovely photo collection of his family."

June Ashby flashed a smile. "You would do that for me? It really is very kind of you." The harsh voice had softened and her eyes twinkled. "Sorry, you didn't tell me your name. You must call me June by the way, I am June to my friends."

"I'm Jim." He held out his hand, but she missed the gesture and he put his hand into the safety of his trouser pocket. "I'll go and see what I can sort out, leave it to me, um... June."

June watched as he left the room. He was the first nice man she had come into contact with since New Dawn House. Perhaps she had found her first friend and she could really put the past firmly behind her.

After chatting with the boys, Jim walked back down the pier. The strong wind had dropped and the sun was trying to push through the clouds. If the weather forecast was correct it was going to be a lovely day. He knocked on the box office door and waited for Maud to go through her keeper-of-the-keys routine.

"Who is it?" said the voice of Maud through the panelled door.

"Charlton Heston," Jim replied, with a laugh.

Maud opened the door. "Leave your chariot outside and come in. Suppose you'll want a cup of tea?"

It was the same every time and it never failed to amuse Jim. Maud was a character, and he liked characters. He cast his mind back to June Ashby; if he wasn't mistaken he had just met another one.

"You'll have to have a Lincoln shortcake with your tea this morning, the Co-op was out of digestives."

Jim accepted the cup of tea and helped himself from the open packet. Maud must have started early. Maud settled herself back on her chair and Jim leaned against the wall. "Things going all right up there?" she said, nodding her head towards the theatre behind her.

"The sets have all arrived but someone has sent the costumes for the dancers to the Sparrow's Nest at Lowestoft."

Maud did one of her sighs. "That's typical of that silly old trout. She is getting right forgetful if you ask me. My sister was telling me about the farce with the pantomime in Gorleston. Apparently she had ordered sailor outfits for the walk down at the end. They were doing Red Riding Hood for goodness sake!"

Maud took a sip of her tea. "Now young Jim, you've something on your mind, out with it."

"June wants her dressing room spruced up a bit. I've got the lads to give me a hand with a quick once over, touch the door frame up, that kind of thing. I wondered if you could lay your hands on some knick-knacks to cheer the place up a bit."

"June is it?" said Maud in a knowing kind of way. It was good to see him with a bit of a spark; a man left on his own was never a good thing in Maud's book. How he had coped with the girl's wedding was amazing. A tear came to her eye as she remembered the speech he had given. Karen would have been proud of him that day and no mistake.

"We don't normally run to this kind of attention, knick-knacks indeed! Are you sure she wouldn't like a grandfather clock, there is bound to be one knocking about somewhere?" Maud tapped her fingers on her counter. "Don't let the management find out or there will be hell to pay. Leave it with me Jim. I'll look out some bits tonight. Now pass me those biscuits before you finish the lot."

***

When Jim returned to the theatre later he could hear music. He stuck his head through the swing door and could see three girls rolling around the stage on over-sized beach balls and if Jim's eyes weren't playing him tricks, they weren't looking very blonde this morning.

A couple of the stagehands had made a start on the dressing room door, giving it a more cheery look. Jim found an armchair in the area beneath the stage and had given it a good dusting. It was red leather, a little worn, but comfy enough. Lilly the cleaner had promised to give the room a thorough going over and had managed to pinch a couple of cushions from the Green Room. All in all, Jim thought, it was going to look the business.

Later that afternoon Jim took a stroll along the pier and he saw the figure of June Ashby seated on one of the many benches.

"Mind if I sit down?"

June turned and looked up and smiled through teary eyes. "Hello Jim, no please do."

"Care for a cigarette?" Jim offered.

"I don't thank you, not any more. It isn't good for my voice." She half-laughed, trying to cover her embarrassment. "Not that there seems to be much left of my voice at the moment, my rehearsals have been awful. Maurice has been very kind and set the songs in lower keys for me, but I am still struggling." She paused as she gazed at Jim's face. "I must apologise for my silly outburst earlier, it's a little bit of the old June coming through. The temperamental artiste, you will have seen it all before."

"I've come across one or two in my time. It goes with the territory. Sorry you are having a bad time. I am sure it will be all right come Monday."

Jim took a long draw on his cigarette. "I know you don't know anyone here so would you fancy a drink later on?" He hesitated before he continued; he had surprised himself by being so forthright. "I usually go along to the New Beach. The company doesn't tend to go in there and I think you'll enjoy it, it might help take your mind off things for a while."

"If you are sure I wouldn't be in the way, it really is very kind of you to ask. I don't expect you'll be asking any of the summer season stars that question."

Jim smiled to himself. "Shall we say seven at the box office; you should be through with rehearsals by then?"

June nodded. "Seven it is and thanks again."

Jim stood up. "You won't recognise the dressing room when you see it tomorrow. I best get on, things to do."

June watched Jim as he walked away, then the screech of a seagull distracted her attention and she found herself lost in troubled thoughts as another tear escaped down her cheek.

***

When Jim walked back through the theatre all havoc seemed to have broken loose on the stage.

"One of my doves has escaped," shouted the voice of Mystic Brian.

A female voice called back from the wings, "Your bloody bird has just deposited a nasty mess in my wig. It will be a bugger to clean; it isn't drip-dry you know. Who is going to foot the bill for that I wonder?"

Jill of the Dean Sisters strutted onto the stage with one hand firmly on her hip and a blonde wig dangling from the other.

"Have you got Lottie in your dressing room?" asked Brian, swaying slightly on his feet.

"We weren't formally introduced so I wouldn't know; all I do know is this wig is going to need cleaning."

Brian swayed a little more. "It's not like Lottie, it could be Caroline. She sometimes has a bit of trouble in that department."

Jim strode forward purposefully, trying not to laugh. "Jill, perhaps I can help, there is a salon in town where they dress some of the wigs for the summer season dancers, when we don't have a permanent stylist on hand. Give it to me and I'll get Lilly to drop it off for you. It will be back for Monday's opening."

Jill flung the wig from the stage to Jim's outstretched arms. "Thanks Jim, you're a doll. Fancy a drink later?"

"Sorry, I'm busy, perhaps another time."

Jill smiled. "Another time would be great."

"Can we get on with this rehearsal please," cried Maurice Beeney from the orchestra pit. "We were hoping to get home some time tonight."

"I can't perform without my dove."

"Sod your dove. For gawd sake get on with it. Right boys, from the top - I've got magic fingers."

The orchestra drowned out the voice of Mystic Brian as he fell into his magic cabinet and disappeared.

Jim shook with laughter. You couldn't make it up, you really couldn't.

***

Maud had just finished some ribbing when Jim appeared at the box office window.

"You look nicely turned out young Jim, haven't seen that shirt before. Going somewhere nice?"

"I am meeting a mate for a drink."

"A word to the wise young Jim, I have it on good authority Don Stevens is paying us a visit tomorrow, so you might want to warn that lot up there to look sharp."

"And who have you been talking to Maud, I haven't heard anything."

"I'm well in with his secretary Gwen. She phoned to see how ticket sales were going and she let it slip. Of course, I said I wouldn't say anything to anyone, you don't count."

Jim grinned. "Thanks Maud. I'll make sure the troops are in bright and early tomorrow, it wouldn't do for old Stevens to come down here throwing his weight about."

"You'll be pleased to know they found Mystic Brian's beloved dove in the laundry basket and everything will need to be laundered again by all accounts."

"Who was the culprit, Lottie?"

"No, it was Enid apparently. Daft name for a bird if you ask me."

"Hello Jim, I hope I am not late."

Jim turned away from the box office window. "No June. I'm right with you. See you tomorrow Maud."

"Mate is it?" said Maud to herself, as she watched them walk away. "Now I wonder where they would be heading?"

***

The New Beach bar was relatively quiet and June and Jim sat near the window looking out onto Marine Parade with The Golden Sands Theatre firmly in their view.

"Do you always drink mild and bitter?"

Jim nodded. "Usually, I steer clear of spirits apart from Christmas. Port and lemon your favourite tipple?"

"I am but a creature of habit. It used to be gin years ago, but somehow it and I didn't agree."

"My late wife Karen used to say that; said it made her depressed for days on end." He stopped, realising it was the first time he had spoken Karen's name out loud in weeks.

"I am sorry you lost your wife, it must have been painful for you," said June, taking a sip.

"Cancer is a dreadful thing. One moment she was well and then within two weeks I barely recognised the woman I had married." There was a catch in his throat as he spoke, but he continued steadily. "It was very difficult for Debbie, our daughter. Her husband Peter had a good job and decided to settle in Huddersfield. The memories were too painful for her here."

"And how do you cope with the memories?"

"I am not sure I do, but you have to get on with things. Life doesn't stand still, however much we would like it to at times. Old Maud at the box office is an acquired taste, but she has a heart of gold, she helped me through the early days, shopped for me, made sure I ate proper meals. Good old friend is Maud for all her bluster at times."

Two plates of sandwiches duly arrived on the table in front of them. "Not much choice here I am afraid," said Jim. "The good old standby of ham and cheese. Are you sure you wouldn't like to go out for a proper meal?"

"This will be fine Jim. I don't eat heavy meals on a show night and there haven't been many of those recently, so it will be good to get back into training for Monday."

Jim just stopped himself from asking why she had been away from the theatre for so long and instead blurted out, "That reminds me, Don Stevens is arriving tomorrow. No one is supposed to know, but I thought..."

"Thanks for the warning. I had better get an early night and make sure my voice is well-lubricated in the morning, otherwise the orchestra is going to have to play even louder than they do now."

"Apparently they can hear them on the Wellington Pier already according to my mate Dave."

June laughed. "I should think they can hear them in Norwich for that matter, the deaf old beggars."

Chapter Two   *"Any Old Wind that Blows"*

Tuesday 29th April

"We are talking professional suicide if you sing live June."
Don Stevens took a long puff on his Havana and coughed.

"But I have never mimed to anything in my life." She knew
she was lying but he didn't need to know.

"Your voice is just not doing the business; click-track is the
only option. One was put together of some of your recordings as
a precaution. It is standard practice at the moment so don't look
so startled. Last year one of my best bill-toppers lost her voice,
but with the aid of click-track performed to an audience that was
none the wiser."

June was not defeated. "Don, I am not performing any of
those recordings in this set. It was agreed, I'll try some new
stuff, new image, new me."

"I know it is hard for you, especially with this being a
comeback of sorts, but it will be much better to give the audience
what they expect to hear. If you sing as I heard you do this
morning, your comeback will be over before it has started. This
may be Great Yarmouth, but news travels fast in the business as
well you know. Besides, do you really think the Dean Sisters
will be singing live at every performance?"

"They had to perform live on Opportunity Knocks."

"Look, singing on live television for three minutes while
balancing on a ball is one thing, but they are doing fifteen
minutes here. They'd have no breath. They are a novelty. If
those kids work hard they could become the new Kaye Sisters.
They sing one song 'live' in their set and the rest is click-track.
Have a chat with them and they will tell you it is a great help."

He paused and looked at June. He noted that she appeared to be under some strain, it was etched on her face, but this after all was his bread and butter.

"The Black and White Minstrels use a click-track and no one questions it. Look, the tapes are with Jim Donnell, he can play them through for you, the orchestrations can be faded out and Maurice and the boys will play live. Maurice and his boys know the score, they have worked this way many a time."

"Don, I am not happy about this and I am not miming, I sing live or nothing."

"Then nothing it might have to be my dear. Now get your arse out there and start doing those numbers. I want you perfect by this afternoon. The alternative is we replace you with Derinda Daniels."

June stood up. Derinda Daniels was a much respected artiste in the business and June knew she was up against it if she faltered for one moment. With her hands in the air she replied with a smile, "Okay Don, you win, I'm rehearsing."

"That's my girl. Ask Brian to come in will you and tell him to leave those bloody birds in the dressing room, I am not discussing business with bird shit down my whistler." He picked up the telephone and dialled. "Gwen, see if you can find me a local vocal coach. June needs some help I think. Oh, and Gwen, if you're stuck you can always ask old Delfont." He smiled to himself. "Good girl, see you next week."

Don looked down at the paraphernalia Gwen had given him on June Ashby. Having never met the lady before he had been taken by her striking looks. Looking at the photographs on the résumé he guessed they must be rather old, June Ashby certainly didn't look so lush close up. Maybe once the slap was on it would improve things, it seemed to work well enough for Gwen who could look quite the dolly bird when she made the effort. He pushed the papers to one side and waited for Brian to arrive.

***

June went to find Jim. He was busy below stage but he stopped what he was doing and smiled at her. "You okay?"

"Suppose I am. I am beginning to think this show wasn't such a good idea after all."

"You want to run through those tapes?"

"I would like to hear them first, as a precaution you understand, and see what the old boy has had put on them. Some of those old show songs I haven't worked with for years. I bet I won't remember the words."

"It will come back, don't worry."

June wasn't so certain; she could barely remember where she was the day before half of the time.

"Come on, let's go and do the deed. The sooner you try the better you will feel."

"By the way, I forget to say the dressing room is great, thanks again Jim."

Jim smiled. "Maud provided all the trimmings, Lilly installed them and the smell of paint on the door will fade soon enough."

Lilly had worked very hard indeed to get the dressing room looking as lovely as it did. She had reflected as she dusted and swept that the dressing rooms were built for practicality not for a home-from-home feel. All most artistes were interested in was to have somewhere to change and get on stage to do their act. Lilly had tutted as she climbed the small step ladder to have a second go at the windows from the inside. No matter how she worked her Windolene, the salt stains on the outside of the glass were still visible. She had done the best she could and if her ladyship wasn't pleased she would have to call in the local coastguard to have a go, there was no way on earth Lilly was going to clamber up the side of the theatre to please a theatrical. With the things that Maud had provided the room had taken on a more comfortable air. Lilly had straightened a cushion one more time and had departed feeling that her job was done.

"I must remember to thank them both. Perhaps I could get them some chocolates or something," said June, smiling.

"Lilly loves Milk Tray and Maud is very much a fan of Weekend."

"My old mum used to like Weekend."

"Used to?"

"She died some years ago, heart attack."

"I'm sorry. Is your father still alive?"

"Somewhere I guess. He upped and left when I was young. I wouldn't know him from Adam."

"Come on, the stage is free. We had better take our chance now; the boys will be installing more of the sets later in readiness for the summer run. Are you ready for this?"

"As ready as I'll ever be." June touched Jim's arm. "I really am very grateful to you, if it hadn't been for your kindness I don't know what I'd have done."

"It really is no problem. It is part of my job, besides I wanted to help."

June walked onto the stage while Jim set the tape.

June's recorded voice suddenly filled the auditorium. Lilly, who was at the back of the theatre stalls dusting a handrail, stopped what she was doing and watched.

Don Stevens entered the auditorium and stood beside Lilly. "Got a fine voice hasn't she?"

Lilly, who had seen it all before and to her mind better, shrugged her shoulders. "If you like that sort of act and many do. I am sure the audiences will love her."

And in the end, thought Don, that was all that really mattered.

Don watched with interest and then moved down the auditorium, he wasn't too impressed, June and the click-track were out of sync, he had seen drag queens mime more accurately. This was clearly going to need a lot of work if this show was ever to succeed. June's movements looked clumsy; her glowing résumé bragged of her 'Ginger Rogers and Fred Astaire dancing'. One thing was for certain, if she carried on in this vein people would certainly be 'a-staring' all right!

Don shouted his command to stop the click-track as he walked onto the stage.

"Jim can we have that from the top please. June I want to see you do that again, from where I was standing you didn't look very comfortable with the material."

June raised her eyebrows. "I did tell you that I hadn't performed some of these numbers for years and I am not happy with this click-track arrangement."

"I am sorry Miss Ashby but from what I just witnessed it would seem you had never performed any of these numbers before. Now I suggest you take five minutes to compose yourself and then get yourself back on this stage ready to work. I expect to see nothing but perfection from my leading lady." And without looking at June further he exited stage left leaving June somewhat lost for words and Jim wondering what the hell was taking off.

Don stopped by the stage door and motioned to Jack. "Okay to use your phone a minute?" he asked. Jack looked up from his paper and nodded.

"Gwen," said Don, just about managing to control his mood, "who the hell exactly have we booked into this show? A West End star, or a West End has-been? You'd better get a couple of the regulars on the blower and ask them to stand by, I have a feeling I might be needing one of them. And cancel the voice coach, I really don't think it would be money well-spent".

Gwen was alarmed; Don didn't normally go off the deep end. "Don please calm yourself down. I did say June had been away from the business for a while, perhaps she just needs time to settle in."

"You'll be telling me next she only performs when there is an 'r' in the month!" And with that he banged down the receiver making Jack leap off his chair and drop his Daily Sketch.

***

Wednesday 30th April.

"Haven't seen you around the last couple of days, what have you been up to?"

Jim looked up from the staircase he was securing at the back of the stage.

"Hello Dave, what brings you down here?"

"I wanted to see my old mate. Besides, the Wellie is pretty dead at the moment. A couple of the lads were telling me you had been busy with the star turn."

"You can say that again, one or two problems, but it's sorted out now."

"So I can expect to see you tonight in The Growler?"

Jim stood up and scratched his head. "Don't know yet."

It wasn't like Jim to be secretive. Dave and he went back a long way.

"Is everything okay with you, not like you to miss a pint?"

Jim hated lying. "Just one or two things I have to do that's all. How about having something to eat at lunchtime in Henry's?"

Dave rubbed his chin. "You normally bring sandwiches in."

"I forgot", said Jim, turning a nasty shade of scarlet.

"Okay then, see you about twelve in Henry's. I'll leave you to get on."

Dave walked by the stage door. "Jack, is everything okay with Jim, do you know, he seems preoccupied?"

Jack looked up from his newspaper. "It will be the doves."

Dave looked puzzled. "Doves?"

"Escaped, caused havoc they did."

"Yeah, right. Thanks Jack see you later."

The pier was relatively quiet with just a few people walking up and down, taking in the view. He arrived at the front of the pier just as a group was walking away from the box office. He tapped on the window.

"Hi Maud me old flower, business looks good."

Maud looked up. "Things are picking up, nearly sold out for Saturday both houses. There has been a large party booking in from the Carlton." She smiled at Dave, she liked old Dave. Good looking, always smartly turned out and very well-mannered. "Been up to see Jim have you?"

Dave nodded. "Seemed a bit preoccupied to me, is everything okay with him would you say?"

Maud guarded her reply. "It will be the doves…"

"Doves! Yeah Jack said. Not like Jim to get worked up over doves though is it?"

Maud folded her arms. "He has had a lot to deal with this last twelve months one way or another. I think he is only now beginning to feel it. Young Debbie up in Huddersfield, Karen barely cold as you might say. These things take time. Grieving is a funny old thing as well I know to my cost."

"Yeah yer right Maud. I suppose I miss the old Jim. Selfish of me I know."

"Give him time love. Now, do you fancy a brew, I've just boiled the kettle."

"Thanks Maud, but I'd better get back to work or they will wonder where I am. See yer later."

Maud waved as Dave set off down Marine Parade. Nice fellah, she thought, shame he had never married. There had been rumours of course, but Maud never took much heed of rumours, he was far too much of a Jack the lad for any substance there.

Maud poured her tea and as things had quietened down she went outside carrying her mug in one hand and a fold-up chair in the other. She set the chair up, retrieved a Woman's Realm and sat down to enjoy the air. For the last day of April the sun had suddenly roused itself and the warm rays were beating down. Maud put the magazine on her head and sat back to enjoy her brew. You had to savour moments like these as during the season they didn't come along very often. When they were busy, Barbara, her second in command, would also be working alongside her and it sometimes got a bit cramped in the small office for the two of them. The work was seasonal and they had to work as many hours as they could to keep them tided over during the winter months. In Maud's case it helped top up her earnings for the winter, as the shop she owned with her sister tendered to be busy during the summer and then for a month leading up to Christmas. Her sister lived above the shop in a small flat, but Maud had a larger home to run on her own and the bills didn't get any smaller because she was on her own. Her sister would sometimes move in for a few weeks, but after a while they both began to get on each others nerves and returned to the status quo.

Maud spotted a couple walking arm in arm along the promenade and hoped they were not heading towards her box office. She was enjoying her tea and didn't want to have to get up. Within minutes the couple were standing in front of her.

"Excuse me love," said the woman with what sounded like a Yorkshire accent, "can you recommend somewhere for a decent cup of tea please?"

Maud smiled. "If you are heading into the town centre there is Matthews in Kings Street or there is a nice coffee room in Palmers department store just off the market and Vettesses down Market Row, they do a good pot. Italians they are and I can highly recommend their coffee."

The woman nodded in thanks. "Come on Joe let's take a walk to the town, I might even go mad and treat you to a cream horn."

Maud laughed to herself. As the actress said to the bishop, she thought, draining her mug. She fancied another one, but the effort of getting up just as she had got so comfortable eluded her. Before she knew what was happening she had closed her eyes and fallen asleep as the music from Joyland wafted over the nearby dividing wall.

***

When Dave walked into Henry's later the juke box kicked off in the corner where a couple of day-trippers were having what looked like a shandy and pork pie apiece. Venus in Blue Jeans boomed out as he approached the bar.

"Mild and bitter mate please." The barman stirred himself into action and by the look of him he hadn't seen too much of that lately, Dave surmised. Probably in his twenties he looked like another drifter from up north, here for the season and then back home after making a few bob.

"Quiet in here," said Dave, attempting to make friendly banter.

"It's been quiet all week. Boss reckons it all happens later on." He put the pint down in front of Dave.

Dave handed over some cash. "We usually have a good season here. I work up at the Wellington Pier. Always a bit quiet until all the summer shows open, then you'll notice the difference."

"I was in Blackpool last year. That was really busy."

"Are you from up that way then?" Dave asked, taking a sup.

"Aye, Preston, born and bred. I fancied a change of scene."

Dave held out his hand. "I'm Dave by the way. You'll see me in here from time to time."

The barman shook his hand. "I'm Dan pleased to meet you. You're the first person who has introduced himself."

"You won't get many of the locals in here; they tend to keep to the town. A bit reserved at first, but once you get to know them, they're not a bad lot."

Dave felt a slap on his back. "Get a pint in then, what's keeping yer?"

"Dan, this is my best mate Jim who works over at The Golden Sands Theatre. Another pint of the same please."

Dan shook Jim's hand. "You another local then?"

Jim smiled. "Can't you tell? You're from up north, am I right?"

Dan grinned. "Preston, the accent is a dead give-away."

"Are we having some thing to eat then?" Dave broke in. "What's on offer?"

Dan winked at Dave. "Depends on what you fancy, ham or cheese sandwich, there's a pork pie. Or if you want something hot, steak and kidney pie or chicken and mushroom from a local bakery they tell me."

They both settled on a steak and kidney and moved to a window table.

"Seems a good sort," said Dave, settling back in his chair.

"Friendly enough, I grant you, and he'll need to be in here, they attract a funny crowd in the season. He'll make a change from Stella turning the beer sour; why Ken keeps her on I'll never know."

"She's a good worker and doesn't take any nonsense from the punters. Had a hard life by all accounts, according to what Maud told me anyway." Dave lit a cigarette. "So what's been happening then Jim?"

Jim had been preparing himself. He found it hard to keep things from his best mate, but he decided caution was probably the best route for now.

"We had Don Stevens down here yesterday stirring things up with the company and by all accounts he intends to stick around. Miss Ashby has been a bit upset, but then it's what you expect from these artists. Old Brian is up to his old tricks, blotto by ten and the only thing he has made disappear so far is two bottles of Scotch. Old Maurice is losing patience with him. Then one of the doves escaped and messed up one of the Dean Sisters' wigs. Nice enough, could put a word in for you if yer like. I get the impression she's looking for some male company."

Dave puffed on his cigarette. "Not the only one from what I've heard."

Jim drank down the last of his beer and stood up. "Fancy another pint?"

It was unlike Jim to have a second at lunchtime.

"Yeah okay," said Dave. "And you can get me a bag of crisps while you're about it, that pie was more air than filling."

When Jim returned, Dave decided not to pursue his line of questioning, the truth would out eventually, as his old mum used to say, and he could wait.

***

"Come on girls, get in line, we don't want Mr Stevens thinking you are not ready for next Monday."

Don Stevens smiled. "Can I have a quiet word please?"

Jenny Benjamin moved to the side aisle where Don was standing watching the proceedings.

"Forgive me mentioning this, but that routine I have just seen, wasn't that in a show we did last season?"

Jenny Benjamin looked puzzled. "I don't think so Mr Stevens."

"How can I put this?" Don began, standing with his legs apart while folding his arms. "Last year the girls did a routine dressed as Indians, I remember the set like it was yesterday. Now here they are togged up as French peasants, with Maurice supplying an accordion. They are, if I am not mistaken, doing the same routine. Somehow, peasants performing what can only be described as a war dance is not on."

Jenny pulled a notebook from her rather worn-looking jacket. "I have most of my routines in here," she said, flicking over a couple of pages.

Don waited as a nervous Jenny read through her notes.

Maurice Beeney popped his head out from the orchestra pit. "If it's any help Don, the piece is the same as last year and if my memory serves me right it was used the year before as well."

Jenny continued to fumble with her notebook.

"Clear the stage please. Get Ted out here now I want to hear his act. Jenny, would you go backstage with the girls and see if you can come up with something fresh. I do not wish to see yesterday's leftovers."

"Yes Mr Stevens," said Jenny, looking slightly worried and feeling it.

Ted Ricer strode on to the stage. "I hope you are ready for this Mr Stevens, I've got some real crackers for you this year."

"Yes Ted I am sure you have, I love Christmas too. Now get on with it man I haven't got all bleeding day." Don looked at his watch and sighed heavily.

June sneaked in at the back of the theatre and stood and listened to Ted's act. There was no doubt about it, the man knew his stuff and she could hear Don Stevens chuckling away. She looked around her to see if anyone was watching and then took a large swig of vodka from the hip flask hidden in her bag. When Ted had finished his act the Dean Sisters came rolling on stage singing Puppet on a String. June watched their footwork on the beach balls and found herself swaying to the beat. She had to admire their technique. They had a fifteen-minute spot which included them juggling, something they had added to the act following their television appearance, and ended with them skilfully rolling the balls up a three-tiered ramp singing Walking Back to Happiness. June knew they were working to a click-track, but that didn't distract from the fact that they were very talented. The act was slick and June had to admit to herself it was very entertaining. She took another swig.

Mystic Brian did his act and for once everything went perfectly, even allowing for a few vocal hiccups coming over the sound system from time to time. Then Don called the dancers back and with a change of pace and some different music, which Maurice appeared to have produced from nowhere, the routine was much improved.

Then it was June's turn to impress him. Don called her and she walked from the back of the auditorium, trying not to stagger as she went up on to the stage; she had drunk more than she had intended.

"June, I wanted to see you in costume, why aren't you wearing it?"

"I'm sorry, I was watching from the back, it slipped my mind."

Don didn't look impressed. "Derinda Daniels is ready to take over any time you say the word."

"Don, I'm sorry, what more can I say?"

"Jim, is the click-track in place? Maurice are you ready?"

"All set," came the reply from Jim as Maurice raised his baton.

The orchestra started to play There is nothing like a Dame and then the recorded voice of June was heard singing Honey Bun from South Pacific. June had played Nellie in a touring production of South Pacific after its West End run which had starred Mary Martin. Her second number was Wonderful Guy, which she mimed badly, and this was followed by a couple of songs from a musical specially written for her entitled The Girl from the Rainbow! and Don concluded that as far as he could see she had gone over the rainbow and failed to return. June danced across the stage and broke into a tap routine, tripping a little as she did so.

"STOP!" shouted Don Stevens, getting up from his seat. "What is the point of doing a tap dance if you are not wearing the bloody shoes?"

June's face crumpled and she ran from the stage.

Jim came on to the stage. "It's okay Mr Stevens I'll get her back."

"Don't bother, I've had enough for one day," replied Don, as he began to walk quickly up the theatre aisle. "Just make sure everyone is here at eight sharp tomorrow morning. I want a full run-through and if Miss Ashby isn't up to scratch she knows what the consequences will be."

"I've lost one of my doves."

"Not now Brian," said Jim, as he marched off the stage.

Jim found June in her dressing room crying. "Come on June, there's no real harm done. You'll be fine."

June wiped her eyes and blew her nose. "Will I?"

"Course you will, you're a pro. Look, I'll go and stall Maurice and the boys; we can run the click-track through again while no one else is here. What do you say?"

"I'll give it a go, but without any click-track Jim; I want to sing the numbers I originally rehearsed for this show if only to prove to Don Stevens that I can still sing."

Jim smiled. "Be on stage in five and don't forget the tap shoes."

As June put on her shoes there was a knock and Ted stuck his head round the door. "You okay?" he asked.

"I'm okay Ted, thanks for asking."

"Don can be harsh at times but it is to be expected, he is a very busy man. Look, if you fancy a drink later I'll be in the bar."

June stood up. "I think I had better give the bar a miss and get an early night. I can't afford to screw up this job. Now I had better go and face the music."

Ted stood to one side as he watched June walk on to the stage. He knew a drinker when he saw one. He had seen her once on stage, it might have been in London, but there was something different about her now and he couldn't put his finger on it. Age he supposed, but no, it was something else. When he telephoned his wife Rita later, he would ask her to find the theatre programme from the musical revue he had seen at the

Fortune and bring it with her if, as he suspected, Rita was planning one of her surprise visits to the resort in the hope of catching him flirting with one of the company.

As Don made his way to the back of the theatre, Lilly stood there holding a bag.

"I found this in the back row."

Don took the bag from Lilly and thanking her went out of the door towards the manager's office. He sneaked a look inside the bag which felt heavy and raised his eyes to the ceiling as the hip flask came into view. "That bloody Brian and his drinking." He did a U-turn and headed towards the door leading to the dressing rooms. He found Brian feeding his birds.

"Brian, yours I think," said Don, holding out the leather bag.

Brian took the bag and looked inside. "I doubt it," he replied, noticing the hip flask and taking out a lipstick, "pink isn't my colour, clashes with my eyes."

***

Freda Boggis poured the tea and handed her friend Lilly a cup. "Help yourself to a biscuit Lil; I have some digestives if you'd prefer them."

Lilly looked at the plate of custard creams. "These will be fine thanks Freed. I can't stop long as I promised old Gut Buster Scott I'd give his office a good seeing to. He's a miserable old sod at times."

"Bob Scott has never been anything else in my opinion. Horrible little git he was at school, always getting into scrapes with the other boys. Never understood how he became the pier manager, he wasn't what you'd call a scholar."

Lilly sipped her tea. "His father was very friendly with old Ernie the last manager; I think he put a word in for Bob when he got sacked from Coopers."

Freda raised her eyebrows. "My Dick would have made a marvellous manager. Let's face it Lil he's had experience in the food and drink business," she said, looking about her.

"Yeah, he certainly knows his way round a bar," Lilly replied, helping herself to another biscuit.

Just then the doorbell rang, it was Muriel. "Hello Lilly how are you? Funny thing, I mentioned you to Barry only the other night. Haven't seen Lilly lately I said, I wonder how she is."

Lilly smiled, she liked Muriel. "Are you coming along to see the show?"

"That's just why I popped in, to see if Fanny here had made up her mind what night we were going. Have you managed to see any of the rehearsals Lilly?"

"One or two, I was just about to tell Freed. Ted Ricer reckons there is something odd about the leading lady."

"Really!" exclaimed Muriel, making herself comfortable on the settee.

"Is Ted the one with the doves?" asked Freda.

"That's Mystic Brian, Ted's the comedian, bit of an eye for the ladies. You must remember him, he has performed here before, I like him."

"Hush Freed, pour me a cup of tea and let Lilly tell us the news."

Freda reluctantly took herself off to the kitchen to fetch another cup and saucer.

"Well," said Lilly, pulling herself up to her full height, "Ted reckons there's something strange about June Ashby."

"You told us that already Lil," said Freda, banging the china down onto the table. "What's strange about her? Is she foreign, what?"

"Well I'm not really sure. I heard him talking to his wife from the callbox at the stage door. Rita, he said, there is something odd about June Ashby. Then he said something about a programme."

"On the telly?" asked Freda.

"I don't know, could have been. The boys were moving some scenery about above and I couldn't catch all of it."

Muriel heaved a sigh. "Lilly Brocket as I live and breath, here we are on the edge of our seats and you haven't got the full story."

Lilly felt herself blush. Snatching another custard cream just as Freda was about to offer the plate to Muriel, she stood up. "Anyway, I'd better be off, I've an office to clean."

Freda showed Lilly to the door and watched her small frame cross the road.

"Now Freda Boggis," said Muriel, "when are we going to this night of a thousand stars? I thought the opening night with the party to follow."

***

June dialled and waited for an answer. Jack was moving around in his office by the stage door, but thankfully the hatch was down. Noises above indicated that the sets were being moved about again and apart from mumbled voices from members of the orchestra, there was no one around to overhear her conversation. It seemed an age before her call was answered and June's palms became clammy with the wait. She could feel her heart beating against her chest and her mouth had become very dry. Then she heard the receiver being picked up at the other end and she spoke quickly and quietly.

"I can't do this, I really can't. You have got to do something to get me out of here." There was a catch in her voice as she spoke and she could feel tears pricking her eyelids. "But I'm not ready for this show; you are going to have to think of some other way."

Jim walked in at the stage door and tapped on Jack's hatch. June hearing the noise quickly replaced the receiver and fled to the safety of her dressing room. Jim ,distracted by the sudden movement, saw June moving hastily towards the stairwell.

Jack opened his hatch with a thud. "Hello young Jim, what can I be doing you for?"

"I just wondered if there had been any post today, only I'm waiting on some blurb for the summer show."

"Nothing today Jim, but I'll give you a shout if I sees anything."

"Thanks Jack," Jim called, as he walked away, his mind now on other things.

Jim could hear sobs as he passed by June's dressing room. He raised his hand to knock, but thought better of it and moved out on to the stage to see if his latest instructions had been carried out. He was pleased to see that they had. The boys had been working hard to get everything in place for the final rehearsals.

"Well done you lot," shouted Jim above the noise of a drill. "There will be a pint in The Growler for you tonight."

The boys waved their approval and continued with the task in hand.

Maurice walked up the side steps from the orchestra pit. "Ah Jim, thought I heard your voice. One or two things I wanted to run past you before the rehearsal tomorrow."

Jim motioned to the wings where they continued their conversation and took down notes as Maurice rattled off his concerns.

Jim nodded. "Don't worry Maurice, I will call an early start tomorrow and run through one or two things before you and the boys arrive at ten."

Maurice patted Jim's arm. "I knew I could rely on you Jim."

Jim smiled. "Well Maurice, I had better get a move on, one or two lighting hitches to check out and then we should be all ready for Mr Stevens."

"I do hope so Jim. I've never seen Don quite as agitated as he was today with Miss Ashby. I know he can be a bit of a worrier, but I thought he was going to throw a fit earlier."

"Maurice, what is your opinion of June Ashby?"

Maurice scratched his chin. "Well, I had heard of her of course, but never seen her until now. The voice seems a bit of a problem, though for a professional it does seem a bit strange to me. It might be nerves of course, but when she ran through a couple of the original numbers I did think the voice had improved. Don's idea of using click-track is ridiculous for a show this small and it is murder for my boys." He paused for a moment recalling something in his mind. "I remember an artiste who worked here one year who had had a problem with his voice mid-season and a doctor had come in and sprayed his vocal chords and he sang as right as nine pence. Surprised Don hasn't done the same for Ashby."

"Probably a money or time issue," Jim replied, taking in what he had been told. "What do you think of her act as a whole?"

"Compared to some of the others on the bill, it seems to be ill thought out. It doesn't flow. The dance routines, such as they are, seem okay, but it all seems a bit higgledy-piggledy to me. Amateurish I would call it. When an artiste has been used to playing musicals with a large ensemble behind them, stepping out in a little show like this on their own is not easy. I do feel for her, but she is supposed to be a professional. If I were Don I would replace her immediately with Miss Daniels. If I had time I would rehearse June myself, but this show opens in a few days and I have enough keeping my boys in hand."

"We must have been thinking along the same lines."

"You should talk to old Ted, he told me he had seen June work in a variety show in London once. He said she was good."

"What about now?"

Maurice smiled. "Best you speak to Ted. You can hear it from him first-hand, I never repeat gossip."

"Jim, you are needed over here," shouted a voice from the back of theatre. "The follow spot is playing up."

"Be there in a minute," Jim responded loudly. "Thanks Maurice. See you later in The Growler?"

"Oh, I think I'll be able to manage a couple of Scotches, it's going to be a hell of a long day tomorrow." And with that the two went about their separate business.

***

Lilly was as good as her word about cleaning the management offices. She set about her task in her usual happy-go-lucky fashion and hummed a tune she had heard on the wireless earlier that day. Setting out her stall of polish and dusters, she began to move a few of the papers on the main desk. The telephone, which had not had much use since the last season, was particularly dusty. Just as she had finished cleaning it, Ted Ricer stuck his head round the door. "Lilly, any chance of using the telephone while old Scotty is not about?"

Lilly folded her arms. "You know the rules Ted Ricer; performers are to use the payphone at the stage door."

"But you can be overheard there Lil and it is a bit personal."

"Another one of your fancy women I suppose. How that poor wife of yours puts up with you and your floundering I will never know."

"It's her I need to speak to, she will be coming down and I need her to do something for me. Go on Lilly, give yer old mate five minutes."

"You'll be getting me the sack Ted Ricer and no mistake. If old Scott found out I'd been letting the likes of you use his facilities he would soon show me the door and I am getting too old to be looking for another job."

"I'll buy you a drink in The Growler tonight and you can bring old misery guts Scott with you if you like," replied Ted, with half a laugh.

"I shall tell him what you said Ted Ricer. Five minutes and not a minute longer and I will have you know I am very partial to a large port."

42

"Try Southampton." Ted laughed as Lilly scuttled out of the office.

Ted waited patiently as the telephone rang out, but it appeared that Rita had gone out. As he replaced the receiver, his eye caught a piece of paper on the desk. The name of Lorna Bright for the production of Summer Frolics was scribbled on it. Ted was puzzled. He heard Lilly clanking her mop and bucket in the hall. Who was Lorna Bright? She certainly wasn't in this production.

He heard the voice of Bob Scott talking to Lilly and quickly made a dash for the door. Luckily Bob's back was turned away from him and he slid out unnoticed and back into the auditorium.

***

June walked down the pier trying to put her mind to other things. The rehearsals were not going well, but she was determined not to work with a click-track. The problem was she couldn't remember half the songs and it was too late to start learning new ones with the opening almost upon her. A stiff breeze was coming in from the North Sea and she pulled her coat tightly around her. There were one or two people walking up and down chatting and laughing. June turned on to Marine Parade and started to head towards the Wellington Pier. A crowd of people were getting off a Seagull coach, having been on a tour of the Broads. Lucky them, June thought, she would do anything to be anywhere other than here right now. She decided to go into a small café on the other side of the parade and have a coffee. She found herself an empty table and sat down. The café was warm; she unbuttoned her coat and reached into her handbag for a bottle of tablets.

"Can I get you some water love?" asked the man who had served her coffee and was now in the process of clearing a table.

June smiled. "That would be very kind."

The man returned with a glass of water and put it before June. "Headaches are the worse things. Been a martyr to them all my life and that wind off the North Sea don't help none."

June, who wasn't in the mood for chatting, nodded and smiled and took two tablets from the bottle. She watched as the man went about his business, smiling and chatting to the few customers that had come in for their afternoon snacks, no doubt before they headed back to their boarding houses for an evening meal.

June was staying in a small hotel in Gorleston, a couple of miles over the river, which meant either catching a bus or paying out for a taxi. She imagined what the town would be like once the season was in full swing. All of the amusements arcades would be up and running and the promenade full of families out to enjoy the sands and attractions. Gorleston was quieter than Great Yarmouth, though she hadn't had time to explore as much as she would like to have done. The seafront was in complete contrast to the one she was on at the moment. There was a yacht pond, a small parade of shops, an outdoor pool and a small funfair adjacent to the Pavilion Theatre, which housed Old Time Music Hall throughout the season. June finished her coffee, thanked the man behind the counter and continued her walk to the Wellington Pier. She crossed the road, managing to dodge an open landau, the first she had seen in operation, and stopped to gather her thoughts while she made fast her bag.

"What are you doing here, aren't you supposed to be in rehearsals?"

June looked up. "God you gave me a fright. I was just on my way to see you."

***

Maud had just settled herself down with her knitting when the familiar tap was heard at the door. "Who goes there?"

"Doctor," prompted the reply.

"Doctor Who?" Maud laughed out loud. "Come in Jim me old darling – bit early aren't you? Just seen June walking down the front, rehearsals finished?"

Jim leaned against the doorway as Maud laid down her knitting.

"Rehearsals are far from finished Maud and the way things are going I shall be surprised if this show opens. A whole week of rehearsals seems excessive. In the normal course of events the artistes arrive here with their acts, the whole process is put together in London. They do a couple of run-throughs, one dress-rehearsal and you have a complete show."

"So there really is trouble at mill?"

"Trouble isn't the half of it. I just can't put my finger on it," said Jim. "June really isn't cutting the mustard. Old Stevens is doing his nut. The routines are all over the place, and even old Maurice is concerned, he said if he'd had time he would have spent some of it helping June, but this schedule is so tight. I have a feeling another artiste will shortly be arriving here, I heard Don make a call earlier."

Maud looked concerned. "Not like you to get so worked up over a pre-season star. You'll have your work cut out when the Delfont lot arrive. I have heard Dora is a lot of fun to work with."

Jim lit a cigarette.

"Don't let old Scott find you smoking in here; you know what he's like when he's on a crusade at the beginning of the season. Told Lilly off the other day for sucking a Polo mint."

"I can handle Scott," Jim replied, with a smile, "but I really can't get my head around this show. Just when you think one thing has been solved, another one comes along. I feel like I am on a crazy merry-go-round."

Maud sighed. "Lilly weren't impressed, and she has seen them all. She said her neighbour's daughter was better in the local panto. Fairy Bow-bells she was, Lilly helped make the frock."

"Well I've done all I can," said Jim, sighing. "I wonder where June was going?"

Maud looked at her friend. "Don't know old love, but I am sure she will be back."

"I do hope so," said Jim, putting out his cigarette.

Maud smiled to herself, Jim seemed smitten and no mistake.

Back in the theatre Jim heard Don shouting. "Where is this so-called West End Star then? This isn't good enough."

Ted walked onto the stage. "Don, please forgive me asking but did you actually meet June before you engaged her?"

"What business is it of yours?"

"Well, let's face it, she has been a cause for concern ever since she walked in here. If you ask me…"

"But I am not asking you Ricer, so button it. Right, I want those bloody dancers back on the stage right now, that finale routine is crap! Ted, shift yourself and see if you can't find some material that Noah didn't write. Maurice – I want to hear the second act opening again. Where's Jenny? Is there anyone actually working here today?"

Jim stood at the back of the auditorium. This really wasn't shaping up well at all. He went out of the door and into the foyer where he came face to face with Rita, Ted's wife. "Hello Rita, nice to see you again, how have you been keeping?"

Rita gave Jim a warm smile. "Hello Jim, it is lovely to see you again. I was so sorry to hear about Karen."

Jim bowed his head for a moment. "Thanks for the flowers Reet; it was good of you and Ted."

"Least we could do. Karen and you are like family, we've known you so long. I wonder we don't just move down here – we seem to spend so much time in Yarmouth." She studied Jim's face for a moment; she could see the sadness there. "Perhaps we can have a proper chat later, right now I've got to find the old bugger and see what he's been up to."

Jim laughed. "Well Reet, as far as I can see, your Ted has been as good as gold so far."

"That's what's worrying, Jim, I think he must be losing the knack, or getting old. I usually have at least one love affair to break up, he is definitely slipping!"

"He's through there," said Jim, nodding towards the door. "But tread carefully Don Stevens is on the warpath."

"He doesn't frighten me," said Rita, opening the door, "I've had better than him for breakfast. See you later love."

Rita moved speedily down the theatre aisle.

"Ted Ricer where are you?" she shouted above the noise invading her eardrums.

"Well if it isn't the lovely Rita," said Don Stevens, walking towards her, arms outstretched.

"And you can cut that out for a start Don Stevens. I had enough of you in Scunthorpe. You don't beguile me old lover, so get that into your head right now."

"But Rita, you know this torch I carry for you," he replied mockingly.

"Well from where I am standing the batteries are rather flat," said Rita, as she brushed by him and walked up onto the stage and exited via the wings.

Don immediately turned his attention back to the dancers who had assembled before him. "Right you lot – I want to see high kicks, not the military two-step. Now Maurice, hit it."

The theatre filled with the tune Variety and the dancers went into their routine as Don's eagle eye watched and Jenny Benjamin sat in the stalls with her fingers crossed looking anxious.

Jim walked out of the theatre entrance and headed sideways toward the stage door. Jack was busying himself with some late mail, but looked up as Jim approached.

"Any sign of Miss Ashby?"

Jack shook his head. "Sorry Jim she hasn't been through here. I didn't even know she had left the building until one of the Dean Sisters mentioned it. She must have gone through the front door."

"Thanks mate. I'll go and see if there is any sign of her on the prom."

Jack went back to his mail thinking, not for the first time, that things were not going too well.

Jim marched down the pier oblivious to the holidaymakers who were walking towards him. "Watch it mate," cried one, "you nearly had me over. What's the rush?"

***

Coming out of the box office to get a breath of air, Maud saw Jim speed by her as he turned on to the promenade. Lilly suddenly appeared beside her. "God love us, he's in a hurry."

Maud turned and smiled. "I think our Jim is smitten with our leading lady."

Lilly raised her eyebrows. "Well he's got competition," she huffed. "She was seen with Dave Grant coming out of the Tower nightclub late last night."

"Lilly Brocket you are pulling my leg."

"Dick Boggis saw them; he was coming home from the Legion."

"You can't always believe what Dick says, he was probably six parts cut. How did he know it was June Ashby?"

"I am fair parched Maud Bennett," said Lilly, licking her lips.

Lilly followed Maud into the box office. "Sit yourself down there Lilly and don't you move until you have told me everything."

"Well," began Lilly, "Dick often does odd bits of work here and there, as you know. Well he was bottling up for the New Beach and he saw our Jim and the lady in question in there.

When he bumped into Jim in the Gents he asked who the lady was."

Maud looked puzzled. "But how would Dave know June Ashby? It doesn't make sense and he is Jim's best mate after all."

Lilly helped herself to a biscuit. "Just because they are the best of friends don't mean they live in each other's pockets. When Karen was alive they only saw each other for the odd night out and when they were working at the nightclub. Karen and Debbie were Jim's life, everyone knew that."

Maud eyed Lilly quizzically. "Lilly Brockett for someone who was brought up on Balliol you weren't last in the queue when they handed out common sense."

Lilly smiled. "I shall take that as a condiment coming from you Maud Bennett. People only see the cleaner, the little old gal that does the scrubbing. I see and hear things."

Maud handed her a cup of tea. "I might go and see our Dave. If what you tell me is right, Jim could get hurt. He is still not over Karen and to see him suddenly taken with another woman, well it doesn't seem right, like he's not thinking straight."

"Men do some daft things when they're not thinking," replied Lilly, knowingly.

"Like what?"

"Bloody magic acts with doves for one thing," said Lilly, with a laugh, and Maud heartily agreed.

***

Jim reached the Marina and slowed his pace, he was feeling tired. His work seemed relentless, trying to keep things in order and keep everyone happy. He couldn't remember it being so difficult in previous years, but then he had Karen beside him. Always a sounding board when things weren't going right. Always there to support him, whatever decision he made.

There was still no sign of June so he sat himself down on the Marina wall and took out his cigarettes. A few sparrows flew down and started hopping around him, looking for an odd crumb or two. He gazed across the road and could see workmen busily putting the finishing touches to an amusement arcade, replacing bulbs on the façade before the busy season kicked off. People were enjoying a walk and taking in the sights. Soon there would be hoards of children with their parents beach-bound with their tin buckets and spades. The beach vendors would be selling their ices and candy floss, and the familiar cry of old Ben, the newspaper seller, would be heard from his carrier bicycle once more.

He remembered when Debbie was small and how much she enjoyed being taken along to Joyland at the side of the Sands Theatre. She loved the snails and the Noah's Ark that dominated the small funfair. Her face would light up when he announced they were having a trip to the circus. Debbie loved to watch the horses and the girl on the flying trapeze, always declaring that when she was big enough, she was going to be the ballerina on horseback. Memories were all he had now.

"Hello mate, what are you doing up this end?" said the familiar voice of Dave Grant.

Jim pulled himself together and got up from the wall. "As a matter of fact I was looking for our star attraction; she appears to have gone walkabout. You haven't seen her have you?"

"Wouldn't know her if I saw her," Dave replied. "Come on, I'll walk back to the Sands with you, I'm finished for the day."

The two sauntered off together, Jim with his mind now clear of all thoughts concerning June Ashby, at least for the time being.

Chapter Three   *"Half a Photograph"*

Ted poured himself a Scotch and offered Rita a glass.

"Ted Ricer it is too early to start drinking, besides aren't you due to go through your act again?"

Ted took a glug of his Scotch and smacked his lips. "I think old Stevens has had enough of me for one day."

"I know how he feels," replied his wife, pulling an easy chair nearer the dressing table, "and I have been here less than an hour. Now Ted, I've done as you asked and brought you this." Rita rummaged in her bag and pulled out a theatre programme, she flicked it open and then showed Ted the photograph. Ted studied it in silence.

"Well," Rita asked, "is it her?"

Ted laid the programme on the table before him. "Of course, this photograph is hardly true, it's dated, but yes it could be her."

"But you are not convinced?"

"There is just something about her that doesn't ring true. I am sure when I saw her on stage she was more vibrant, alive!" Ted studied the photograph again.

Rita took her powder compact from her bag. "Is she around, I'd like to meet her? I saw that show too, I would soon know if it was her."

"Hasn't been seen for the best part of the afternoon, seems to have gone walkabout." Ted paused. "I watched her this morning in rehearsal, the dance routines were a little rusty and she couldn't lip sync for toffee. Mind you, I was watching Dusty on some pop programme back at the digs and you could tell she was miming."

"Well, Ashby hasn't worked for a while, maybe she just needs some more time."

Ted banged the programme down on the table. "She is supposed to be a professional. You can't tell me she has forgotten the words to some of the biggest musicals since Me and My Girl. I asked Don Stevens today whether he had actually met her before he signed her up for this show and he avoided answering the question."

"I bet I could get an answer out of him, he has a bit of a soft spot for old Rita."

"He has a bit of a soft spot for most women," said Ted with feeling.

Rita laughed loudly. "Ted Ricer, if you could only hear yourself."

Ted grinned and squeezed Rita's knee. "I have a reputation to keep up old gal, mustn't let the mask slip."

"If they only knew what an old queen you were," Rita replied. "You'd have the likes of Jim and his stagehands running a mile."

"But you haven't regretted it have you Rita?" asked Ted softly.

Rita reached across and squeezed his cheek. "Of course I haven't you old bugger. We've had a good marriage, you and I, though it doesn't do for others to know that." Rita went quiet for a moment reflecting on what had gone before. "You were my knight in shining armour Ted Ricer. You rescued me from my father and showed me that there was such a thing as a kind and caring man. My poor old mum, God rest her soul, never had a moment's peace from that old tyrant."

Ted's eyes were moist. "But you always wanted kids Rita and I…"

"Don't go beating yourself up over that old chestnut. You've been a bloody good husband. Kids, well they would have got in the way. How could I have gone out on tour with you with a couple of little ones hanging around my neck? No Ted, life is just fine the way it is and despite your hankerings, I love you and I always will."

Ted picked up his glass and gazed into it. "Here's to the best wife a man could ever have."

"Give me some of that you old sod, I'll drink to that."

Just then there was a knock on the door.

Rita got up and opened it. It was Brian. "Oh hello Rita," he said, smiling, "I heard you had blown into town. Is the master at home?"

"Come in Brian," shouted Ted, "and don't bring those bloody birds with you."

"Old Stevens is looking for you," said Brian, giving Ted one of his toothy grins. "He's been like a bear with a sore head today. He's quite upset my aura."

Ted got to his feet. "Don't tell me, another one of your doves."

Brain looked at him perplexed. "Ted them doves are my life — I lives them, I breathes them."

"One day Brian you'll stick some feathers up your arse and fly off with them. Now let's go and see what old misery guts wants."

Rita guffawed as Brian meekly followed Ted out of the dressing room.

Don had assembled the company on the stage, minus the leading lady and as Ted and Brian walked on from stage left he addressed them.

"I have a few things to say. Firstly, the whole show needs tightening up. We are over-running by at least thirty minutes. The dancers are slack; I want to see a big improvement by tomorrow, the finale routine is still crap!" He turned his attention to the Dean Sisters. "Cut the stalling with the balls girls, after three attempts the audience will be well aware you can roll to the top with no problem and one of the numbers has got to go."

The girls looked at each other and groaned.

"Brian, the act needs to lose at least five minutes, you are doing two spots and for gawd sake please get those birds under control. If one more little bastard makes a dash for my head I won't be held responsible for my actions."

"They get a bit anxious," Brian mumbled.

"Great!" said Don, flicking a stray bird feather from his sleeve. "So now we have birds that should be in therapy. Why oh why I ever came into this business I will never know. I should have gone to sea like my old dad wanted." Don sighed heavily. "Maurice, you and the boys are doing a great job, keep up the good work". Maurice nodded his thanks as a bead of sweat ran down his face. "Ted, I saw your lady wife earlier, I hope she has brought you some new material? Your stuff is good, but half of this I've heard before."

"But the audience won't have done," said Ted, defending his corner.

"As most of the audience will be about a hundred and three, I would have thought it to be a strong possibility," Don replied, getting agitated.

Rita strode onto the stage. "Don Stevens don't you dare say anything against my Ted's act. He has never been out of work in all the time we have been married." She handed Ted a wad of papers. "Ted here's the new gags you asked me to bring."

Ted winked at her. Good old Reet.

"Rita, as much as I love you, would you please get the fuck off my stage. Unless, of course, you are planning on giving us one of your turns?"

Rita walked to the edge of the stage and down the side steps; she walked over to Don and planted a big kiss on his lips. "Don Stevens, you sure do know how to sweet-talk a woman." And with that she swept up the aisle and out of the theatre.

The company cheered and even Don managed a sly grin to himself.

"Now where is our top of the bill, anyone know?"

There was silence. Don grimaced. "Oh well, I'll deal with her separately. Well that's all for today. I want you all here at 9am sharp for a complete run-through. If you need to change any orchestrations, see Maurice before you leave here. Don't forget to drop one of those numbers girls – lose Puppet on a String."

The company started to break up and Don headed for the exit.

***

It was a somewhat downhearted June who sauntered onto the pier an hour later, her meeting hadn't gone as she had hoped and she found herself going over and over the conversation in her head.

The company was just leaving the theatre for the pub. Brian spotted her first. "Eh up Jim, look what the wind's blown in." He walked jauntily over to her. "You're for it and no mistake, old Stevens is going to have your guts for garters, he doesn't like being kept waiting."

"Okay Brian leave it," said Jim, stepping in. "You go along with the others I'll catch up with you in a minute."

Brian shrugged his shoulders and went off to join the Dean Sisters who, after arguing between themselves about Puppet on a String against Walking Back to Happiness, were skipping gaily out onto the promenade.

"You okay?" Jim asked.

June kept her eyes firmly down studying the boarded deck. "I'd prefer to be on my own if you don't mind."

"If that's the way you want to play it. But I really think you owe these people some kind of explanation. They have been working really hard to pull this show together and the one person who should have been there let them down."

"I'm sorry," June mumbled, "but there are things you don't understand."

"Then try sharing them with someone. Come on June, I've tried to help you since you arrived."

June raised her head; Jim could see that she had been crying. "And I'm really grateful Jim; really I am."

"Don is buying the company a drink in The Growler, come and join us."

"I don't think I could face it."

"Look, I know he can be a funny beggar at times, but after a couple he is a different person. You can chat to him over a drink, work something out."

June turned away and looked out to sea. Ted and Rita came hurrying out of the theatre with Jack in tow.

"Hey Jim you going to The Growler?" Ted shouted.

Jim raised his hand. "Be there in a minute Ted, see you in there."

"Who's Jim talking to?" Rita asked, catching Ted's arm.

"The famous June by the look of things, do you recognise her?"

"Not from the back view," she replied. "Don't worry lover, there'll be plenty of time."

They walked on with Jack rambling about his win at Haydock that afternoon. "It came in at twenty to one."

"Yeah so you said about three times." Rita smiled. "You'll be able to get a round in." Jack suddenly went very quiet.

"It's up to you June, you can stay here with your thoughts or come and join the gang. The Growler is just off the market place, it won't be a late night, and there is a 9 o'clock call tomorrow."

June turned back and looked at him. "Maybe later Jim, you go on."

Jim put his hands in his pockets and went to catch up with Ted. June turned again and looked back out to sea. She had been gazing out for some time when she heard a familiar voice say, "You won't find the answer out there."

June swung round. "God, you really are taking some risks today, what if someone was to see you?"

"There's no one here, the theatre is dark and all the visitors have gone back to their boarding houses for their evening meal. And you, lady, need to pull yourself together and go and join the others. Everything will be okay, trust me."

***

The Growler was quite busy and the company moved away into the back bar where there was a little more room and the promise of a pie and sandwich laid on by Don, who was at that moment enjoying a rather good meal in the Star Hotel.

"He sure knows how to push the boat out," said Sue, one of the Dean Sisters, helping herself to a steak and kidney pie. "I'm starving. Hey barman, are there any chips to go with these?"

"Sorry love we only do pies, crisps and sandwiches. I've got some HP if you'd like."

Sue shook her head. "Thanks mate but I'll pass, I have enough sauce of my own."

Rita took a couple of ham sandwiches and put them before Ted, who had settled himself down with a large Scotch. "Get these down you before you start hitting that stuff. I am not carrying you back to the digs."

"She's a real lady your missus," said Brian, supping his pale ale. "She puts me in the mind of that Elsie Tanner in Coronation Street."

"Don't tell me that Mystic Brian watches Coronation Street," Ted replied, tucking into his sandwich.

"I like to watch something when I'm on me own with the birds in digs. Off to St Anne's after this stint, working men's club. What about you."

"I have landed a summer season in Scarborough and old Reet likes the bays there. She will come down and join me for a couple of weeks."

"Keep an eye on you more like, you randy old git."

"Are you referring to my husband by any chance?" asked Rita, as she sat down with a cheese sandwich and a port and lemon. "What's he been up to now?"

Jill had latched herself onto Jim as soon as he had walked through the door. "I've been waiting for you. Thought you and I were going to have a drink together?"

"Sorry love, been very busy. Has anyone got a round in?"

"Money behind the bar from Don," Jill replied. "And what's your pleasure?"

Jim unhooked himself from Jill's arm. "Right now a nice pint of twos, I'll catch you later," and he moved swiftly to the bar and ordered his poison.

Jill knocked back her gin and tonic and went and sat with Sue and Dawn.

"All the bleeding same these men, they lead you on and then leave you high and dry."

"How many of those have you had?" Dawn asked. "You want to go easy, we've got to be up early in the morning."

"Give it a rest love and let your hair down for once. You are too bloody sensible for your own good sometimes."

Dawn gave Sue a nod. "No three guesses for who will be carrying her home tonight. Best get some food down her."

"Well I don't recommend the steak and kidney," Sue responded, "it keeps repeating. I don't know about steak and kidney, it's probably one that fell at Haydock."

"Come now girls, do I sense some tension in the air?" Maurice Beeney butted in, peering down at them through his half-moon glasses.

"And you can sod off you miserable old fart," said Jill, finishing off her drink. "Go and put some money in the juke box and let's hear a bit of Englebert."

Maurice moved away and went to find Jenny. She was always good for a bit of pleasant conversation.

Jim surveyed the company before him. Get a couple of drinks down them and you never knew what you would end with. Old Ted would have everyone in stitches, with darling Rita egging him on. Maurice would go all posh as if he had been educated at Eton, Jenny would get a fit of the giggles and her girls would nod and smile afraid to say boo to a goose, while Brian would become maudlin and worry about his birds. The Dean Sisters were a new entity and he could already see how they were shaping up. Where was his mate Dave when he needed a bit of company?

Just then Don Stevens came through the door. "Hi everyone," he called out. "Barman, more drinks all round."

"You're in a good mood," said Jim, welcoming Don at the bar.

"Nothing to be in a bad one about," Don replied. "I like to see people having a good time and this is what this is in aid of, a good time."

"You won't be saying that when they all turn up with hangovers in the morning."

"Look Jim, I've been in this business a long time, too long. I know show business people like I know the back of my hand. Sure, I can be the hard task master, but you have to relax the ogre act sometimes, and if that means this little lot turning up with heads banging, so be it. They will all be saying what a good night they've had and work all the harder for it. I know most of them, they are my friends, but don't tell 'em I said so."

Jim slapped Don on the back. "You're not such a bad sort after all."

Don handed out the drinks, working his way round the group and saying a few words here and there. As anticipated, Ted was in fine form and had the others rolling around laughing, even Brian managed a titter and seemed to have forgotten all about his beloved birds for once in his life.

"Any sign of her ladyship?" Don asked Jim.

Jim told Don about his encounter with her on the pier earlier, trying to plead her case.

"The fact is Jim old lad, she is not up to it. What am I supposed to do about her?"

Jim downed his second pint and didn't answer.

Rita excused herself from the table and went through to the main bar in search of the Ladies. As she was returning she overheard a woman at the bar asking where she could find the company from the Golden Sands Theatre.

"Excuse me love," said Rita, smiling, "I am Ted Ricer's wife Rita, the company is through the back bar. You are?"

"June Ashby," said June, holding out her hand to shake Rita's. "Jim said they would all be in here, I got a bit caught up so I'm a bit late."

"Follow me love, it's just through here."

June followed Rita. "Jim is just over there love, at the bar. You're welcome to join Ted and me if you'd like, though I do warn you he and Brian are a little bit over the eight."

June smiled. "I'll just go and have a word with Jim, I can't stop long."

Don, who had moved away from the bar to join Maurice and some of the boys from the band, saw June enter but decided against going over to speak to her. Best leave things like that until the morning he decided.

"So you made it," said Jim, as June sidled up beside him. "Would you like a drink?"

"Vodka and orange, but let me get these, I owe you," said June, taking her purse from her bag. "Barman, vodka orange and a pint of twos please."

"I thought you were a creature of habit," said Jim, but June ignored the remark.

"Do you want to sit down, we could move into the other bar perhaps?"

"No, thank you. I will be fine here, besides I won't stay long. I really came to apologise for earlier."

"No need to apologise, I was concerned about you that was all. Look June I don't know what is going on and it is really none of my business, but if you ever need a friend."

June handed over some money to the barman. "Thanks Jim, but this is something I am going to have to see through myself."

"Forgive me butting in but I need another drink," said Rita, moving in between the two. "Quite warm in here isn't it. That's the trouble with these back rooms they never open enough windows. Honest, you could suffocate in some of them I swear." She studied June's face for a moment, motioned to the barman for some service and carried on. "It's really nice to meet you at last June; Ted has talked so much about you. Say, where's my manners would you two like a drink?"

"Just got one in thanks," said Jim, coming to the rescue.

"How long have you been associated with Don Stevens then?"

"Not long," said June. "In fact this is my first show for him."

"Bet he auditioned you up in the Smoke. He always insists his artists travel to him, he never goes to them, stingy old beggar. Good sort though, he has given Ted lots of work over the years. What did you think of his Regent Street suite then?"

June blushed. "I've never been there."

"What, never? Don't tell me old Don actually came to see you."

"Well no, I mean yes. Gosh it is rather hot in here, would you excuse me I need to get some air," said June, lifting her bag from the bar.

"Dear, you do look a bit flushed, I hope you're not sickening for something," said Rita, showing concern.

"No I'll be fine, just need some air." June hurried away out of the room.

"Jim, best go after her, make sure she is all right. Get her a brandy or something; she did look a funny colour."

"Yeah, thanks Rita. I'll be back in a minute I'm sure it's nothing serious."

Rita paid for her drink and went back to Ted and Brian who were in deep conversation about the price of a new motor.

"Ted, a word."

"In a minute Reet, Brian's just telling me about his Vauxhall."

"It'll keep," said Rita, picking up her drink. "Watch my bag lover, I'm just going to go and have a word with Don, that's if I can drag him away from the gorgeous Jenny Benjamin."

Rita pushed her way through the gathering and gave Don a nudge.

"Rita my darling you are looking particularly lovely tonight," said Don, putting his arm around her waist.

"Is that you or the drink talking or a combination of both?"

"Rita, don't spoil an old man's pleasure. Can I get you a drink?"

"Later. Can I have a quiet word please?"

Don looked at the group before him and swayed slightly. "My friends, I have to part for a small moment, but have no fear I shall return."

Rita moved him to the back of the bar and into the bay window, which had just been vacated by a couple of the dancers.

"Now Don me old darling tell me about June Ashby."

"There is nothing to tell Rita my dear, but between you and me she is not very good and it's my bloody name presenting her."

"Why didn't you audition her in your Regent Street offices?"

"Didn't I? What a silly boy I was."

"Don concentrate, there's a large one in it for you," said Rita, giving his arm a pinch. "How did she come to be on your books?"

"Rita my lovely you ask so many questions." He coughed. "Right, let me see, I was asked to put together a show for the Golden Sands, last minute it was. I was going to engage one of my old stalwarts but there was a problem, he died two months ago and no one told me. You remember old Benny 'a song and a half' Bolton?"

"Yes, yes, but who put you on to June? Surely you would have wanted to see what she could do?"

"I asked Gwen to pull together as many of my regulars as she could, but I needed a name to carry to the show and with old Benny gone... I remember now, we placed an advert in The Stage and got several responses. One was from an agent by the name of Wendy Patterson, she said she had June Ashby available but she was also on offer to someone else so if we wanted her we had to act quickly. She gave a rundown of June's previous form to Gwen. I think I had seen Ashby years before in a musical or some other trifle, but I could be mistaken I have seen so many. Gwen pressed me to book her."

"Has Gwen ever met June?"

"Not to my knowledge. She keeps saying she's going to come down here, but she has been tied to the office. Believe it or not my agency still generates business."

"Did you ever speak to Wendy Patterson?"

"Rita are you with the secret service or something, this is worse than No Hiding Place!"

"Don please answer my bloody question."

"No I never spoke to Wendy Patterson, Gwen handled everything. I was in the middle of getting a showcase together for a couple of holiday camps, this show was a bonus and I might say a very fortunate one. Business was a bit slack last season, there were one or two unexpected cancellations."

"And this Wendy character hasn't been in touch with you, or come down here to see how things are going?"

Don scratched his chin. "Come to think of it, no she hasn't. What is all this about Reet, is something afoot?"

"Don, I am going to come back to you on that one, but for now I don't want you to discuss what we have talked about with anyone, not even your beloved Gwen."

"Gwen? Beloved?"

"Oh come off it Don, you've been knocking her off for years. It's no secret."

"Oh, Reet please!"

"Look out Maurice is coming over. Now remember Don, not a word. I'll go and get that drink I promised you."

As Rita reached the bar, Jim came back. "Where's June?"

"She has gone," replied Jim. "Said she needed to get to bed."

"Probably not feeling well, I said she didn't look well."

Rita smiled at the barman. "A double Scotch, port and lemon and a pint of twos."

"Rita, what you said earlier, what did you mean?"

"About what love?" said Rita, getting her cash ready.

"All that business about June going to Don's offices in Regent Street, I got the impression you were after something."

Rita smiled. "I was just taking an interest that's all. The Dean Sisters were talking to me earlier at the theatre and going on about how plush Don's office is. I was interested to hear June's impression of the place. Quite frankly, Ted said he always finds it nauseating, but then a woman has a different perspective on these things. I have never seen it for myself, though Ted has shown me a photograph. A bit gaudy for my liking, red plush drapes and Queen Anne chairs, fake of course, but Ted said they looked real enough to the novice. There's a drink there for you Jim."

"Thanks Rita." Jim eyed her closely. Rita was quite an open person, spoke her mind about things, but he somehow felt she was holding back on something. "What's your opinion of June Ashby?"

"Opinion?" said Rita. "I don't know that I've have had time to form one. I saw her work many years ago. I only met her this evening to speak to, why do you ask?"

Jim lit a cigarette. "Well you always seem to be such a good judge of character, I just wondered."

"I've certainly met a few characters in my time, you can't be connected to this business and not meet them. Take Brian over there, he likes everyone to believe his life revolves around his act and his doves. Not true. When he is away from this show business world he returns home to a cottage down in Torquay and to his adoring wife Brenda and their five kids. Bet you didn't know that, Jim Donnell, and you've been around him on more than one occasion. He plays the fool, because that's what he thinks people expect, a sort of Tommy Cooper; though nowhere near as talented. I met Brenda years ago when the kids were small. Ted was doing a season in Newquay and Brian was brought in as an extra turn. She is a lovely person and she adores him. She shies away from the limelight, likes to keep in the background. He goes out and makes the money; she stays at home and plays the doting wife."

Rita paused and took a sip from her glass. "My opinion of June Ashby, for what it's worth, is that she seems a nice enough woman, but not, I suspect, a very strong one. At least not as strong as one would expect considering her, well, tabloid past.

Observing her this evening, I would say she was nervous and perhaps a little frightened like she is hiding something."

"Interesting. Frightened of what, hiding what?"

Rita sighed. "We are given to believe that she has been away from the business for five years or so and now here she is being put through her paces in a small variety show. According to my Ted, she has hardly sung a note since she arrived and as for dancing, Ted said she was at sixes and sevens. Frightened? She is frightened of what will be written about her if this little show is not a success. Every thespian's nightmare, a bad write-up. Hiding? I am not sure what but it is sure to manifest itself eventually."

"You know Don had her working a click-track," said Jim, stubbing out his cigarette and lighting another.

"No shame in a click-track, the Black and White Minstrels have used one for years, providing, of course, you know the words and again according to Ted she can't even remember those. Come on Jim, a famous actress, a singer who can't remember the words to a song from South Pacific? Even I know the words to most of them."

"Do you think she has had a breakdown?"

"She may have, but then I am not a doctor and, as I say, I only spoke to her briefly. What do you think of her Jim?"

"I really can't make my mind up about her; in fact everyone I speak to about her has a different opinion."

"But you do fancy her don't you?"

"I thought I did," Jim reflected for a moment, "when I first met her, but I think I was feeling lonely. I miss Karen terribly. There, that's the first time I have openly admitted it. Perhaps fancy is too strong a word, I think maybe I felt sorry for her."

"In other words, you wanted to protect her from whatever it was you thought she needed protecting from."

Jim nodded. "I suppose so. It is too soon after Karen for me to start thinking about any kind of relationship and I have Debbie to consider."

"Debbie is married now and has a husband of her own to take care of her. You have to cut Debbie free, she has moved on, but that doesn't mean she loves or cares for you any the less or you for her. Jim, you have a great capacity to love and one day, when you are truly ready, you will love again. Give yourself time to grieve properly first, don't get carried away with the first female who gives you the time of day, you are worth more than that. And besides, you owe it to Karen to make the right choice."

Jim looked at his watch. "I really ought to make a move. I've enjoyed our chat Rita; you've helped me put a few things in order. I really needed that. I usually go to Maud Bennett when I am in a fix, but listening to you has really helped."

Rita was flattered. "Sometimes someone who is slightly removed from the situation helps. Maud is there all the time, she's like a mother to you I know, but Jim, if you ever need me you know how to get in touch and let's face it Hull is hardly a million miles away and you'll always be welcome."

"Thanks Rita, that means a lot, I might take you up on that. Can I get you another before I leave?"

"No Jim you're all right. I had better get this over to Don and then return to my husband before he thinks I have deserted him. Remember what I said, any time."

Jim bent down and kissed Rita on the cheek. "Good night Rita and thanks."

Jim said his goodbyes around the room and Rita watched him with a smile. She picked up the drinks and made her way back to Don and his entourage. She spotted Lilly in a corner with Bob Scott and made a mental note to go and rescue her at some point during the evening.

There was a slight chill in the air as Jim walked along the market place. He decided to walk over Haven Bridge rather than catch a cab from outside the Regal. He needed the fresh air and a clear head for the following morning. He turned into Regent Street and just as he reached the Quay, he saw a familiar figure come out of the Star Hotel bar, he wasn't alone.

"Dave mate, what have you been up to?"

Dave walked over to Jim. "Hi Jim, me old mucker, I have just been having a couple of bevvies with Dan here. You remember Dan, he works in Henry's."

Jim held out his hand. "Yeah of course I do."

Dan seemed rather the worse for wear and half-winked in reply.

"We were just going on to the Tower, fancy coming Jim; we haven't been out for ages."

"Not tonight Dave, I've got a lot on in the morning."

"Oh yeah I forgot, the pre-season. I prefer the proper season shows, them others are too much like hard work."

Jim grinned. "I know the feeling. I'd better get along and if you'll take my advice Dave you ought to see that my laddo there gets home. I don't think they'll let him in the Tower in his state."

Dave looked at Dan, who was staggering around trying to light a cigarette.

"Yeah you're probably right. Catch up with you at the end of week, perhaps go for a few jars?"

Jim slapped his pal on the back. "See yer Dave, you take care."

Dave grabbed hold of Dan's arm. "Now look here, you've got to pull yourself together. I'm taking you home, right?" Dan attempted a reply, but it came out totally inaudible. "Call yourself a barman and you can't hold a few drinks? Come on let's make a move."

When Jim reached the other side of the road he turned and watched as the two figures weaved their way into Regent Street. He smiled to himself and remembered when he and Dave had been in much the same state many years before. He turned on his heel and began to walk over the bridge. There was quite a bit of traffic about and the buses were ferrying their usual mix of locals back to Gorleston, Bradwell and Belton. He crossed the road opposite the old South Town Railway Station, now sadly disused thanks to Beeching, and walked towards home. He pondered on what Rita had said and made the decision to give Debbie and Peter a call over the weekend and try to get up to see them. Once the show was up and running he could sneak off for a couple of days and leave it to run its course. He would have to clear it with old Scott, but he didn't think that would be a problem. He felt he needed to make more of an effort with Peter. There was nothing wrong with the man, he was honest, hardworking and in his heart of hearts he knew he looked after Debbie very well, but being the father that he was he hadn't liked his little girl going off with another man. There should have been more children, but Karen miscarried twice and then had to have a hysterectomy and that put an end to any further family plans. They had talked about adoption once, but when they had sat down and discussed all that that entailed, had decided that having one child wasn't such a bad deal. Debbie was a model daughter and had done well at school. She worked hard and always listened to her parents. She never gave them cause for concern.

He put his key in the lock of number sixty-six and went in. He had left the small hall light on. It was an overhang from when Karen was alive; she always left that light on and sometimes the radio. She said it always made it feel like you weren't coming home to an empty house. Jim had tried the radio theory for a few weeks after her death, but it upset him, for when he opened the living room door he always expected Karen to be sitting near the fireplace listening to her favourite radio programme. He walked through to the kitchen and turned on the light. He had left everything tidy, his mug stood near the kettle in readiness for his return and he flicked the switch. A brew before he turned in would we most welcome and it would help take away the beery taste. While the kettle boiled, he picked up the post he had left on the side earlier and opened them. A letter from Aunt Sally telling him all about her latest ailments, an electric bill and the obligatory prize-winning letter from Reader's Digest inviting him to purchase a long playing record set of all the favourites from the fifties. He laid them to one side and put a teabag in the mug. Karen had always favoured 'proper tea leaves', but since he had been on his own, the thought of dealing with a tea strainer and leaves blocking the plughole somehow did not appeal.

He yawned loudly and stretched his arms outward. He hadn't realised how tired he was. He leant over the sink to pull the curtains and caught sight of his neighbour Bill putting his teeth in a glass of water. He laughed to himself. For years Karen had been going on about removing the small fence and having a proper wall built, but somehow he had never got around to it, though his neighbours were more than willing to help with the cost. He waved to Bill who waved back, showing his gums. Life was a funny thing, he thought, as he poured the water into the mug, you never knew what was around the corner and perhaps that was just as well or you would never get out of bed in the mornings.

***

"Come on old lover," said Rita, pulling Ted to his feet. "Let's make a move, everyone else has gone. Why do you always have to be the last to leave? We are keeping that young man from his bed." She smiled at the barman who was looking across the bar anxiously.

Ted staggered to his feet and Rita led him towards the side exit. "Goodnight old love," she called. "Thanks very much, see you again."

The barman hoped very much that he would never see any of them again, they were a strange bunch. He had had his ear bent listening to tales of rolling balls, doves and some of the worst jokes he had heard since he had last pulled a Christmas cracker.

He placed the two complimentary tickets he had been given at the back of the bar and made a mental note to pass them on to an unsuspecting punter the very next day.

Once Ted was in the fresh air he seemed to come to and straightened himself up. "Sorry old gal had a bit too much tonight I think."

"Don't worry, you enjoyed yourself that's the main thing. Now are you up to walking to Nelson Road, or do you want me to grab a taxi?"

"We'd better walk," said Ted, leaning heavily on his spouse.

"Come on then," said Rita, "let's get ourselves across the market place; we'll do the scenic route via the seafront. Your head should be a bit clearer by the time we get back. Nice crowd you've got there, even old Jenny surprised me. I had always imagined her to be quite stuffy, but a few 'sherries' soon loosened her tongue. Did you know she had once danced for Miss Bluebell?"

"What, old Jenny!" Ted exclaimed. "Pull the other one it's got bells on, bluebells!"

"Bluebells, indeed! I hate to disappoint you old lover, but it's true. Maurice Beeney backed up the story. Apparently his late wife was in the line-up with her."

They carried on at a steady pace and were tooted at as the Dean Sisters passed by in a mini. "Well, I'm glad one of them is sober enough to be driving. Can't imagine what that Jill would be like in the back of a taxi. Dead common she is Ted Ricer; in fact she lets the other two down. I'm coming along to rehearsals tomorrow I want to see her rolling on a beach ball with the head she is going to have in the morning."

Ted laughed. "You're a sadist Rita so you are."

"More to the point I want to see Swoon June in action."

"You spoke to her then?"

"I most certainly did Ted Ricer, and if that is June Ashby, I mean the real June Ashby… No Ted, I think that woman is an impostor and what's more I intend to prove it."

Ted stopped and looked at his wife. "What do you mean old gal?"

I am driving back to Hull tomorrow after the rehearsals, there are some more photographs I want to collect."

"Photographs, photographs of what?" asked Ted, slightly intrigued.

"You'll see soon enough," said Rita, with a smile. "I had forgotten about them until a couple of hours ago. Don mentioned something and it triggered a memory."

"I wish I knew what you're going on about Rita; you've always had a bit of mystery about you."

Rita laughed out loud. "That's probably why you asked me to marry you. Come on Ted or we will be arriving with the milkman and Mrs Haines wouldn't like that."

Ted was going to add his own thoughts on the landlady from hell, but decided against it as it wouldn't be gentlemanly to do so in front of his lady wife.

Chapter Four *"Too Many Rivers to Cross"*

Thursday 1st May

It was five o'clock when June Ashby looked at her alarm clock, an anxious feeling causing her stomach to have butterflies. She turned on the bedside light and got out of bed and made her way to the small en-suite bathroom where she ran a bath. She went to the wardrobe and pulled out a blouse and some dark slacks which she laid on the bed. She had ordered a breakfast tray for five-thirty, courtesy of the late night receptionist. She needed to be out of the hotel by six to ensure she wasn't late for her meeting. The thought of going through yet another full dress-rehearsal filled her with dread and her hands trembled as she endeavoured to assemble the rest of her attire. She felt she needed a vodka to steady herself and tried to put the temptation out of her mind.

***

On the other side of the river Dave awoke to face his day. Sets were due to arrive for the forthcoming summer season show, new spots were to be installed and the cleaners would arrive in force to blast the theatre into a pristine condition ready for the summer season show. Dave turned to face his sleeping companion and wondered how best to handle the situation. Things had happened the night before and, though he was fully in control, he realised that Dan in his drunken stupor might awake with regrets. He got out of bed gently and went through to the kitchen and switched the kettle on. Tea and a cigarette first of all, then he would tackle the rest with his normal tact and humour. After all, he told himself, he had been here before, but maybe, just maybe, things could be different this time. He was fed up with one-night stands and having to lead a double life, but living in a small town like Great Yarmouth left him little choice. He knew there were other blokes like him out there, he had popped over to Norwich a few times to the Studio Four, but his encounters had led nowhere other than to a state of depression. He lit a cigarette and waited for the kettle to boil. He had often thought of moving away to London, but it was probably too late for that now, he was too set in his ways and, besides, he didn't want to leave his friends behind. Often he had wanted to sit down with his best mate Jim and tell him, but he wasn't sure what kind of reaction he would get. If Karen was still alive, he felt he could have told her, now he wished he had tackled the subject when he had had the chance, but it was no good going down that road. He made a pot of tea and put two mugs on a tray with a sugar bowl and milk jug.

Sod it! He thought. I'll wake him now, best get it over with.

He went into the bedroom and put the tray down on the bedside table and drew the curtains. The sky was lighting up gently and it looked promising.

He went over to the bed and gently tapped Dan's exposed shoulder.

"Morning sleepy head, I've got some tea for you."

Dan opened his eyes, which were somewhat bleary and blood shot. At first he didn't respond, and then he beamed a pearly white smile at Dave. "Hello handsome, I really thought you had been a dream. God my head is banging, what the hell did I have to drink last night?"

Dave laughed, the earlier tension he had felt, gone. "What didn't you have to drink would be a better way of answering. Did you sleep okay?"

Dan nodded and sat himself up. "Are you coming back to bed?"

"It's very tempting, but I have an early start today. I'll fix us some breakfast in a minute and run a bath for you if you'd like."

"Are you always so bloody organised in the mornings?"

Dave smiled and poured the tea. "Do you take sugar?"

"Sweet enough already, but I could murder a fag and a couple of aspirin."

Dave threw a packet of cigarettes across the bed. "Ashtray in the locker beside you, lighter somewhere on the top there and you'll find some aspirin there too."

Dan lit a cigarette and took a mouthful of tea.

"Do you remember what you said last night?" Dave asked, making himself comfortable on the edge of the double bed.

"Of course I do. Want me to repeat it word for word?"

"No need, it's all in here," said Dave, tapping his forehead. "Look, you know the score, I have to play things down here, but if you want to go on seeing me I will take the chance and get you a key cut, say in a month's time. After we have seen how it goes, then you can come back when you want to. It will save all the cloak and dagger stuff."

"Thanks Dave, that means a lot."

"I promise you there are no skeletons in my cupboard. I have never had a serious relationship, mainly because I have never met the right person and when I thought I had, they weren't. I like you Dan and I hope we will get to know each other better in the weeks to come. I am fed up running away. I want to be with someone."

"Would you consider moving away?"

"I don't know, it's too soon to say, but who knows, I might be persuaded by the right person." Dave got up. "I'll go and run that bath and start some breakfast."

Dan finished his cigarette, popped a couple of aspirin in his mouth and drank some more tea. He smiled to himself. He really hoped he and Dave would be able to make a go of it. He was willing to try and Dave's speech had already confirmed his willingness to do the same. Moving down to the East Coast was turning out to be better than he had hoped.

***

Marie Jenner had been preparing her day ahead and as she put egg and bacon in front of Sara, who was her usual grumpy self, she thought it was time she spoke her mind. "Sara I really could do with some help in the shop, can't you see your way to finding some time please?"

Sara looked at her mother through sleepy eyes. "Oh mum not that again. I am working all the hours I can at the factory. I told you, I want to make something of myself and get away from this place. Why don't you employ someone part-time?"

"Have you any idea the paperwork involved employing someone and besides I am trying to put something away for my own retirement, I get no help from your father."

"But you expect me to come and work in that pokey little shop for nothing. I get good overtime where I am."

"When have you ever done anything for me for nothing? I have always given you pocket money, even as a little girl you had everything you wanted and more. You live here for practically nothing; do you think the couple of pounds you give me towards your keep pays for very much?"

"Oh here we go, get the violins out. I'll start looking for my own place if you want to let my room."

"And a damn sight more I'd get doing so. You really are an ungrateful girl at times. Don't you worry about your mother; I'll carry on doing the long hours. When you are set up in your own place you won't find things quite as cushy my girl. You can clear your own breakfast things and when your father comes down you can give him his breakfast. I'm off out."

Sara watched her mother pull on her coat and leave by the back door. Her mother had never behaved like that before and it surprised her.

"Where's your mother off to so early?" said Alf, as he entered the kitchen in his dressing gown.

Sara huffed. "If you want any breakfast dad you'll have to get it yourself, I'll be late for work."

"And a good morning to you," said Alf, irritated at the thought of having to cook his own breakfast. He had a good mind to go to the greasy spoon, but on second thoughts the Sporting Life would come through the letterbox any minute and he fancied settling down with that. With a hearty yawn he wandered into the kitchen.

***

In a small mobile home, one of the Dean Sisters was waking to a morning chorus of dustbin men emptying bins on the Caravan Park.

Jill groaned out loud. "Give it a rest; my head has got enough banging going on without you lot as well."

"Are you ever going to get out of that pit," said Dawn, joining in the din by banging about in the kitchen area. "I ain't cooking breakfast for nothing."

"You've no mercy," replied Jill, attempting to lift her banging skull off the pillow.

"Serves you right for drinking so much," Sue added, as she came back through the main door from the park showers. "Water's freezing; think they forgot to turn on the heater. Do you good to get your head stuck under a shower my girl, that would wake your ideas up."

"You sound just like my mother."

"Pity she isn't here. She wouldn't stand for any of your nonsense."

Jill groaned again. "What's that smell? Oh gawd it's making me feel sick."

"Sausages and fried bread," Dawn replied. "Put hairs on your chest."

"I'm starving," said Sue, making herself comfortable at the table and buttering a piece of toast. "You're a whiz at cooking breakfast Dawn, if show business ever gives up on you, you could open a café."

"I wish you two would give it a rest, can't you see I'm dying?"

"You'll be dead if you muck up rehearsals today lady and no mistake," said Dawn, wielding a spatula. "Now get up, get some grub inside you and stop your belly-aching."

***

Jim had been up since six, had had breakfast, watered the plants, read the newspaper and put the rubbish out. He had made the bed and hoped he would be able to come home at lunchtime, providing rehearsals went according to plan. He picked up his car keys, locked the front door behind him and placed the small bunch of flowers he had picked from the garden earlier on the back seat and headed off to the cemetery. He liked to visit Karen at least once every two weeks, more often if time allowed, it gave him a lot of comfort to tell her all that had been going on. If she had been sitting beside him she would have listened, nodded and then added her usual words of support and, oft-times, wisdom. He removed the dead flowers from the urn, replenished the water from the stand tap and set about arranging his new offering as best he could. All the time he talked and for a moment he cried. He tidied up and stood head bowed and said the Lord's Prayer. He bid her goodbye, promised to come again soon and headed back to the car.

***

Rita was applying her eye makeup when Ted emerged from the bathroom washed and shaved. "We don't want to be late down for breakfast otherwise all the cornflakes will be gone again."

"Why she doesn't put out enough in the first place is beyond me. Proper management, that's what this place needs," said Rita, looking around her. "That bedspread looks like some one's shaved it, half the tassels are missing and that carpet won't stand much more hoovering, half of it must have disappeared up the crevice tool."

"Next time I'll book something better. Should have gone to Mrs Steer but couldn't remember the telephone number. Anyway it's only for a couple of weeks."

"They said that about Colditz and we all know how that ended."

Rita combed out her hair and lacquered it, sending a mist in the direction of Ted who was adjusting his collar. "Reet, what the hell is that, it stinks!"

"It's Love in a Mist, if you must know."

Ted laughed. "I'm not surprised it's missed, no bugger would want to find it."

Rita smiled to herself, Ted was never off stage, but she wouldn't want him any other way. She slipped on her court shoes and stood up.

"Come on lover, let's go and see what old Spitfire Haines has got to offer this morning and I bet a smile won't be on the menu."

"It is difficult to smile if you happen to be sucking on a lemon and your teeth are in a glass."

"Ted please behave or I'll not get through breakfast for laughing."

Arm in arm the two went down to the dining room to face whatever fate had in store for them.

***

June arrived at her destination with only moments to spare; she pressed the buzzer and waited for the door to be answered.

"You'd better come in. Did anyone see you?"

"No, the taxi driver dropped me at the top of the road."

"Do you want some coffee?"

June shook her head. "No thank you, I feel like my eyes are on stalks now, coffee will only make it worse."

"You know what we agreed."

"But I am not up to it. I've told you from the start, I am not ready for this. People are looking at me as if I am mad. I am having trouble remembering the words to some of the songs. If Don Stevens screams at me one more time I know I am going to crack." June fumbled in her pocket and pulled out a packet of cigarettes. "Don't look at me like that, I need one. I've bloody earned it."

"You haven't been smoking in front of the others have you?"

"Don't be so stupid, of course I haven't. I gave up ages ago didn't I?"

"Have you listened to the tapes I gave you?"

"Every spare moment I've had. But I can't play them when I am in the theatre. I can't even make a phone call, there is always someone around."

"Look, I fished these out of my suitcase; they are scores of songs you will be more familiar with. Perhaps they will agree to you using these instead of the stuff from the musicals."

Taking the music sheets gratefully, June sighed. "It's worth a try, but at this late stage who is going to write the band parts? Anyway, thank you."

"Is the hotel okay?"

"It's my salvation. The room has a lovely view overlooking the pier." She took a long, satisfying drag. "I watch the fishermen with their little stools and tackle making their way down the pier every morning. They always sit in the same spot, habit I suppose."

"How are you getting on with Jim?"

"Fine, why do you ask?"

"It's important that you get along with people, especially Jim. By all accounts he is the one that keeps the place ticking over backstage. What about the others, do they say much to you?"

"Ted has been to see me a couple of times and offered me comforting words. The Sister act seem okay, but they are young and I am not really on their wavelength."

"You see how relaxed you are now? You were like a coiled spring when you first came through that door."

June looked at her cigarette. "This has helped."

"Better make sure you have got some mints with you."

"No one is going to get that close, don't worry. Even good old Jim has cooled off."

"Look, we have time to run through a couple of those numbers I gave you, I think you will remember them. Let's try Apple Blossom Time and that funny ditty How Much is that Doggie."

As soon as June heard the melody being played on the piano she found herself singing in the right key and with confidence.

"I told you you could do it."

June smiled. "Thank you, that's the kind of tunes I am more familiar with."

"Time is getting on, you really ought to be making a move. You must not be late, it won't look good. Besides, you don't want to upset the applecart any more than you already have. Take these with you they might help your nerves."

"Bit late to start taking pills, they won't help me now."

"Stop worrying, you will be fine. Remember what I showed you."

June stood up. "I'd better be off then, wish me luck."

"You will have to catch a bus from the top of the road; it will only take a few minutes."

June looked at her watch. "It's okay, I'll walk. The air will do me good."

***

Jim went through the stage door and said good morning to Jack, collecting his mail as he did so.

"Morning Jim, good night last night wasn't it?"

"Hello Mr Stevens, yes I think the company enjoyed themselves. Let's hope it has put them in a good frame of mind for today's rehearsal."

"I was chatting away with old Rita last night, do you know she's even funnier than her old man, surprised she never trod the boards."

"But she did," replied Jim, tearing open an envelope marked urgent. "Before she met Ted, went by the name of Moira Clarence. She worked abroad mostly, and by all accounts had a great singing voice and told some very funny stories."

Don scratched his chin. "Well I'll be blessed, all these years in the business and I never knew that. She has never said anything to me and we've spoken enough times over the years."

"Ah, well Don, that's a woman who puts her man first. Story goes, when she met Ted she gave up the business and put all of her efforts into making him what he is today."

"You'll be telling me next she writes his material."

"Well you were there when she handed Ted over a wad of papers yesterday and it's my belief she didn't get them from any library."

"Say no more Jim. I don't think my heart can stand it. There she was, mine for the taking. Why, her and Ted could have toured together in one of my shows. Now I understand why she is always so firm with me and so defensive of old Ted. He's a lucky man."

"He knows that well enough because he has told me often enough. Don't you tell her I've said anything."

"Don't worry Jim I'll be discreet, though I might let slip the name of Moira Clarence into the conversation and see what response I get."

Jim began to walk away. "Good luck, and remember she has got a very swift and firm left hook."

"Thanks for the warning."

Don made his way to the auditorium and sat himself in his usual seat, third row centre. He took the tools of his trade from his large leather briefcase: pen, paper, running order, lighting sets, choreographed routines and orchestrations. He had made several notes against each, but his main concern was concentrated on the star of the show against whom a large exclamation mark was placed.

Jenny Benjamin walked out from the side door by the stage and approached him. "Sorry to interrupt you Don, but I just wanted to say a big thank you for last night. The girls really enjoyed themselves and I can honestly say there is a spring in their step this morning! They are warming up downstairs in readiness for today's run-through."

Don acknowledged Jenny with a smile. "I am very pleased to hear it Jenny. Please come and take a seat for a moment there is something I want to talk about while the others are not around."

Jenny sat herself down in the row in front so that she could maintain eye contact; she always felt this to be of great importance when dealing with Don.

"You have been in this business a number of years. I have had the pleasure of working with you and your troupe on more than one occasion when I have been producing shows and cabaret in the area. I wondered if you had made any plans for the future, someone to take over the reins when you retire."

Jenny looked more than slightly surprised. "I've never thought of retiring. Dancing is my life, the girls are my life, and the theatre is my..."

"Yes, I get the picture," Don interrupted. "But you have to realise that times are changing. Why, you only have to turn on the television and watch the Cilla Black Show, for example, and there you can see the different kinds of dancing troupes that are coming to the fore."

"I don't understand what you are saying," said Jenny, removing her spectacles and rubbing them on her velvet tunic.

"You have to admit that your routines are rather staid. I mentioned only the other day about recognising a routine I'd seen last season. The fact is that for the last five years there has been nothing new, nothing exciting."

"What are you suggesting?" she asked, with a pained expression on her face.

"You need new blood; you need to hand over to someone younger. Jenny, what I am trying to say, rather badly, is you need to step down."

"You're sacking me!"

"No I am not sacking you. I cannot sack you from your own business. But I feel it is only fair to tell you that when the curtain falls on this little show, I will no longer be engaging your services. I am very sorry, but I believe that you and I have reached the parting of the ways."

"Oh!" was all that Jenny could manage as she excused herself and went back to the dressing rooms.

Don sighed and admitted to himself that he felt like a complete bastard, and maybe he had not handled it as tactfully as he might, but that was show business.

The company was beginning to assemble backstage. Jim was visiting each dressing room to ensure the internal tannoy was working. Ted was in fine fettle considering the state he had been in the night before; Mystic Brian was talking to his doves and reassuring them that everything would be wonderful when the magic music played. Two of the Dean Sisters were putting on their pumps, while the third was throwing up in the sink, and Maurice Beeney and his boys were tuning up in the pit. There was no sign of June.

Rita walked into the auditorium determined to watch the dress-rehearsal through before heading off to Hull. Don spotted her. "Rita darling come and sit beside me I'd value your opinion on this morning's proceedings."

Rita sat herself down and smiled. "Well Don, I am honoured. You just keep your eyes on the action and your hands firmly on your pen and paper."

Don laughed. "Rita I don't know what you can be thinking."

"Just remember, Don Stevens, I've got your number. Have a Polo, it will help you to focus."

***

Dave was just walking past the Sands box office when Maud Bennett spotted him as she was crossing the road.

"Dave," she shouted, "wait a minute love."

Dave stopped in his tracks and waved to Maud who hurried over to him. "Have you got time for a brew?"

"Not this morning Maud me old love, I've got a lot on. All the gear is arriving and I am already late."

"None of my business I know, but how well do you know June Ashby?"

"June Ashby!" Dave exclaimed. "You're the second person who has mentioned her to me. Apart from the photograph in your box office window, I have never as much as seen the woman, why?"

"Someone thought they saw you with her coming out of the Tower the other night."

Dave laughed. "Dick Boggis! He asked me who I was with, I wouldn't say. Did your source also tell you that Dick was as drunk as a lord? Yes, Dick did see me with a lady, well a lady of sorts. It was Alan from the Tower nightclub."

Maud suddenly felt embarrassed. "Alan?"

"You might know him as Lana, one of the best female impersonators ever! You should catch the floor show some time, strictly for adults you understand. He was in costume. I was walking him across the parade to his car. Alan was on his way to do another show in Lowestoft."

"Oh Dave I am so sorry."

"Don't lose any sleep over it Maud. Some people have got nothing better to do than make idle gossip."

Maud was mortified. Just wait till I see that Lilly, she thought to herself.

"Dave I really am sorry. The only reason I mentioned it was because I thought that if you and June were seeing each other, it might upset Jim."

"How does Jim fit into the equation?" Dave asked, pushing his hands deep into his jeans pockets.

"I think Jim might be sweet on her."

"Sorry Maud, but I've heard enough. I know you are a great friend of Jim's, as indeed I am, but I think he is old enough and wise enough to lead his own life without any interference from either of us." And without saying a word of goodbye he walked off in the direction of the Wellington Pier leaving a rather shamefaced Maud to open her box office.

***

June had meant to catch the bus, but she found herself walking into town having lost all sense of the time. She gazed in the window of Arnolds, the department store, and was tempted to go inside. It had been a while since she had looked around shops of any kind. The store was reasonably busy and she took the caged lift to the first floor. The lift attendant nodded at her as she left and pointed her in the direction of the ladies fashions. She picked up several blouses and looked at them in great detail, trying to decide in her mind if she had anything in her wardrobe that would go with any of them. A sales assistant walked by and offered help, but June smiled, politely declining. She moved away from the section and looked at summer dresses and found her mind drifting away to wooded picnic areas with a cloth laid out on a grassy patch with food and drink.

Her train of thought was interrupted by the voice of another sales assistant. "Did madam require any help?"

June, half-dazed, gazed into the face of the woman in front of her and opened her mouth to reply, but she couldn't find her voice.

"Is madam all right?"

The hanger June was holding slipped from her fingers and she stood rooted to the spot unable to move.

"Perhaps madam would like a chair, you are looking very flushed." She motioned to another assistant nearby to bring over a chair and helped June sit down.

"Julie, some water for the lady please."

June gripped the glass tightly and raised it to her lips, but as she did so felt her hold loosen and the water splashed over her as the glass fell to the floor.

"Julie, ask Mrs Mason to call a doctor, I think the lady is ill."

June suddenly became aware of her surroundings and on hearing the word doctor stood up and ran down the staircase and out of the store, her heart pounding. Panic gripped her and the passers-by in her view became blurred, disorientating her for some minutes. She took a deep breath and tried to steady herself and wiped away the beads of sweat on her forehead with a handkerchief she had tucked in her sleeve. It took a few moments before she felt able to walk and, with slightly unsteady steps at first, she began to head towards Regent Road, just managing to get out the way of an oncoming bus that tooted at her, pulling her senses firmly back into place. Not for some time had she experienced such a severe attack. She turned off Regent Road, taking the back streets so that when she eventually reached the promenade she was outside the little café, far enough away from the Golden Sands Theatre as to feel out of sight of anyone who knew her.

The same man who had served her before came out from behind the counter and greeted her with a smile. "Hello, what would you like today? It is nice to see you back again. As you see we are little quiet at present, but soon we fill up with the early morning rush."

June sat herself down and ordered a coffee and some toast. She lit a cigarette.

"What time is it please?" she asked Mario, as she now knew his name to be.

"Ten-thirty, give or take a few minutes, I must change the batteries in the clock," he replied, glancing up at the clock above his counter. "I never wear a watch; I work my day by the sun as I did back home in Italy."

How could it be ten-thirty? Where had the time gone and, more worryingly to June, where had she been? She thanked Mario and drank her coffee; she was now very late for rehearsals. She requested another coffee and ate the toast. She felt very hungry. Mario placed the second cup of coffee before her and removed the empties. He studied June and was just about to say something to her when a voice yelled, "Hey Mario, I have a message from your brother, he will be arriving in London today."

Mario turned and went to greet his best friend, leaving June with her troubled thoughts.

"Mario the lady, look!"

Mario turned back to where June had been seated and saw her lying on the floor; he rushed to her and bent down.

"Giuseppe call for help," he said, feeling June's pulse, "she doesn't seem very good."

Mario took June's bag which had fallen to the floor and opened it to see if he could find any identification. He found a card with the name Lorna Bright on it and a London address but the telephone number in the corner of the card had become worn and he was unable to read it. There was a flyer advertising the show at the Sands Theatre, some makeup, a handkerchief, a quarter bottle of vodka and a small bottle of white pills.

"The ambulance is on the way," said Giuseppe. "Do you know who she is?"

"She has been in here a couple of times. I found this card, Lorna Bright it says."

Mario lifted June's head and placed a cushion from one of the chairs under it. "She is not breathing very well."

"The ambulance will be here soon Mario; they will know what to do."

Chapter Five   *"Whose that Lady?"*

Jim walked along the aisle to where Don and Rita were sitting. "Sorry to be the bearer of bad news, but June Ashby is not in her dressing room and nowhere in the theatre to my knowledge."

Don took off his spectacles; his neck had begun to redden which was always a bad sign.

Rita took his arm. "Now Don, please calm yourself, take a deep breath. Jim, could you get Don some water please?"

"I don't need any bloody water," said Don through gritted teeth. "I want the person whose name appears on posters all over this town to be in her dressing room getting ready."

"I've checked with her hotel, they said she left hours ago," Jim replied. "Shall I give Derinda Daniels a call?"

Don shook his head. "I think she has taken a booking for a club in Manchester. I can hardly blame her, I really thought Ashby was going to do the stuff so I released Derinda, fool that I am. My own instincts should have told me differently."

"The girl could be ill," said Rita. "Has anyone thought of that? She might be lying in some hospital bed somewhere."

"I'll check with the General and see if they have had any admissions," said Jim, moving away. "I won't be long."

"There must be a solution," said Rita. "I cannot believe the great Don Stevens hasn't got another trick up his sleeve."

A grin suddenly came to Don's face. "If only I knew where to get hold of Moira. Now, whatever was her last name...?"

***

During the winter Lilly worked full-time at the General until the season got under way at the Sands when she reduced her hours to work between the two. She had been doing it for so long she could never remember which she had started with first. Cleaning hospitals was hardly the job she had mapped out for herself back in her youth. Though considered by her teachers to be promising, she had never been allowed to pursue her dreams and was forced into the work by an overbearing mother and a father whose fists were ready more often than not to give young Lilly a clip round the ear if she didn't obey orders. A job cleaning a big house in the town had been her first job and, as word spread of Lilly's hard work, she soon found herself being sought after by others. Lilly had really wanted to be a librarian and consoled herself by joining the library and touching the pages of books she one day hoped to own for herself. Lilly was a secret reader. As a young girl she would smuggle books into her draughty bedroom and read them by torchlight under the bedclothes. She was particularly fond of history and historic novels, reading about the courts of King Louis of France and King Henry VIII. Words fascinated her and through her own determination she overcame the earlier reading problems she had had and found help in an old lady she cleaned for, a former English teacher who in turn for some household chores taught Lilly all she needed to know about reading and writing. To the outside world Lilly remained the Lilly everyone had come to know. Her parents died totally unaware that their daughter had hidden talents.

An ill-fated marriage to a childhood sweetheart left her a widow at the age of just twenty-five and she had never remarried or expressed any interest in another man. She struck a lonely figure of fun in her overalls to those who knew her as she confidently went between the jobs of her daily routines. But when she went home to her small council home, Lilly became the person she had always wanted to be. She would lay her books out on the large dining room table and study. In her bedside locker there was a handwritten draft of a story she had been working on secretly for years and that one day she hoped to see published. Lilly had visualised that day so many times in her mind's eye, her book on the bookshelves of the Jarrolds store and her friends gaping in wonder when they read of their friend's success in the world of literature.

Every Tuesday evening as regular as clockwork Lilly took the bus to Lowestoft where in a church hall she attended a small writing class. She had found out about the class quite by accident some years previously while helping to set up a jumble sale and had seen a small poster advertising it.

At first she had been wary of bumping into someone she knew, but the class consisted of a couple of elderly ladies who wrote articles for the church magazine and a small group of middle-aged women who were very much into poetry. The tutor was a Polish gentleman who had seen a few of his own works published during his sixty years and was eager to help others and from whom Lilly had learned a great deal. It was the part of the week she looked forward to most.

Lilly clanked her bucket along the hospital corridor and into the cupboard allotted to her. She emptied the water down the tiny sink and cleaned away her utensils. It was time to be getting off to the Sands to do her daily stint there before setting off home to braise some stewing steak she had got cheap from her local butcher. Enough there for two days she had surmised, and a few more pennies to add to the savings account she had set up for herself.

As she passed though Emergency on her way out she noticed the face of the woman on the trolley that had just been wheeled in. Lilly did a double take, surely that was June Ashby lying there? She grabbed the attention of the receptionist. "Lizzie, the lady on the trolley, is that June Ashby?"

Lizzie looked up from her paperwork. "Hello, Lilly my love. No, according to this it is someone called Lorna Bright. Why, do you know her?"

"Well I thought I did, sort of. She's in the show at the Golden Sands, but I know her as June Ashby, I am sure it is her."

"Don't they use different names on the stage?" said Lizzie, tapping her pencil on her admittance book. "You know, like that Engelbert Humperdinck. I'm sure that can't be his real name, I mean, what mother would call her son Engelbert?"

Lilly watched as the trolley was wheeled away. "I'll mention it to Jim when I get to work."

Lizzie put down her pencil and ran her fingers through her hair. "How is Jim these days?"

Lilly picked up her bag. "He's fine as far as I know."

"Tell him I was asking after him."

"I will," said Lilly, as she made her exit. Lizzie was always the same, after anything in trousers.

***

"I cannot see Moira Anderson wanting to come along to Great Yarmouth at short notice. Come on Don, I think you are in dreamland now."

Don took Rita's hand. "My dear I wasn't thinking of Moira Anderson. I have heard tell of a Moira Clarence."

"Who is that? Must be before my time," Rita replied, pulling her hand away.

"Rita, I know."

A memory long buried came flooding back to Rita and she felt a tear prick her eyelids. She turned away so that Don wouldn't see. "Moira was a long time ago," she said quietly. Taking a few moments to compose herself she turned to face him again. "And no, Don Stevens, Moira Clarence is not about to make a comeback," she said with her usual confident air.

"But why ever not?" Don exclaimed, seizing the moment. "Think what a great headline it would make in the local press."

Rita smiled. "Oh yes, I can see it now and you're right of course, it would make a great headline and lift this little show out of the depths it finds itself in at the moment. Moira Clarence was never going to be a household name Don and I have never fooled myself into thinking otherwise. But Moira did think that with some help she could make the name of Ted Ricer become one. Well she nearly succeeded; it was only Hughie who put the mockers on that."

"Old Ted on Opportunity Knocks?"

"He never got past the second audition. Been in the business too long, knew the ropes, Hughie wouldn't have been able to mould him. Look at the Dean Sisters; they pay homage at every given chance. I read an article about them and how they owed everything to Uncle Hughie."

"Well the Bachelors haven't done so badly."

"Call it sour grapes if you like," Rita continued, "but my Ted had the talent and a helping hand in the right direction could have delivered his own television show."

Don reflected for a moment and smiled at Rita. "I respect your wishes Rita. I will not mention the name of Moira Clarence again, but don't ever lose sight of your talent."

Jim approached the two. "No luck with the General. Sorry Don I cannot think were June might have got to."

Don sighed. "Well, let's see what we have got and then deal with what we haven't after. I can't keep Maurice and the boys waiting any longer, he has been holding that baton for far too long, I am surprised he hasn't joined a relay race. Poor old sod."

Don stood up and moved to the front of the stalls and picked up the mike connected to the tannoy system. "Right you lot, we are going to do a run-through. Miss Ashby's playbacks will be heard without the lady herself, she has been held up. Everything is to happen exactly as if she were here. We will start in five minutes so be ready as soon as Maurice and his boys strike the first note."

Rita moved to the side of the auditorium where Jim now stood.

"A fine mess this is young Jim and no mistake."

Jim shrugged his shoulders. "If he cuts Ashby's numbers, he'll be knocking a good forty-five minutes off the show. The punters won't stand for being short-changed and it will leave a hell of gap between the two houses. I've exhausted all the places I can look for her, where the hell can she be?"

Rita squeezed his arm. "I don't know old lover but I've a feeling she will turn up yet."

***

"You're in a hurry Lilly Brocket," said Maud, as she emerged from her box office to stretch her legs.

"Morning Maud can't stop. Catch you later," huffed Lilly, tearing along the pier.

"You want to be careful Lilly or they will be entering you in the Donkey Derby next month and no mistake."

"Hi there Maud."

The voice of Dave Grant made her turn round quickly. "Oh Dave, you gave me a start."

"Where is our Lilly going to in such a rush?" he asked, lighting a cigarette.

"Well, she says she can't be late. Doesn't start for another half hour to my reckoning, never been late in her life, maybe she wants to get finished early. How are things up at the Wellie?"

"Coming along nicely thanks," Dave replied. "I was thinking of bringing a friend along to see this here show one night, any chance of a couple of comps?"

"Of course there is," said Maud.

Taking the olive branch that he knew Maud was offering, Dave followed her into her office. "Normally, Jim gives me some freebies to hand out, but I haven't seen so much of him lately."

Maud switched the kettle on. "Dave, I've wanted to say…"

"No need Maud. It isn't worth getting worked up about, words between mates that's all."

Maud was relieved. She hated bad feeling.

"How are the bookings going?" Dave asked, making himself comfortable on a stool.

"Not bad as it happens. It seems to be pretty busy. The seasonal show is booking very well too, I love the summer shows. I know you can watch some of the stars on the telly, but seeing them live on that stage is really the best."

Dave nodded in agreement. "Bit of drama at Mario's this morning by all accounts. One of the boys called by and apparently they had had an ambulance there, some woman had collapsed."

Maud's face lit up, she liked a bit of gossip from time to time. "Anyone we know?"

"Don't think so. Probably a holidaymaker, Giuseppe is hardly the most reliable source of information at the best of times. He has the attention span of a gnat. I was quite surprised he'd actually remembered anything."

Maud poured boiling water into the teapot.

"He comes from a nice family. I knew his mother, we used to see each other at bingo. I wonder who the woman was."

Just then someone appeared at the box office window.

"Pour the tea Dave, there's a love. I'll just help this lady. Now my love which performance were you interested in?"

***

The lady leaned heavily on her walking stick as she made her way slowly along the pier. The dark glasses and tightly knotted headscarf kept much of her face hidden. She wore a smart, dark navy blue coat and low-heel court shoes. Each step was a painful one, not only in body but in memory. She sat down on the first bench she came to and caught her breath. The sun was particularly bright and made the rippling sea glisten. There were a few people walking along the seashore and one or two young children playing and collecting pebbles in tiny tin buckets.

She looked towards the theatre, which seemed an endless walk away, but she knew it had to be done and had prepared herself for the reception she would receive and whatever outcome it would bring.

The lady shivered at the thought.

Her memory recalled the hum of an audience as they made their way to their seats and the smiles of the usherettes selling programmes. An orchestra tuning up played through her head and she felt the giddiness and excitement of the thrill it had given her. She pulled herself up and placed her handbag on her arm. Placing her walking stick firmly in front of her she continued her pilgrimage along the slatted pier. She stopped from time to time to catch her breath and to drink in more of the wonders around her, transporting her back to the days of yesteryear when everything in her life seemed to be mapped out and was there for the taking.

***

The train had just reached Acle as Debbie glanced up from her Woman's Weekly. She had often travelled this line with her mother to Norwich on one of her shopping trips. They were always a special treat and as a little girl Debbie had loved watching the cows and horses from the train window as it went on its way.

Today her heart was heavy. Her marriage to Peter had hit a problem and the move to Huddersfield had proven to be a disaster as far as she was concerned. Her job wasn't going too well and she had become homesick for Great Yarmouth. The realisation that she missed her father more than words could say didn't sit easy with her. Peter and her had argued over petty things and it was he who finally suggested she take a trip back to her hometown to see her father for a few days. She still had her own key to the house and planned to take her small suitcase back there first before setting off to the seafront to find her dad. What a lovely surprise it would be for him. She knew how much he still pined for her mother and that her own breaking away from the family home had been too soon, not only for him, but also for her. She opened her purse and took a small photograph of her mother from it. Even when her mother had been ebbing away, she had always given Debbie hope. Hope that she would pull through, hope that Debbie would one day make someone a wonderful wife and hope that if the worst did happen, they would again meet in a different world.

The train pulled out from Acle station and began the last leg of its journey to Yarmouth Vauxhall. Debbie adjusted her hair and put away her magazine. What if her and Peter couldn't make a go of it in Huddersfield? Would he agree to move back here? What if he wouldn't? What if they parted? So many 'what ifs'. Her mother would have understood what she was going through, but her mother was no longer around to ask. Perhaps her father would be able to give her some advice. If not, she would seek out Auntie Maud; she was always ready to listen and offer words of wisdom.

Debbie got off the train and walked out of the station. She couldn't decide whether to take a taxi or walk over the bridge to Southtown. It really wasn't that far, but she felt hot and the small case seemed to weigh a ton, so she got into a taxi and settled back in her seat to enjoy the sights of the place she had missed so much. The fleet of local blue buses could be seen lined up near the Town Hall and a solitary red bus on its way to Lowestoft was ahead going over Haven Bridge. She could just see the Eastern Princess and the Golden Galleon moored at the quayside awaiting the busy summer season ahead when the holidaymakers would flock to them to take a trip around the Norfolk Broads. The memory of her first trip out to Scroby Sands to see the seals was as clear now as it had been then. The familiar sight of the Two Bears Hotel came into view as the taxi went over the bridge and the realisation that she was just a few minutes away from home filled her heart with happiness.

***

"Lilly whatever is the matter?" said Jim, catching hold of her.

Lilly looked fit to drop.

"I've got something to tell you," Lilly panted. "It's something very important."

"We are about to start rehearsals, can it wait until after then?"

"Not if you want to know where June Ashby is."

Jim went straight over to Don. "Don can we halt the rehearsal for a moment, Lilly has found June?"

"So where is she?" he asked. "Hiding underneath Lilly's skirt?"

"Look, perhaps we ought to move to the back of the theatre Don, out of the way of listening ears."

"Okay Jim, give me a minute, I'll make an announcement and join you."

"I would suggest the office but Scottie is in there catching up on some box office receipts."

Don waved his hand and Jim took Lilly to the back of the stalls. "Let's sit down here Lilly. Get your breath and Don will join us in a minute."

The rehearsal was stalled for another half hour, much to the relief of Mystic Brian, who had lost a dove, and one of the Dean Sisters whose costume had come unravelled at the edge and needed some stitching. Maurice Beeney raised his hands in despair and went off to find solace in a cup of tea and the cream horn he had been saving for later.

Rita was backstage doing her best to comfort Jenny Benjamin and trying to reassure her that her career hadn't come to an end just because Don Stevens said he wasn't going to employ her any more. Ted was running through some new material given to him by Rita and two of the backstage boys were trying to rectify the walk-down staircase that had mysteriously decided to come adrift in the middle and become two instead of one.

Don seated himself beside Lilly. "Now Lilly, Jim here says you know where we can find June, is this true?"

Lilly nodded, turning first to Don and then to Jim. "She is in the General. I saw her with my own eyes on a trolley in Emergency."

"But I phoned the General myself and they had no record of June," said Jim, puzzled.

"That's because it is Lorna Bright, my sister. I am June Ashby."

The three of them turned to see a lady swathed in a tight headscarf, wearing dark glasses and leaning on a walking stick.

Don stood up. "I am sorry madam, but who did you say you were?"

The voice though cracked was steady. "I am June Ashby, the person who has been masquerading as me is my twin sister."

"I don't think I understand," Jim said, looking quizzically at Don. "June Ashby has been rehearsing here all week…"

The lady became impatient in her reply. "You are not listening to me. I am June Ashby."

"I think you had better explain," said Don.

The lady nodded. "I would be happy to. But not here, somewhere a little more private if that could be arranged." There was a certain command in her voice which immediately made people sit up and listen.

"I'll see if Bob will vacate the office for an hour," said Jim, moving down the aisle.

***

Debbie paid the driver and turned the key in the front door. The photograph of her mother stood on the sideboard where it had always been and the one of Debbie when she was six, with her front tooth missing, sitting on her first tricycle. She put down her suitcase and picked up the frame and gazed at her mother's photograph. She could not stop the tears welling as she thought of the days long past. The image of her mother patiently showing her how to knit a scarf for her doll, rolling pastry on her very own board and the excitement when her mother had taken her jam tarts from the oven and put them on a plate for tea for when daddy came home. Going to the seafront to play on the beach and learning to swim at the pool. Shopping in the market place and helping her to read her favourite story about the little people who lived beneath the floorboards in a big house. There were so many happy memories and so many happy days.

She went through to the kitchen and filled the kettle. Her father's newspaper lay on the table together with his reading glasses. Everywhere was clean and tidy, it was just as her mother would have had it. She ran up the stairs and into her parents' bedroom. The double bed had been made and her father's pyjamas lay neatly folded on the pillowcase, again as her mother would have done.

She went into the second bedroom and everything was just as she had left it. It had been dusted, the carpet hoovered and the bed made up ready.

She went back down the stairs and made herself a coffee. The fridge was well-stocked. Debbie stirred her drink, feeling very proud of her father. He had managed to cope. All of the things she had worried about had been taken care of. If her mother was looking down from heaven she felt sure that she would be very proud too!

***

Bob Scott didn't need much persuading, anything to get away from the accounts. He made himself scarce and the small party seated themselves down in the reasonable comfort of the office.

June Ashby removed her dark glasses and headscarf. Her eyes were heavy with dark circles and the little hair she had was sparse and white. She wore no makeup and her face was slightly wrinkled as if exposed to too much sunlight.

Lilly was riveted; she couldn't take her eyes off her as she began to speak.

The lady appeared to drift into another world and began speaking from memory, with no further reference to the statement she had made earlier and she didn't wait for any kind of introduction from the group sat in front of her.

"My twin sister and I went to a stage school at an early age. We used to do a variety act involving singing and some magic. I would front the show and a member of the audience would seal me in a box on stage from which I would disappear. Lorna would immediately enter the auditorium from the back and it would seem to the audience that some kind of magic had taken place. The act was called One and One. No one, apart from our agent, knew there were two of us."

"But surely the stage crew would know?" Jim queried.

The lady looked at Jim and smiled. "My good man you are interrupting me. I do not like to be interrupted. May I continue?"

Jim blushed and nodded.

The manner in which she was speaking reminded Don of a story he had once heard tell about June Ashby, that she could put someone down with the mere flutter of an eyelash. The June he had been working with seemed mellow by comparison.

"We toured the act for a couple of years until my aunt, our agent, felt that we had exhausted all possibilities. Lorna's voice wasn't as strong as mine, but she had some talent and I didn't want to see it go to waste. My aunt, a clever lady indeed, came up with the idea of launching me as a solo artist. Theatre history will tell you how well I succeeded and I won't bore you with the details here. Lorna became my understudy, of sorts."

She coughed. "Some water please, I am very dry."

Lilly, trying desperately not to take her eyes off the lady, moved to the sink and filled a beaker with water.

"Lilly, perhaps you could arrange some tea for us all?" Jim said.

"No fear. I'm fascinated," said Lilly, sitting herself down again and taking up her position of an observer.

The eyes of the lady moved around and looked at each of them individually. "I am sorry if this is rather a long-winded way of explaining things, I will try to keep it short, you have a show to rehearse."

"Please continue," said Don, reaching in his pocket for a cigar. Damn it, he had left them in the stalls.

"Unfortunately, an infection of chicken pox in her late teens left Lorna with a nervousness that could only be controlled by medication and she was greatly relieved not to have to perform regularly. She did, however, always learn all of my lines and rehearse all of my songs." She turned and looked Don straight in the eye. "I believe you came to see a performance of that musical Mr Stevens."

Don nodded.

A smile passed over the frail-looking mouth. "You also saw me in a review at the Lyric."

There was a long silence. Lilly continued to stare and Jim fidgeted trying to make head and tail of it all, while Don racked his brains trying to recall any of the stories he had heard of the lady in front of him and he knew there had been several over the years.

"I am feeling rather tired so I will move ahead and bring you up to date. Just over five years ago I was told I didn't have long to live, cancer." She turned her attention to Jim for a moment. "I was sorry to hear that your wife had died of cancer, it must have been a terrible blow for you. Cancer is a terrible disease."

Jim nodded a reply and stared at the floor.

June continued. "However, I agreed to take a musical in London that had been written for me, little realising how ill I was to become. Hence my sudden departure from it. In an attempt to keep the story quiet, my aunt released a statement saying I was exhausted. It only ever made the London papers and the show faded without a trace." She paused. "I know what you are all thinking, why didn't Lorna take my place?"

Lilly nodded.

"Lorna had become heavily reliant on medication, sometimes the demon drink, and for her own safety was admitted at great expense to a private clinic. Then my aunt died suddenly."

The lady opened her handbag and took two photographs from it and handed them to Don. "One is me, the other is Lorna. If you look very closely you will notice a small mole on Lorna's forehead, normally hidden by makeup. You will notice I do not have such a mole and I am wearing no makeup at all."

Don studied the photographs and then looked at June. Satisfied, he handed the photographs to Jim and Lilly.

"There is such a lot I don't understand. Both yourself and Lorna have been, are terribly sick, why put her through the ordeal of another show?"

"Lorna came out of New Dawn House some three months ago and she certainly seemed to be more like her old self again. I, on the other hand, as you can see for yourself, have not fared so well. I love my sister dearly, neither of us ever found happiness with a member of the opposite sex, me because I never entertained the idea and Lorna always met the wrong kind. Another reason I suspect that she took to drinking heavily. Gwen, your PA, was known to me and used to visit me often and she told me of this show you were planning for Great Yarmouth. Just one more time I wanted to see my name at the top of the theatre hoarding before I went to meet my maker. But I also wanted to see Lorna shine again and give her back the confidence she will need once I am gone, my days are numbered now. After all she has never known anything else. However, the plan went horribly wrong when Mr Stevens here insisted on introducing songs that, quite frankly, I would have trouble remembering now. As for the ones from South Pacific, we desperately tried to work on them, but Lorna didn't have the strength or courage to pull them off. A voice ruined by vodka and twenty Capstan full strength a day. Funny really, that I should be the one who ended up with the cancer." She paused for a moment and then continued. "Even with all my coaching I couldn't get her to lip-synch properly. The idea of using a click-track was a prayer answered of sorts but it appears she is struggling with that. Only this morning I gave her some sheet music of songs more familiar to her, if you use these in place of show tunes you may find the voice in better form. My sister cannot be trusted with tablets. I think Lorna may have tried to kill herself today."

The conversation seemed to veer from one thing to another and it became clear that the mind was muddled and somewhat confused. June then broke down in heavy sobs. Lilly came to her rescue and gave her a fresh handkerchief.

"I'll get you some more water," said Jim.

Don wiped the beads of sweat from his forehead, not being able to get his head around what he had heard. He was incredulous that all this time Gwen, his trusted secretary and part-time lover, had been hiding a secret from him.

June dried her eyes and continued. "I know how it must look to all of you, but I wanted Lorna to have the chance I knew I would never have again."

She took a long drink of water.

"Gwen is at the hospital checking things out. I have been renting a house here and the telephone number was found in Lorna's bag. The hospital rang and Gwen went straight to her."

"But Gwen was in London when I last spoke to her," said Don.

"She certainly was, but she has since called you here in this very theatre. She was calling from my rented accommodation."

"Can I just cut in here," said Jim, getting to his feet. "We are writing Lorna off as if she is dead. She may just be okay. I don't profess to know much about June, I mean Lorna, but the woman I spent quite a few hours with never struck me as someone who would take her own life."

June nodded. "You have a point, of course, but you don't really know my sister. Until we hear from Gwen we won't know the situation."

"What makes you think she has tried to take her life anyway?" Jim continued.

"She was very low when we met early this morning, I assumed she might try, she has once before."

Lilly had listened and up until then had kept relatively quiet. "I think you all need to take a deep breath and wait to hear what the situation really is. Lorna could still fulfil her sister's wish and perform."

The company turned and looked at Lilly in surprise, the pussy cat had roared.

"Lilly has got a point," said Jim, agreeing. "But what we have heard must never go any further."

"Are we all agreed then?" Don asked. "As Jim suggested, this conversation goes no further than the four of us."

June sighed. "I came here expecting to be lynched. Thank you; thank all of you for your support."

The door suddenly opened and Rita came in. "Oh, I am terribly sorry I was looking for Bob."

"Rita my dear come in," said Don, standing up. "Following our conversation the other evening there is someone, with permission from those present, I should very much like you to meet. Rita can be trusted I assure you."

107

***

Freda looked at Muriel's purchase. "How much did you say that cost?"

"Twenty-nine pounds," said Muriel, looking at the expression on her neighbour's face. "Don't you like it? I thought I'd wear it to the Sands."

"Twenty-nine pounds Muriel, you could have got one on the market for much less than that. In fact, you could have got two, even three."

"My Barry likes to see me wear a bit of class when we step out."

"Well my Dick wouldn't know if I was wearing class or not. It's very nice I must say. The colour suits you and not everyone can wear green."

"It's emerald."

"Emerald, green, it's all the same to me."

"What you going to wear then Freda?"

"I thought I'd give my floral print an outing."

"Is that the one with the big roses?" Muriel asked.

Freda nodded. "It is."

"That's the one your Vera's Mary was sick down at the fête last summer wasn't it?"

Freda blushed. "It came up lovely with a bit of Daz. I'll have you know Muriel Evans, that dress is a hundred per cent polywossname."

Muriel winced at the thought. "I suppose Dick is going to come? Only the other day when Barry was talking to him he said he was in two minds."

Freda laughed. "He's never in the right one, let alone two. He will be coming don't you fret. I wonder if Lilly is going to bring someone with her. It will be a nice evening out that will be and there's the party to look forward to afterwards. I hope they do sausages on sticks."

"I've no doubt they will, and pineapple and cheese as well," replied Muriel, as she raised her eyes to the ceiling. "Oh, they know how to push the boat out." Muriel made a mental note to pack a couple of decent ham sandwiches and a pork pie apiece for her and Barry. None of that party fare for her, not after spending so much on a new frock!

***

When Dave walked into Henry's Dan was just finishing serving a customer.

Dave winked. "Hi Dan, pint of best please and one for yourself."

"I didn't expect to see you in here today."

"I've just been along to see Maud and make my peace with her. I don't like there to be bad blood between us. I've managed to nab us a couple of comps for the show. I hope you can get a night off, I'd like you to come along with me."

"Steady on mate," said Dan, putting the pint of beer down on the counter. "You'll have the natives talking."

"Sod the bloody natives," said Dave, taking a swift gulp of beer. "I am beginning to think that life really isn't worth living if you can't relax and be who you really are."

Dan smiled. "Let's just take things one day at a time shall we?"

"Sounds like the old me talking," replied Dave, lighting a cigarette. "Well, this is the new me and the others can go hang themselves."

Stella walked through from the back bar. "Hello Dave, haven't seen you in a while, been keeping you busy have they?"

"Hello Stella, nice to see you. Yep, the theatre is looking pretty good at the moment. I was just asking Dan here if he'd like to come along and see the show at the Golden Sands, I've got a couple of comps. I thought seeing as he is new in town it would be a good opportunity for him to meet some of the locals afterwards."

"You're very thoughtful Dave, you really are," said Stella, with a smile. "I am always happy to change a night shift with you Dan if you'll do my lunch stint. Just let me know what day and we will sort it out."

"Thanks Stella I really appreciate that."

"Old Ken won't mind, I'll square it with him. As long as I am able to get to my hairdresser at some point and get my roots done."

Dan kissed Stella on the cheek. "You're a pal, I won't forget it."

"Yeah thanks Stella," said Dave in agreement. "Get Stella a G and T Dan."

Stella gave one of her gravelly laughs. "Gin and tonic at lunchtime, oh you boys will have me tipsy. Make it a large one Dan, but only charge for a single."

Dave grinned at Dan. "And while you're at it you can put another one in there, I'm feeling lucky today."

Dan smiled at Dave. Great Yarmouth really wasn't a bad place to be.

***

June looked at Rita and smiled. "Well I'm dashed!"

Rita walked over to June and shook her hand gently. "I am very pleased to meet you, at last."

"I wonder if you would mind leaving Rita and me alone for a few minutes."

Lilly, Don and Jim exchanged glances and left the office.

Intrigued, Rita sat down opposite June.

"You are Moira Clarence aren't you?" said June, looking Rita in the eye.

Rita blushed. "How do you know, has Don been gossiping?"

"No my dear, I knew it was you as soon as you walked into the room. My Aunt Bernice saw your act on a cruise ship once and offered you work with her agency. She thought you had a wonderful talent and wanted you on her books. I saw you on her recommendation and agreed."

Rita tried to recall the moment. "I am very sorry, but I don't remember your aunt, are you sure you have got the right person? There was a Moira Moraine, perhaps you mean her."

"The agency was called ABP – Aunt Bernice Presentations, she would have introduced herself to you as Bernie Bernard."

Rita thought for a moment. "She smelt of lavender water."

"You've got her in one. Her big hats, feathers, she was completely over the top. I am almost convinced that Danny based his act on my aunt. She would have been wonderful on the stage. Strange how it's the lavender water that always sticks in people's minds above all else."

"Old-fashioned isn't it, lavender water," said Rita, congratulating herself on how she had pulled that one out of the hat. She had certainly heard of Bernie Bernard but knew she had never met her.

June took a small bottle of lavender water from her bag and showed it to Rita. "I always carry one as a reminder of the old gal."

There was an agreed silence between them as if they were paying respect to Aunt Bernice and then June continued, "I fear that Don and co will be waiting for news of my sister, the other June Ashby, and what can be done to save the show."

Rita eyed the lady in front of her who held herself well despite her slight disability. She reminded Rita of those old Hollywood film stars, and that was something that didn't sit well with Rita. This lady was obviously a good actress. How could this person be a twin, a sister possibly but, a twin, never. Just like the previous June she had met, Rita was not convinced, but for the sake of whatever charade these two were playing she chose to go along with it, for now!

***

Lorna opened her eyes. Gwen was looking at her. "It's okay Lorna you are in hospital."

"What happened?"

"You fainted that's all, you had one of your turns."

Lorna's face looked ashen. "I haven't been feeling myself."

"Look, they are going to let you out in a couple of hours. Your sister is at the theatre now explaining things."

"Oh God, why has she interfered, she didn't want anyone to know?"

Gwen squeezed Lorna's hand. "It was bound to come out sooner or later. The plan is to keep it out of the press. I need to ask you a question Lorna," said Gwen, after a brief moment. "Did you take any tablets from your sister's cabinet this morning, only there are some missing?"

Lorna shook her head gently. "I haven't taken anything I swear. She gave me a couple of tablets this morning to steady my nerves and I always carry a bottle of aspirin, but I swear that is all."

"Don't worry your head about it. Let's concentrate on getting you out of here and back on your feet."

"I want to do the show for my sister. I promised her I would and I will see it through."

"We can discuss that later. I am going to have a word with the doctor and then I will pop over to the theatre and let them know the score. I'll be back soon."

Lorna lay in troubled thought; the well-thought-out plan wasn't exactly going as rehearsed. It would only be a matter of time before people began to suspect that something wasn't quite right.

***

June Ashby sat at the back of the stalls beside Rita and watched the rehearsal of the show. Hearing the voice on click-track come over the loudspeakers sent a tingle down her spine and her foot tapped gently in time to the music. For those few minutes at least she truly imagined she was on the stage performing songs from a well-known repertoire and dancing across the boards in sweeping chiffon gowns that glittered from head to toe. She heard the applause that had met the performances all those years ago and the thrill she had felt.

Rita kept a weather eye on her, concerned that it would all be too much for her to cope with. But somehow she felt deep down that this actress would handle matters with aplomb.

At the end of the rehearsal Don walked on to the stage and made a speech.

"Well, congratulations to all of you. That is the best run-through I have seen since I got here. Jenny, I know it was difficult to perform the routines without the input of Miss Ashby, but I have to say that your girls pulled it off magnificently. Perhaps you and I could have another chat later. On the subject of Miss Ashby, I am pleased to inform you that she will be here for opening night. It will be necessary for June to run through the routines with the girls again, perhaps tomorrow afternoon would be okay, Maurice and the boys have agreed to come in. As for the rest of you, you can enjoy a well-earned day off tomorrow and I look forward to seeing you all on Monday afternoon for the final technical run-through. We have a great little show and once again congratulations and good luck to you all."

There was applause from all those present on stage as Don made his exit down into the auditorium to rejoin June and Rita.

"Well, what did you think?" Don asked June.

"It was very good and I for one cannot wait to see the opening on Monday evening."

Don glanced at Rita and winked. "I am sure Rita would be happy to join you."

June touched Rita's arm lightly. "If Rita isn't busy with anything else, I would be most grateful, no, delighted if she would."

"I need to go and catch up with Jenny. I'll see you both later."

"Don, go easy on her, this is all she has," Rita called after him.

Don turned and smiled. "Don't worry Reet, everything will be just fine."

***

Jim made his way home, needing to put as much distance between him and theatre as he could. It had been a strange day with more to come tomorrow. He would need to be on hand when Lorna rehearsed, if only for some kind of moral support. He decided to stroll up Regent Road, briefly through the town and over the bridge to home. A walk always helped him clear his head.

He bumped into Dave coming along King Street who, if he wasn't mistaken, seemed a little worse for drink.

Dave blurted out some kind of mumbo-jumbo at him and Jim managed to catch the names Dan and Stella and something about a new beginning. He patted his old mate on the back and sent him on his way, promising to catch up with him after the opening on Monday. Right now, home beckoned and he thought a nice fry-up with a cup of tea would go down a treat. He waved to a couple of people he recognised at the bus stop and began his walk over the bridge. The traffic was picking up as Saturday shoppers drove their cars home and the buses would soon become packed with shop workers as they headed home after another long day on their feet. It wouldn't be long before the town became even busier with the hustle and bustle of the summer visitors packing into the many guest houses and hotels.

As Jim opened his front door he was greeted by the smell of bacon cooking. For a fleeting moment he thought Karen had come back. He snapped out of his momentary thought when he heard a voice shout out, "Dad, is that you?"

He went through to the kitchen and saw a smiling Debbie with outstretched arms and went to hug her. "Debbie, what a lovely surprise!"

"Egg and bacon okay?" she said, turning her attention back to the cooker. "I phoned Auntie Maud at the box office and she said you were on your way. I told her not to say anything to you. I wanted it to be a surprise. Sit down and I'll pour you a cup of tea and then you can tell me all your news. Oh Dad, it is really great to see you."

They ate their meal in relative silence at first, Jim reflecting on his day and Debbie wondering how best to broach the subject of her marriage. Jim helped himself to more bread. "Why isn't Peter with you?"

Debbie was cornered, she should have known that her father had guessed she hadn't turned up out of the blue for nothing and the fact that she hadn't mentioned her husband was a dead giveaway. She stumbled on her words at first, but finally managed to give Jim a fair, she hoped, picture of the situation.

Jim listened, nodded in the right places and let his daughter get whatever was troubling her out into the open without interruption. He tried to recall how Karen would handle things if she were in the room right now. When Debbie had finished he poured himself another cup of tea, pushed away his empty plate and leaned back in his chair.

"What would your mother have to say about all of this if she were here?" he began, reaching for his cigarette packet. "That's what I have been thinking. She would probably say this – firstly, every marriage in the early stages goes through a settling period when you find things out about each other which weren't evident before. There will be some things you like about each other and there will be one or two things you dislike, but because of your feelings for each other you either learn to live with them or, if they bother you so much, take the get-out route." He lit the cigarette and continued. "No marriage is

115

perfect. When me and your mum first started dating everything was sunshine and roses. The hard bit was living together. Like us you and Peter had never shared a roof together. That step is a difficult one, the honeymoon is over and real life kicks in. You have had the added problem of moving away and making a new life in Huddersfield. To Peter that is home, the place he grew up in, home for you is here in Great Yarmouth. It is a shame Peter couldn't find suitable work down here, but then he would be going through what you are going through now. You have to ask yourself a question, do you love Peter enough to want to make it work and if the answer is yes then you know what you must do. If the answer is no then, Debs, you and Peter are facing a difficult time."

"What would you do Dad?"

"I loved your mother with all my heart, but it wasn't all easy. We had to work hard at it. If you and Peter are as committed as we were you must get your heads together and work out a compromise. It is too early to give up because you fell at the first hurdle."

Debbie stood behind her father and bent down and hugged him. "Thanks Dad. Now I really know why mum loved you so much."

While Debbie busied herself clearing away the dishes, Jim picked up the telephone and dialled. "Hi Peter it's Jim. Look, I was wondering how you would be fixed for getting down here for a couple of days. The show at the Sands has its opening night and it would be great if you and Debs could be there together. There will be a first night party afterwards, old Dave is coming along and one or two of the boys, it should be a laugh. What do you say?"

Debbie hummed to herself as she washed up. Things weren't so bad after all.

Jim replaced the receiver and smiled to himself and congratulated himself on a job well done. And Karen would be smiling to herself wherever she was.

***

When Marie Jenner returned home she was greeted with a laid tea table and her daughter Sara hovering over the stove stirring something in a saucepan.

"What's all this?" she asked, taking off her jacket and hanging it up.

"Soup okay?" Sara asked. "I managed to get some bread from Mrs Rolling and she says it was fresh in today. Dad's gone down to see some of his mates on the jetty."

"You still haven't answered my question."

"Look mum, I'm sorry I haven't given you a hand with the shop but I really am trying to save up for my future. I can't stay here in this town; I want to try something else."

"Sara, you have to understand that the money coming in from the shop is all I have. Your father's retirement fund isn't great and I also have myself to think of. If you could see your way to giving me a bit more housekeeping it would be a great weight of my mind. Why should I have to take a job in the winter stacking shelves in Fine Fare and then spend all the hours God sends running a gift shop during the summer just so you and your father can live off the fat of the land? I am tired Sara, in fact I am sick and tired." And with that Marie Jenner burst into tears.

Chapter Six   *"A Hole in One"*

When Gwen returned to the hospital she found Lorna waiting for her beside the reception desk. She seemed better than she had done a few hours previously and the doctor had shown concern about the prescribed drugs she had been using. He recommended she stopped taking them for the time being and return to her own GP to have the situation reassessed. He gave her a milder prescription drug so that she wouldn't have any withdrawal symptoms. As Lorna had experienced panic attacks and fainting fits before, it seemed fair to say that her collapse had been little more than that, given the pressure she was currently under.

Her blood pressure and temperature were normal and, apart from being told to get as much rest as she could, she was released from hospital on the understanding she return should it happen again.

Gwen started the engine. "Where would you like me to take you?" she asked.

"I think I would like to go back to the hotel first and have a proper bath. Then I intend to put some practice in before I face my nemesis."

"It won't be that bad Lorna. You have a lot of people behind you. Now that your sister has explained things to one or two people it will make it much easier for you."

"The so-called June Ashby," said Lorna with a hint of sarcasm in her voice.

"Now Lorna, none of that, you know the rules," said Gwen firmly. "You must keep to the story."

"Which seems to be unravelling quicker than a ball of three-ply! I am determined to do this show whatever it takes, if only to see the look on old sour puss's face. It might be possible to get them to open the theatre very early tomorrow morning so I could get some time on the stage to myself. They must be cursing me, you tell me everyone else has been given the day off."

Gwen turned out of the car park and onto the road. "I think Don thought if you had extra time with the dancers and orchestra tomorrow it would help you. He really isn't as black as he has sometimes been painted."

"There speaks the woman who has fallen in love with him," Lorna replied and the rest of the journey continued in silence.

"Would you like me to come up to your room with you?" Gwen asked, as she parked the car. "Perhaps I can give you a hand with something."

"Thanks Gwen, but you have been more than helpful already. You go off and enjoy the rest of the day, I will be fine."

"Don't forget these," said Gwen, holding out a bottle of tablets. "You know they work better than all that stuff the doctors keep giving you."

Lorna took the bottle and put it in her bag and watched as the car drove off. Tapping the bag she muttered to herself, "My bottle of magic pills."

Pulling off her coat, Lorna poured a large vodka and tonic and then ran herself a bath and had a long hot soak. Sipping the drink she swallowed a couple of the tablets Gwen had given her and sighed heavily. Sinking back into the warm water she rested her head and began to relax.

Some hours later and feeling much revived by the bath she ordered room service to bring her a tray and as she replaced the receiver the telephone rang.

"Hello, yes the coast is clear you can come in, I've just ordered some food. The staff here must think I am such a pig. See you in a minute."

Lorna checked herself in the mirror and went to open the door.

***

Lilly had been in a whirl ever since she had sat in on the news concerning June Ashby. It really was quite thrilling to think that she, Lilly Brocket, had been involved in such a revelation. Maud had seen her coming down the pier and commented on the bouncy step of her old friend.

"Lilly, I have never seen you looking so... I can't find the words. Have you had a win on bingo?"

"Can't a woman look happy without someone making something of it?" replied Lilly in her usual tone.

"If I didn't know better I'd say you had a fancy man."

"And what would I be doing with the likes of one of them?"

Maud looked at Lilly in her little brown jacket, her brown stockings, brown ankle boots, no makeup to speak of and wisps of mousey brown hair poking out from beneath her brown beret and couldn't help wondering the same thing herself.

"Time for a quick chat?"

Lilly was tempted, but needed time to digest everything properly in her own mind and store it with all the other things she didn't tell of.

"Not just now Maud. I think I'll take myself off to Arnolds and treat myself to something to wear on Monday evening. I know Muriel has bought something new. Are you going along?"

Lilly, a new outfit, the mind boggled. "When I've closed the box office I will come in to see the show and attend the party afterwards. Are you going to be bringing anyone with you Lilly?"

"I did ask my neighbour, but she hasn't been very well so it looks like I will have a spare ticket. I'll be sitting with Freda and Muriel I expect."

"Tell you what Lilly, I'll see if I can get Barbara in to cover me from six and if you like you and me can go and have something to eat and come on here afterwards. I'll sort out some seats so that we can all sit together. I'll give Muriel a call later and arrange it."

"That sounds really good," said Lilly, unable to contain her excitement. "It's been ages since I went out for a meal."

"Nothing fancy, just one of the restaurants in Regent Road," said Maud, "it won't break the bank."

"Thanks Maud. I had better get on and you've got some people at your window, see you later."

Maud went back into her office and above the heads of the queue which had formed could see Lilly bounding up Regent Road swinging her handbag. What had got into the woman?

Lilly came out of Arnolds department store with a carrier bag swinging on her arm. She had selected two nice dresses and had been allowed to take them on approval as long as they were back within three days. She hadn't been able to decide on the one she liked best. Both were inexpensive but to Lilly, who had little in her wardrobe, they were the best.

She put down the carrier bag in the bedroom and her eye caught the photograph of her late husband standing on the dressing table. She picked it up and rubbed the glass with her sleeve, gazing at the face that haunted her memory still. For some moments she stood entranced as days gone by danced before her eyes. Opening the top drawer she took out an envelope yellowed with age. The small photograph inside was the only one she had, it had been taken when the baby was just four days old, a little boy who they had called Alfred. Two days later, Alfred had died and a year later her husband Cyril had gone too. She kissed the photograph gently and put it back in the drawer. With a sigh Lilly took the dresses from the carrier bag and hung them with care inside the wardrobe wondering how things might have been.

***

"Come on old lover, it has been a long day and I need a nice walk along the seafront," said Rita, picking up her bag.

Ted had changed back into his normal attire, a pair of smart trousers, jacket and blue shirt. "I can't believe we won't be needed here for rehearsals tomorrow, not like old Don to let us off so easy."

"Well, it really was a very good show you all put on today, even the dancers were in line. I kept an eye on those Dean Sisters and I swear that Jill was suffering from the after-effects of too much booze, but she didn't let the other two down."

"I think they are a pretty sound group, but I can never make out who is the leader. With the Beverley's it's obvious Joy is in charge, the eldest is usually the boss. No, they are not a bad little act, though how long they will stay together is another matter. They might be better going into the circus with their skills."

"Never mind about all of that, let us get out of here."

They both nodded to Jack, who was busy on the telephone as they went through the stage door. Walking hand in hand along the pier in relative silence they saw Lilly in the distance heading off and Maud going into her office.

"Fancy an ice cream old gal?" said Ted, putting his hand in his pocket.

With a vanilla cornet apiece they walked along the promenade. It was reasonably warm with no breeze to speak of.

"Who was the woman you were sitting with?" Ted asked, as they stopped to watch a couple playing crazy golf.

"Woman?" said Rita, stalling for time.

"You were at the back of the stalls; I caught a glimpse of you both when I popped out into the auditorium to speak to old Don."

"Oh yes, some agent from London Don asked me to take care of for him."

"What was her name?"

Rita bit into her cornet trying to think of something to say. "Whatever was it? Jean something or other, I can't really remember. She was very quiet; we didn't speak much. Oh look, there's Brian over there going to play golf, shall we go and give him a run for his money? Come on old lover, I'll pay."

Swept away by his wife's sudden enthusiasm for fun, Ted followed her intending to show Mystic Brian what an expert he was at golf, crazy or otherwise!

***

June was quite alone. A taxi had brought her home and Gwen had not been seen since she had reportedly gone to collect Lorna from the hospital. She made herself a coffee and took it through to the small lounge. Trying to manage a cup and saucer while using a walking stick was just one of the problems she had learnt to overcome, refusing to have any form of assistance other than that offered by Gwen, whom she trusted. She would manage as long as she could, but had resigned herself to the fact that as she became weaker she would eventually have to give in. The mere fact that she had outlived the doctor's original prediction was a miracle in itself, but the pain and the medication had taken their toll and she felt that she needed to work fast to put her world in order. She tapped the pocket of her jacket in the sure knowledge that the bottle of tablets she had removed from the cabinet earlier was still there. The coffee was bitter, some nasty brand left by the landlord as a welcoming gift. She intended to stay a few more days and then return to her Kensington home where she would get in touch with her solicitor. They had had words some months ago and her endeavours to secure the services of another lawyer had been fruitless. She could not bear young men who were too wet behind the ears to understand the respect she demanded. Willard

Right, for all his funny mannerisms, was one of the old school and knew how to treat a client properly.

She had settled herself in the bay window so that she could place her handbag and coffee on the small table while she observed the comings and goings of those that lived nearby. The television had remained turned off since she had arrived, but she occasionally liked to listen to a programme on the wireless thoughtfully provided by her landlord. There was sometimes a good play on in the afternoons and often the thought had crossed her mind that instead of wasting away at her home she should have engaged herself in some radio work. She reflected on the rehearsal she had seen and how she had wished Lorna could have been on the stage singing instead of listening to vocals. She wondered what quality performance Lorna would turn in on Monday evening but it was too late to worry, the die had long since been cast and she would have to live with the consequences.

She opened her handbag and from the zipped compartment took out a letter. Now ravaged by time it was a copy she had made of an original that was kept in a safe deposit box. She opened the folded paper and read again the contents as she had done many times before. The letter was from her father. His family crest was barely visible now. The handwriting was neat, clear and concise. Her father was from a landed family and her mother and he had been lovers for many years before she had conceived.

The fact that their parents had never been married had, at first, horrified her when the letter was eventually given to her by Aunt Bernice who had kept it on promise to her sister to be passed to the girls when they were older and she herself dead. Neither the letter nor its contents had ever been shared with Lorna, but now perhaps the time had come for it to be. The letter, written to the both of them, spelt out the sadness it had caused their father to write. He had always ensured that money was in plentiful supply in the hope it would keep his daughters fed and clothed until they could make their own way in life. Their mother had set up a trust fund for them with some of the money given to her and when she passed on had left her own savings to Bernice, her trusted sister.

June liked to read the letter because it expressed with regret why their father couldn't be their daddy in the true sense of the word. When she had first read it many years before it had upset her greatly and she had taken the decision not to distress Lorna as well, feeling it was better for her to think the story their mother had told them to be the right one. There had been nothing to stop her from trying to make contact with her father once the letter was in her possession, but why should she ruin the happiness of others for one fleeting moment of her own? She returned the letter to her bag and, taking a couple of the magic pills Gwen had obtained for her, she drained the remainder of her coffee. She sat quietly looking out of the window until her head began to nod and she dozed off.

***

Alf Jenner returned home to find his wife sitting in the dark. He had clearly been drinking and went to the kitchen to get a glass of water. He turned on the light and saw that Marie had been crying. Just like a woman, he thought to himself, blubbering about something she had seen on the television no doubt.

"Where's the girl," he asked, "gone up to bed?"

Marie looked up, her eyes sore from sobbing heavily. "She's gone Alf, packed her bags and gone."

"Gone where?"

"I have no idea Alf Jenner; she went up to her room and reappeared with a suitcase. Said she had had enough of this place and was off. She never even kissed her own mother goodbye; she just walked out of here and threw her keys on the table. There they are exactly as she left them."

Alf swayed in the kitchen doorway and looked at his wife; he didn't know what to say. He stared at Marie and wondered how long it would be before she too was gone.

***

Ted had settled himself down with a book for the evening in Mrs Haines' lounge room and no persuading from Rita was going to shift him.

"I thought I might pop over and see Jim. I heard from Maud that young Debbie is back, it would be nice to see her."

Ted looked up from the comfort of the settee. "You ought not to go bothering them tonight, I expect they will have lots to talk about. If you are that bored why not go along to The Growler, you are bound to find one or two of the others in there."

"Are you sure you don't want to come?"

"Reet old gal I am fair worn out after the skinful I had last night. I am quite happy here as long as old Haines don't come in here bothering me. You go out for a couple of hours, do you good."

"Okay old lover, if I can't persuade you."

Rita went up to their room and collected her jacket and bag. Mrs Haines was in the hallway when she came down the stairs. "Off somewhere nice are you?"

"Just to see a couple of friends," said Rita, pulling on her jacket and making for the front door.

"Mr Ricer not going with you?"

"No," said Rita, "he is staying in and reading a book."

"Oh," said Mrs Haines, as Rita made quick her escape, "I might just pop in with a cup of hot chocolate and keep him company."

Rita went over to the telephone box on the corner. She looked in her purse for the correct change and took the paper from her pocket and dialled the number carefully. It seemed the phone rang for an age but eventually a somewhat tired voice answered.

"Hello June, it's me, Rita. I wonder if now would be a good time to have that chat you mentioned, I am at a loose end. What did you say the name of the road was again, please? I'll get a taxi to bring me there don't worry, see you soon, bye."

***

Over a drink in a hotel bar Gwen and Don sat and discussed Lorna.

"I think she just might pull it off," said Gwen, knocking back her second gin and tonic. "She has been in her sister's shadow for so long that the woman has never been allowed to find her true self."

"What amazes me is how they managed to get away with it all these years. They must have been seen together, people would have made a connection."

"Not necessarily. Their agent helped to dream up that little scheme and believe me she made sure everything was covered."

Don was very confused and he wasn't sure whether it was what he was hearing or the large Scotches he had been drinking. He studied Gwen for a moment; he wondered why she had decided to speak of this now. He had always felt he could trust Gwen, but now he wasn't so sure. Don's instincts told him there was more to it than Gwen was letting on. She was indeed a fine looking woman. For a thirty-five-year-old her figure was trim, her hair and makeup were always well-kept and she had been a good secretary to him over the years. He was going to have to do some serious thinking. His marriage was a good one, his wife Elsie had always been there for him and supported him through the lean times. She worked part-time for an estate agent. They had a nice home in Richmond. No responsibilities, children had never been seen as a priority. When he summed it all up he had been an old fool to fall for the flattery of a woman young enough to be his daughter. He wasn't sure how he felt about things as more and more doubt began to seep in.

"You're very quiet."

"Sorry, I was just thinking about June and Lorna. There they were two sisters who never spent time together, that is what you were telling me earlier. They must have gone to each others homes?"

"Not according to reports, the Bloomsbury flat is fully paid for by June, the car Lorna drives purchased by June and replaced every couple of years or so, she also takes care of all her living expenses. It is only recently that Lorna has been able to put her hand in her pocket and call it her own. And that is mainly thanks to a woman she met while in therapy who left her some money. I know that because Lorna told me so and I have seen the evidence to back it. June, however, doesn't have a clue about that. She had her home in Kensington and liked to keep herself to herself."

"More secrets," said Don, attracting the barman's attention for a fill-up. "I've heard more today than I think I have ever heard before."

It seemed to Don that Gwen was reading from a very well-rehearsed script, word perfect. She never faltered in her telling. Either she was genuinely getting things off her chest for the first time or she was a very good actress. Most people would um and ah when regaling a story that wasn't their own to tell, but not Gwen it seemed.

"If you compared the two side by side you would have to agree that Lorna is the better actress."

The word 'actress' brought Don back from his thoughts.

"Funny you saying that, someone else commented on Lorna's acting ability today. I was convinced I was dealing with June Ashby until I met the other one. Now there is an actress. Lorna seems mellower by comparison."

"That will be the drugs June has been feeding her," said Gwen, acknowledging the arrival of another drink. "The hospital doctor was slightly worried at the medication Lorna had been taking. When she first came out of New Dawn House she was as bright as a button. I have noticed a change in her, she is quieter than I remember, less animated. I mentioned the fact to June, but she said I was imagining things. I discovered prescribed drugs in the name of June which I later found out were being given to Lorna."

"June really is controlling her by the sounds of it."

Gwen took her lipstick and compact from her handbag. "Now, while I go and tart myself up in the little girl's room you can reserve a table in the restaurant. I don't know about you but I'm starving."

"Actually I am not feeling hungry my dear. Why don't you go and have something to eat. I think I will go out for a breath of air."

"Give me a jiffy and I'll come along I can always grab some fish and chips outside."

Don finished his drink and stood up. "I'd prefer to be on my own if you don't mind. I'll just go and settle the drinks bill and sort you out in the restaurant."

"Okay, as you wish," she replied, a little alarmed. She had never known Don to turn her down before and it bothered her.

Don was lost in thought. Why had Gwen spent so much time with Lorna following her stint in New Dawn House, she wasn't Lorna's nurse and yet the way she had spoken you'd have thought the opposite. It did explain, however, why when he called the office Gwen wasn't always there.

***

Rita left June shortly after 9.30 and made her way by taxi to The Growler. The evening had been an interesting one. June recalled her days in musicals and the many well-known artists she had worked with. Rita in turn had talked about her cabaret work abroad and on cruise ships. The subject of Lorna was barely touched on as the two reminisced. Rita's mind began to work overtime. There was something that didn't ring true in the tales June had been telling. Rita was blessed with a good memory for names, faces and times. She had suspected something at their initial meeting. As Ted's wife and guiding hand she had become a source of information that many would have dismissed but being able to call on her memory bank had proven to be a useful tool. Over the years she had had to make sure Ted was where he was supposed to be and also get herself acquainted with the management and artists he would be working with. One, to ensure he wasn't signing a worthless contract and two, to help keep up the front of a woman wronged in marriage by a husband with a roving eye. This opened doors to many sympathetic ears and confidences. If Ted was having a hard time or not enjoying a season, one word from him would bring Rita to the rescue. She would arrive on the pretence of having heard that Ted was 'playing away' and use this to gain the trust of others so she could investigate further. This time Ted had alerted her to his suspicions about June Ashby and he knew that if anyone could get to the bottom of something, his darling Rita was the best there was.

Rita went through to the back bar and sure enough, as Ted had predicted, found some of the gang there.

"Rita, how lovely to see you," said Maurice, getting up from his chair and greeting her. "No Ted tonight?"

"No, he has decided to make himself comfortable with a book. He had a little bit too much last night."

Rita sat herself down next to Jenny, who was giggling away in conversation with a couple of boys from the band. Brian, after his loss at crazy golf with Ted and Rita, was finding comfort in a pint of Guinness and keeping his own counsel.

A couple of the stagehands were at the bar with Jack and then the voice of Maud Bennett boomed across the room as she entered after a visit to the Ladies.

She greeted Rita with a kiss and pulled up a chair hoping for a good old gossip. Maurice organised a round of drinks and the scene was set for another night of fun in The Growler, much to the dismay of the young barman.

"Rita, are you sure you won't have anything stronger than a lemon and lime?" said Maurice, placing the glass in front of her.

"No thanks Maurice. When I've done here I have to make a quick dash to Hull and back. Ted needs some other outfit to wear for the finale. An oversight on my part I'm afraid."

Maud sighed. "You are an angel and no mistake. I'd be blowed if I would drive all that way and back for any man."

Maurice weighed up the conversation and made a suggestion that he hoped would change Rita's mind about leaving the little party so early.

"Rita, Ted is about my size I could lend him something from my own wardrobe," said Maurice, making himself comfortable on a leather armchair that had seen better days.

"Thanks all the same," Rita smiled, "but old Ted is a funny beggar, won't have anything someone else has worn. He has all his gear made for him by Jimmy Dazzle of Carnaby Street."

"Must cost him a fortune," Maud chipped in.

"No," said Rita, her eyes misting over slightly, "they have been friends for years. Ted and Jimmy have a special arrangement."

Rita finished her drink and made her farewells. The sooner she set off to Hull, the sooner she would return. And knowing that the roads were less busy at this time of the night, the trip should be an easy one.

Again Rita's thoughts troubled her. June Ashby, Lorna Bright, twins? You could see one was older than the other. No!

thought Rita, and not for the first time. Things just didn't add up.

Chapter Seven   *"A Meeting of Minds"*

Friday 2nd May

Jim tiptoed downstairs not wishing to disturb his daughter who, after talking into the early hours of the morning, was fast asleep. He could have done with a couple more hours himself but he knew he must do right by those who relied on him.

He had a quick wash and dressed himself while waiting for the kettle to boil. He put a couple of slices of bread under the grill and mentally planned his day.

Open up the theatre and get June, no Lorna, settled. Pop back here to make sure that Debbie was up in time enough to meet Peter from the station and to organise lunch for all of them. Go back to the theatre after lunch for the arrival of the orchestra and dancers and get them anything they needed. Visit Karen's grave to give Debbie and Peter some time alone. Finally return to the theatre to lock up and maybe grab a beer with Dave if he could track him down.

The smell of burning bread brought him back to his senses and he settled down at the table to eat his burnt offering and drink a cup of very strong tea.

***

Dave had also woken early and looked at the empty pillow beside him. He sat up, lit a cigarette and relaxed against the headboard. His head felt like he had little men inside with hammers banging against his skull, but then that was his own stupid fault. He just hoped he hadn't said anything he shouldn't to embarrass Dan in front of Stella, or indeed anyone else as Henry's had been particularly busy. He hated not being in control, but the change he had felt in himself over the last few days had got the better of him and he had wanted to party. A bath, some breakfast and a couple of pain killers would hopefully put him right again.

He finished his smoke and staggered out of bed and pulled the curtains open. It looked like another promising day if that morning sky was anything to go by.

***

Alf came downstairs to find the kitchen empty. A note propped against the kettle told him that Marie had gone off to the shop to sort out some more stock. Not used to getting his own breakfast, Alf popped some bread under the grill and turned on the kettle. This wasn't how he had imagined retirement to be at all. He thought of Sara and hoped she was all right. It must have been difficult for her having parents who were much older than those of her friends when she went to school. But Marie had had trouble conceiving and just when they had both given up on the idea, along she came. His head was hurting and he wished he hadn't drunk so much; he opened the kitchen cupboard in search of some aspirin but had no luck. That was the trouble with women, they hid things.

***

Jim arrived at the theatre to find Lorna waiting for him at the stage door with a man beside her who greeted him with a polite, "Good morning."

He was early forties, tall and slim, smartly dressed, with well-groomed dark hair. He had obviously been educated at a private school by the sound of his plummy voice and put Jim in mind of the dashing cavalier type that women fell for in films like The Scarlet Pimpernel.

"Hello Jim," said Lorna, "thanks for agreeing to do this. I would like to introduce you to Robin Preston, a friend of mine from the Smoke."

Robin nodded at Jim as they shook hands. "Robin has come to give me some moral support."

136

Jim unlocked the stage door and they went inside. He looked at Robin who was rubbing his hands together. "Sorry, it will be a bit chilly in here until the sun comes up properly. The theatre has no heating as such, but the stage area should be warmer once the lights are on."

Robin smiled. "It's a long time since I have been in one of these old pier theatres."

"This place certainly has some history behind it," Jim replied. "When I think of all the famous television and variety stars that have played this theatre it really is quite incredible. If only these walls could talk."

Lorna took hold of Jim's arm. "I hope, with Robin's help, to surprise my sister on Monday evening by singing 'live'. She gave me songs that are much more suited to me. Robin has agreed to rehearse me with the piano."

"Sounds a wonderful idea," said Jim, moving away and leading them on to the stairwell.

"I would be grateful if you didn't say anything to anyone."

"I'll just get everything ready; I am really not supposed to leave anyone alone in the theatre. Bob will be in his office today and Jack will be at the stage door in about an hour, we are expecting a delivery. Will you want to use the click-track?"

Lorna took off her jacket and laid it at the side of the stage. "Won't you be staying?"

"Not unless it is absolutely necessary. My daughter is down here with her husband and I really should spend some time with them. I haven't seen them since they got married and moved away. Maurice and the boys are due here by two-thirty, along with the dancers, and I will call back then."

"I can always use my tape recorder if I need to, but I am hoping with Robin's expert help that won't be necessary," said Lorna, pushing her hair back and fastening it with a grip. "What I really want to work on are these old favourites." Lorna waved the sheet music in the air like an excited child.

Jim smiled to himself; he had never come across anyone quite like Lorna before. He nodded at them both and left.

Robin sat down at the piano and began to play, Lorna suddenly came alive and burst into tuneful song, and her confidence seemed to return with every note.

Jim walked slowly down the pier, hands in pockets enjoying the air. He wondered how Debbie and Peter would fare and really hoped they would be able to sort themselves out. Things weren't the same as when he and Karen had got together. All that courting and Sunday tea with her parents, there was no hope of sex before marriage and any attempt at a fumble in the cinema brought a quick rap of the knuckles from Karen. The day she had worn white down the aisle she had worn it with pride and Jim wouldn't have changed any of it for the world.

He could see Jack ambling his way onto the pier and glanced at his watch. It wasn't like Jack to be up and about this early, but at least he could rest easy knowing that Lorna and Robin were not alone in the theatre. He wasn't sure why, but he felt uneasy about the whole thing.

***

When Rita arrived back at Mrs Haines' Ted was already tucking into his breakfast. "I wondered where you were," he said, buttering himself a piece of cold toast. "I must have hit the pillow hard last night, I didn't even realise you weren't beside me, just thought you had got up early for a walk. I know how you enjoy the promenade early in the morning."

"I've been back home to retrieve these," Rita replied, banging a folder down on the table and making the cruet set bounce and fall over.

"What is it?" Ted asked, as she sat herself down.

"Pour me a cup of tea and I will reveal all."

"Not in here you won't," said Mrs Haines, as she came into the room to clear some dishes from another table. "I keep a respectable house."

Rita laughed. "Good morning Mrs Haines, I was just about to show Ted some old photographs and programmes."

"Is that all?" said Mrs Haines, folding her arms. "Suppose you'll want a cooked breakfast?"

Rita smiled. "If it's not too much trouble."

Mrs Haines huffed. "Should have finished those fifteen minutes ago, but I'll make an exception for you."

"You are an angel Mrs Haines," said Ted, with the biggest smile he could muster. "And do you think I could have some fresh toast while you are at it?"

Mrs Haines gave a girlish giggle and headed for the kitchen.

"And what did you get up to with old Spitfire while my back was turned old lover?"

"Just worked a little of the old Ted magic."

Rita laughed. "I bet you did you old rascal."

After they had eaten they went up to their room and Rita sat herself down by the table at the window and opened the folder.

"Now Ted, I want you to look at these very carefully and for goodness sake put your spectacles on," she said, handing him some old theatre programmes.

Ted sat himself opposite Rita. "What am I looking for?"

"June Ashby of course, look at them closely and see if any of the pictures in those programmes look anything like the person you have been working with."

Ted fumbled for his spectacles and looked at the old black and white photographs.

"At a glance old girl I would say they do look like her."

"That's what I thought and then only yesterday I was introduced to someone who claims to be the real June, only these photographs don't look like her either."

"Sorry love but I am confused. What other June?"

"Long story old lover and one I really cannot go into at the moment without revealing too much."

"You always do things like that to me," said Ted, gazing at the photographs again and tutting, "you start a story and never tell me the end."

"I am not sure what the end will be yet," Rita replied, flicking through some more photographs. "But I have some more work to do on this one and then I shall play my trump card."

Ted looked at his wife and raised his eyebrows.

"And you can stop looking at me like that old lover," said Rita, without looking up. "One day the wind will change and you'll stay like that."

A knock at the door interrupted the conversation. Mrs Haines stood in the doorway arms folded. "There is a telephone call for you Mrs Ricer, long distance."

Rita blushed slightly. "Oh Mrs Haines, thank you, I should have mentioned I had given this number as a contact, I hope you don't mind."

Mrs Haines gave another one of her huffs. "I don't run a telephone service here as a rule but seeing as it's you…" she looked longingly in the direction of Ted.

Rita brushed past Mrs Haines' ample figure and kissed her on the cheek. "You are a marvel Mrs Haines, Ted is always talking about you. Ted please see to it that you arrange some comps to the show, I am sure Mrs Haines has some friends she would like to bring along one evening."

Mrs Haines smiled. "Telephone is in my sitting room, first left at the bottom of the stairs, please take your time. I'll just have a chat with Ted."

Rita's mouth broke out into a large grin as she went down the stairs. If only the old girl knew. She went into the sitting room and picked up the receiver. "Hello, this is Rita, thank you so much for getting back to me. Let me explain my earlier enquiry."

The call went on for some time, with Rita making mental notes of dates and times. She scribbled reminders for herself on the pad beside the telephone; the pieces of the jigsaw were beginning to come together.

"Do you have a telephone number in France, will she take calls?"

The voice at the other end was calming and confident. "I am one of the few that know her well, we were the best of friends and I helped her find a new life away from the limelight. I will call on your behalf and see how the land lies. I cannot promise you anything, but I am sure that once I tell her the story you have told me it may just interest her enough to make a move."

"You have been really helpful and I am most grateful," said Rita.

"There is something you should know, they are all related. The Bright sisters have the same father as the real June. The elder one who you say is claiming to be the real June is really Veronica Bright, she has always been in charge of the younger one, Lorna, who, let's be honest here, is something of a loose cannon. There is some talent there undoubtedly. But not in the June Ashby league by any stretch of the imagination. Veronica Bright is a dangerous lady; take very good care when you are around her Rita."

"How do you know all this?"

"Please trust me. I will call you once I have spoken to June. If I cannot get you on this number I will try the number you gave me for the theatre office. Incidentally Rita, how did you find me?"

"In an old scrap book of mine, you had signed your autograph and put your telephone number beneath it. You had a crush on me in those days Wally Barrett."

Wally laughed. "I thought I knew the voice, couldn't place the name – Rita wasn't your stage name."

"Moira Clarence."

141

"Of course, you married old Ted."

"The very same and we are still together," said Rita with a certain amount of pride in her voice. "You broke a few hearts Wally I seem to remember."

"Yes I did," said Wally with some regret. "I broke June's once and I have never forgiven myself."

Rita paused before replying, she could hear Wally choking back tears.

"Wally, it's okay love, we all do things in this life we live to regret. I have had my fair share over the years. I heard about June and the baby she lost, you were the father weren't you?"

"Oh goodness Rita, you don't know how long I have waited to talk to someone about it. When I helped June relocate to France after her miscarriage I thought we might be able to make a new life together. June shut me out for a time, but I never lost touch with her. We speak on the telephone and write the odd letter, but we never meet. That is her choice. She turned in on herself for a time and the vibrant talent that lit up many a stage diminished. How did you know about the baby?"

"I have moved around a lot over the years Wally and I have heard things. I knew people in the business that had known June well. Just the other day I was talking to someone and they let slip the reason June had hastily departed from her last show in London and that isn't the story that June – Veronica - gave as the reason. I think that Veronica didn't know about the baby situation."

"June kept it very quiet, especially from the sisters." There was a pause and then he continued, "It would be nice to meet you and Ted again and catch up on old times."

"But first Wally I need to try and sort out this mess with the June impostors."

"Yes, yes of course. I am sure June will be furious when she discovers that her so-called siblings are trying to cash in on her name. It amazes me how they thought they would never get caught out. However, one thing is true in all of this, Veronica Bright was June's understudy for a time, but June dismissed her after a year, Veronica was unreliable, not turning up, that kind of thing. She is obviously seeking some kind of revenge due to her current illness and using the tale to bring Lorna into the equation, a girl with some talent if what you have told me is true. Look, I'll ring off now and get on to June. As I said earlier, I cannot promise anything, but I will do my best for an old friend."

"Before you go Wally, does the name Wendy Patterson mean anything to you?"

Wally laughed loudly. "Not that old chestnut. That name was used when acts who didn't have an agent wanted others to believe they had. When an unscrupulous artist turned up we would always say, 'I bet she's with Wendy'. Speak to you later."

Rita was puzzled as she replaced the receiver. Gwen had used the name of Wendy Patterson to Don Stevens. Gwen was obviously in on this too.

Rita returned to her room and heard the giggles of Mrs Haines from across the landing. "You two sound as if you are having fun," she said, as she entered the room.

"Oh your husband is a card and no mistake," said Mrs Haines. "My sides have been fair aching."

Rita thought it was nice to see a smile on the old trout's face for once. "Mrs Haines…"

"Oh call me Lucinda please," said Mrs Haines, smiling at Rita like they were old friends.

Rita swallowed a chortle she felt coming on. "Lucinda, I am expecting another long distance call, it will be from the same gentleman you spoke to earlier. If Ted and I are not here would you take a message and remind him he can contact me at the theatre."

Lucinda Haines touched Rita's arm. "No trouble at all. Now I was just about to make myself some coffee, would you two care to join me?"

Ted looked at Rita and winked. "Lucinda, that would be lovely," he replied.

***

When Jim arrived home, Debbie was preparing some vegetables. "Don't forget Peter's train will be in soon, do you want me to give you a lift to the station?"

"No thanks Dad, you'll want to get off to the cemetery. You will have lunch with us won't you?"

"Wouldn't you two prefer to be alone for a while; you have a lot to talk about. I can grab a bite at the pub; maybe meet up with Dave if he isn't doing anything. I have to go back to the theatre later anyhow."

Debbie laid down the knife and smiled at her father. "Have I ever told you, you are the best dad in the world?"

Jim smiled. "I think you may have mentioned it, several times."

While Debbie finished off her preparations, Jim went into the garden to pick a small posy of flowers to take to the grave. A couple of early summer roses would set it off a treat.

As Jim walked over to Karen's grave, he saw Maud Bennett coming towards him. "Hello young Jim, visiting your Karen?"

Jim nodded. "I expect Debbie and Peter will come up later, she is meeting him off the train."

Maud nodded knowingly. "You've nothing to worry about there my lad. I've told you often enough, Debbie has the same characteristics as her mother and this Peter will see her right."

"You really think so Maud? I do hope you are right."

Maud squeezed Jim's arm and walked on. "See you later Jim, give my love to Karen."

Jim filled the vase with some fresh water and removed a couple of dead stems, replacing them with the roses he had picked. He knelt for a few minutes, his thoughts were all over the place. The show was giving him grief, he needed to know his daughter was settled and he wished he had Karen there to discuss it with. He spoke to her often enough when he was on his own, but the graveyard was quite busy for a Friday morning with a couple of funerals taking place and he didn't want to disturb others who were visiting their loved ones. He said a silent prayer and blew a kiss at the headstone where Karen's name was etched. For a moment it seemed that a stream of sunlight made the lettering twinkle. He stood up and whispered, "See you later," and walked back to his car feeling slightly better.

***

"You didn't come in last night," Gwen said to Don. "I waited up for you."

"I needed to be on my own Gwen," Don replied steadily, looking her in the eye. "I booked into the Imperial for the night, I had some thinking to do."

Gwen looked worried. "Thinking, about what?"

"Us, and I am very sorry to say that we have reached the parting of the ways. I was foolish to embark on our affair in the first place. I don't need a lover at my age, I need some comfort."

"You needn't think you are getting off that lightly Don Stevens, I have given you the best years of my life. Handled your shady deals and fought off the debt collectors. I wonder what Mrs Stevens would have to say if she found out about our little arrangement over the years?"

"Elsie knows everything Gwen, so you'll get no joy there. She knows every sordid little detail."

"I don't believe you."

"You can believe what you like. I confessed everything, not that I had to, Elsie is a clever woman, she knew about you from the off, she told me as much. So if you were planning a bit of emotional blackmail you would be wasting your time."

"But I thought you loved me," Gwen wailed, fighting back the tears.

"I did love you once I don't deny it, but it wasn't the same love I felt for Elsie. It has taken me some time to admit that to myself."

"What about my job, my future?"

"I need some time to think about that, as for your future that really is for you to decide."

Gwen covered her face to hide the escaping tears. "I love you Don, with all my heart, I love you."

Don shook his head and left the room feeling he couldn't watch the charade a moment longer.

***

Dave whistled as he walked along Marine Parade. He was feeling particularly chipper this fine morning. No work today, a new person in his life and the chance of moving flat was on the cards after speaking to a couple of mates of his. A larger place with a good sized kitchen, dining and lounge area, bathroom complete with shower, and two double bedrooms, all his for the asking, but he wanted to discuss it with Dan first. He saw Marie Jenner taking more stock into the shop and went over to give her a hand.

"This really is very kind of you Dave."

"You should be taking a day off, every time I pass by you are in here doing something," said Dave, placing a box of postcards on the counter.

"I wanted to keep busy, besides I have decided to open up tomorrow, might do some early trade while there are people about."

"No hope of your daughter giving you a hand then?"

Marie turned away as she began to cry.

"Eh up, whatever is the matter?" Dave placed a comforting hand on her shoulder.

"She's left home," said Marie, wiping her eyes and turning back to face him. "Up and left and I have no idea where she has gone to. We had words about her not helping out here and me needing a little more in the way of housekeeping. I don't know why I said anything, but there it is. She needed some home truths, but now I wish I had kept my mouth shut."

"You know what these youngsters are like; they don't know when they are well off. Give it a few days, she'll be back, you'll see."

"I hope you are right Dave, really I do."

Dave wished there was more he could do to help, but Marie had persuaded him that she would be okay and he headed off. He heard Jim call his name and he stopped and turned on his heels. "Hi Jim, how's tricks?"

Jim smiled at his best friend. "Not too bad considering. The show is still giving me the run-around, but in a few weeks from now it will be a distant memory. Debbie is back at home for a few days and Peter is coming down to join her today. You should pop round and see her, she'd like that."

"Bit busy today friend, new flat in the offing."

"I thought you were happy where you were."

"This place has two bedrooms. You remember Nigel and Janice; well they are taking over his mother's old house now she has passed on and they offered me the rental of their old place. It will only be a couple more quid than what I am paying now."

"What do you need a two-bedroom flat for, you'll be rattling around like a ball in an empty tin?"

"I was thinking of asking Dan to muck in with me, he lives over the shop and is a bit fed up being at the landlord's beck and call. Besides, he will get more wages living out."

Jim scratched his chin. "Steady on Dave. How well do you know this Dan, he's only been in town a couple of weeks and you've known him what, days? Besides, you know these seasonal staff, they are off as soon as the summer is over and you'll be left with a two-bedroom flat that you can't afford to keep going in the winter. Our wages at the club aren't that great as well you know. I have said before, if you want a room I have a spare one at my house, you'd be welcome."

"I know what you are saying Jim but think about it, you and me sharing your house, we would be arguing in no time, we would be in each other's pockets. No, thanks all the same but it would ruin our friendship. I have been thinking things through and sometimes you have to take the bull by the horns and run with the race."

Jim wondered if Dave had been on the sauce early. There was something about his manner, his enthusiasm; Dave didn't get excited about flats or homes. Perhaps Dave had met a girl and fallen in love, but by the state of his friend's antics a night or so previous, he didn't think so.

"Jim mate, you look puzzled."

"Sorry Dave, my mind must have been elsewhere. Fancy a jar at lunchtime; I am trying to keep out of Peter and Deb's way to give them some time alone."

Dave looked at his watch, he had to play this carefully otherwise his best mate might suspect something was going on. "I could make one-thirty in the Greyhound if you like?"

"We normally go in the New Beach."

"Fancy a change of scene. Tell you what, I'll meet you in the Barking Smack, they do a fair ploughman's in there."

It was ages since Jim had set foot in the Barking Smack and maybe Dave was right, a change of scene. "Okay Dave, I'll see you in there and lunch is on you."

Dave grinned. "Okay, see you later."

Jim called at the box office and found Maud at her knitting.

"I have no idea why they want the box office open today, I can't see there being many queues, not a soul about when I came along this morning," said Maud, tutting to herself as she dropped a couple of stitches. "Dave called by earlier, he was full of beans for a Friday morning."

"From the look of old Dave, you'd think he was in love or something," Jim replied, taking a seat. "Thinking of moving, he told me."

"Well I can't think why. He seems so settled. Old Madge will hate to lose him as a tenant."

Jim laughed. "Maud Bennett you are a mine of information, I'm surprised you don't have a column in the Mercury."

"Don't you be so cheeky Jim Donnell."

***

Lorna's rehearsals had started off well enough and progress seemed to be being made and she definitely sounded better than she had done. But things began to slide again when she discovered the bottle in her bag, a full one!

"I will have to try that again," she said, knocking back vodka. "The others will be here soon and I am nowhere near ready."

"What are you going to do about Veronica?" Robin asked, pouring another measure into her glass as he had been instructed to do.

"Shh! Someone may hear you," Lorna replied, finding her knees a bit wobbly.

"There is no one else here. Anyway, who would connect Veronica with June?" said Robin, moving the bottle of out of sight.

"Even I don't call her Veronica; I always have to call her June. We have to keep the pretence going. I have to remember it like a play. I was getting quite confused being known as June. The great June Ashby, managed to fool most of them until..."

"Well, I think it must have looked pretty stupid when first you were June and then your sister announced she was. The people round here must think you are both crazy."

Lorna gave Robin a steely look. "Don't you ever use that word again."

"Look, let's try that number with the piano again. I thought you nearly had it the last time."

Lorna put down the glass and with the all the effort she could summon, did her best to master the song that had sounded promising at the beginning of the rehearsal.

Jim walked in from the back of the auditorium and found to his surprise that Don Stevens was sitting in the back row. Jim had noted the goings-on on the stage and was slightly concerned to see Lorna staggering around. He sat down beside Don.

"What is going on up there Jim?" said Don managing to keep his voice low. "How the hell can we allow her to open on Monday?"

"She looks as if she has been drinking and heavily to," Jim replied. "I have known her to take a drink, but never to excess, at least not in my company. I thought her friend Robin was here to help her."

"I wondered who the bloke was, he has been fart-arsing around like some hired help, but he certainly has not been any help to her apart from pouring her another drink. Mind you, give him his due, he's very good on the piano, like a young Russ Conway. It's like he is helping her to self-destruct and from what I've seen this week, she needs little help in that department. Let's go into the back office Jim, we need to put some plans in order. We will leave Laurel and Hardy up there to it."

The two sat down at opposite sides of Bob's desk and Don put his head in his hands. "Jim, I don't like being taken for a mug, and I get the distinct impression that I have been."

Jim nodded in agreement, but let Don continue. "What was all of that confession stuff from that Bette Davis character who claims to be the real June Ashby? Something Rita said to me the other day got me thinking. One, I have never met the agent who claims to represent June, who suddenly was brought to my attention by my PA. Two, Ashby hasn't been heard of in the last five years or so. I don't understand how she suddenly surfaced and I find myself putting her in a show. How can I have been so dumb? Derinda Daniels could have headed this bill and I know for a certainty that I would have had no problems there, a professional from top to toe."

"Can I say something Don?" said Jim, lighting himself a cigarette. "Whose idea was it to put June in the show at all, Ted Ricer is so well-known in these parts you didn't need a named top of the bill, though I do take on board your comment about Derinda Daniels. You know as well as I do that Ted has headlined these pre-season shows around the country. When I first became aware of the line-up I did wonder how the box office would pay for a West End star."

Don wiped his brow and pulled a cigar from his top pocket. "I wish you and I had had this conversation weeks ago. When I was asked to pull together a show quickly I asked Gwen to contact my old faithfuls first; Ted, Brian and even, gawd help me, Jenny and her dancers. I have to say, and I am not making excuses here, but my mind hasn't been on the ball lately and I allowed Gwen to make decisions I should have made for myself. What a bloody mess. If you ever fancy coming to work for me in London you would be a great asset to me."

Jim handed his lighter to Don and stood up. He walked over to the window and stared down the pier. He thought for a few moments and then turned back to face Don who was barely visible through a foggy haze of cigar smoke.

"You cannot allow Lorna to open on Monday night," said Jim firmly. "I am no expert in these matters, but I see professional suicide if you do. The local press would have a field day."

"You are right, they would," Don agreed. "So what do you think should be the plan of action? Speak to me Jim, you are the only one making sense here."

Jim was flattered, he moved closer to the desk. "Let Lorna continue to rehearse today. It is too late to call off the dancers and the orchestra and, besides, you need to keep this quiet for as long a possible. See if you can persuade Derinda Daniels to stand in or find someone else. I know you said she had taken other work, but it's worth a try. An announcement can be made at the beginning of the show that due to the indisposition of Miss Ashby, Miss Daniels has kindly stepped in."

"What do we say to Lorna and her sister?"

"We say nothing. Let them believe that everything is going ahead as planned. We can keep Lorna in her dressing room and the other one will be in the audience if she plans to witness this circus." Jim was thinking on his feet. "Perhaps Rita can give us a hand, she's a good sort and if my judgement of character is correct, she is good in a crisis. Don, get on the phone and see if you can fix up Derinda first, and then have a quiet word with Maurice. Whether it is Derinda or someone else they are going to need band practice. This Robin chap will have to be dealt with, we don't want him hanging around the theatre tomorrow night he could put a spanner in the works."

Don puffed on his cigar. "I am impressed Jim, you seem to have got it all worked out, thank you, thank you very much. I will give Derinda a call now and I won't have to worry about band practice she has her own band. I might be lucky, if not, I will get on to an agent I know in Norwich, he may be able to help an old friend out."

Jim's mind was racing overtime. He was meeting Dave later and he suddenly thought of a plan. If he could get Dave to take Robin out for a few bevies tomorrow and get him slaughtered it would keep him out of the way. Failing that, he wondered if old Maud might be able to play a hand, it was always best to have a plan B, just in case.

"Derinda hello, Don Stevens here, how are you my darling? I need a big favour but I am willing to pay you over the odds for your trouble. It's like this my dear..."

Jim paced the office in deep thought. Don's telephone conversation was a muffled background noise and it wasn't until the big man boomed out his name that he came back to the real world again.

"We are in luck Jim, Derinda will be able to stand in for us on Monday evening, longer if we need her. The job she was offered wasn't really her scene and as she hasn't signed a contract she is a free agent."

"That's a start," said Jim excitedly. "I am sure the show will succeed after the initial opening with or without June Ashby."

Don nodded. There's always Moira Clarence, he thought to himself. "Right Jim, let's make a positive plan and we must try and keep this as quiet as possible."

Jim sat down and the two of them worked on their proposed plan.

***

"Hello Gwen," said Rita, "out for a walk?"

Gwen stopped. "Sorry I was miles away. You are Ted's wife aren't you?"

"That's right me old lover," said Rita, eyeing her up and down. "I can't wait to see how the show takes shape Monday evening, will you be there?"

Gwen nodded. "Yes, Mr Stevens has asked me to be present."

"There have been one or two problems with the top of the bill."

"One or two I believe."

Rita opened her handbag and took from it a small book and pen. "I am pleased I bumped into you Gwen, I wonder if you could do me a favour."

"I will try."

"I am after the telephone number of an agent; I am thinking that Ted really needs to spread his wings a little. I have heard the name of Wendy Patterson mentioned do you have her number by any chance?"

Gwen's face paled. "Wendy Patterson?"

"Yes Wendy Patterson, someone mentioned she looked after June Ashby."

"Yes, she did for a while, but I think June uses someone else now."

Rita didn't give up so easily. "But surely you would know Wendy's number, you did use her when June was engaged for this show didn't you?"

Gwen became flustered. "Well yes, but not exactly."

"Oh, I am sorry, I must have been misinformed, but if you do come across Wendy's number at some point I would like to give her a call, not only for Ted's sake but for my own."

"I don't understand."

"I am thinking that I may like to go back on stage again and if I can find a decent agent of my own it would be a great start. So, as I say, if you find the number and get back to me I would be most grateful."

Gwen played with her jacket buttons nervously. "It's probably back in the London office. I don't carry numbers with me and I am such a muddle-head at times for telephone numbers, but I'll see what I can do."

"I am most obliged Gwen, thank you. Now I had better get on my way I am meeting an old friend and I mustn't be late."

Gwen nodded and Rita watched her walk down the promenade. There goes a woman with something to hide, she thought to herself.

Gwen scurried across Marine Parade and took exit down a side street. This had not been on her agenda, she had been on her way to find Don, who had headed off in the direction of the theatre, to try to salvage their relationship. This sudden turn of events with Rita requesting the number of Wendy Patterson had thrown her. She turned into Nelson Road and headed as fast as she could to the rented home of Veronica (June Ashby) Bright.

The fresh air had cleared Rita's head and as she ambled back to Mrs Haines' guest house she picked up a newspaper for Ted. The promenade seemed to be coming alive with coach parties that had arrived for a day at the seaside. A few of the amusement arcades had opened their doors for business and the machine noises could be heard. The clip-clop of the posse of ponies was audible above the hum of the light traffic as they arrived to take up their stands in the hope of attracting people on what promised to be a fine day. There was already a couple playing crazy golf and the bowling green looked as if it was going to see some action as a group of men in white coats did an inspection of the ground. Shutters were being removed from many of the ice cream parlours hoping to catch some early summer trade. Rita loved the smell of seaside towns and always planned that Ted was able to spend part of the season at the costal resorts. It made up for all the winter bookings in Leeds, Huddersfield, Birmingham and the like, which Rita found quite depressing and didn't visit as often as she might have, leaving Ted to his dalliances safe in the knowledge that there would be no reprimand.

Mrs Haines greeted her as she entered the front door. "Message for you to call Wally, number's on the pad. I'm just out for a loaf if I am lucky enough to find the corner shop open."

Rita thanked her and headed straight for the telephone wondering what news Wally might have for her, if any.

Rita listened to Wally's report. "This is more than I could have hoped for. Is there anything you want me to do this end?"

Ted walked into the sitting room and laid his hand on Rita's shoulder. "I thought I heard your voice."

Rita reached over and tapped his hand gently. "Thank you so much Wally, I shall look forward to meeting you soon. Not to worry, someone will pick her up from Norwich on Monday 5th May, probably me. Bye for now."

"What was all that about?" Ted asked, as his wife turned round to face him. "You look very excited."

"Ted, I hardly know where to start, in fact I am in two minds who I should tell first. I will need to speak to Jim."

"Well you won't have to wait long," Ted said. "He arrived here a few moments ago, he is in the dining room, says he needs to speak to you quite urgently. My quiet day off is turning into a web of intrigue, so much for having a day off."

Rita took Ted's hand. "Let's go and see what Jim wants and then I will tell you both."

Just as they reached the dining room door, Mrs Haines came through the front door clutching two loaves of bread.

"I wonder, Lucinda, if I could trouble you for three coffees in the dining room," said Ted, with a beaming smile and a wink. "A colleague from the theatre has turned up unexpectedly for an urgent chat."

She smiled at Ted. "Of course Ted. Give me five minutes and I'll put some milk on and I might be able to rustle up a few biscuits."

"Thanks Lucinda."

"I am going to have to watch you two," said Rita, trying not to laugh. "You pair are turning into a right Jeanette McDonald and Nelson Eddie; it's like Rose Marie all over again."

Ted tapped his wife's bottom as she entered the dining room. "That's enough from you Rita rascal; now let's see what Jim wants."

***

"This is a surprise, what brings you here Gwen; I thought you'd be with lover boy."

Gwen threw her handbag down onto the sofa and stomped across the room. "Don has called it off, it's finished."

"Don't be so stupid you have all the ammunition you need, threaten to tell his lovely wife."

"Give it a rest Veronica, he's already told her." Gwen banged the back of the sofa with her fist.

"You know the rules, you address me as June, and calm yourself for goodness sake."

"You and your stupid games, how long do you think it will be before someone rumbles the truth? That Rita woman is asking for the telephone number of Wendy Patterson, what the hell am I going to tell her?"

Veronica sat down near the window, steadying herself on her walking stick. "Why would she want the number?"

"Says she is thinking of returning to the business or some such story, wants Ted to spread his wings a bit. I don't know, some rubbish."

"You leave Rita to me. She is taking me to the show; I can soon sweet-talk her round."

Gwen reached into her bag for some cigarettes. "I don't think you're her type dearie!"

"Oh, is Gwen feeling hurt because old Don has blown her out?"

"Don't rub it in. It was bad enough agreeing to pursue him on your terms, I never once thought I would actually fall for him."

"You haven't done so badly out of it. Regular money paid into your account every month, plus whatever he was paying you."

Gwen took a long drag on her cigarette. "That's a point actually. There hasn't been any extra money in my account for the last two months."

"I told you, there have been cash flow problems. I'll see you right as soon as Lorna's first pay cheque comes in."

"I should live that long. She is useless. If you really think she is going to pull it off, I think you're in for a rude awakening."

Veronica frowned. "Why, what have you heard?"

Gwen laughed. "For a starter, that Robin bloke of hers has blown into town and by all accounts she is drinking heavily again."

Veronica pushed herself up on to her feet. "I think I had better pay a visit to my sister."

Gwen moved towards her and pushed her back down again.

"My heart," Veronica gasped. "You're upsetting me."

"You haven't got a heart you silly old cow, it's a swinging brick that keeps you going. I'll make some tea and you, lady, had better calm down, we wouldn't want you popping your clogs before the big night would we?" And with that she moved quickly into the kitchen, tapping her jacket pocket to ensure that the tablets were still there. They might come in handy later on if things got out of hand.

***

Jim found Dave at the bar of The Barking Snack. "Sorry I'm late, had to sort something out for tomorrow. Is there any food still on offer?"

Dave nodded to the barman. "A couple of pints of best and two ploughman's mate, when you're ready."

"Let's take the window seat over there," said Jim.

Dave carried the pints of bitter to the table and sat down opposite his friend.

"So young Dave, what's all this about moving to a bigger flat. Have you asked your mate Dan?"

"I've mentioned it," said Dave, taking a sup of his pint and lighting up. "I popped into Henry's just before coming on here. Mind you, I have taken note of what you said about him possibly sodding off at the end of the season."

158

"You hardly know the guy and somehow I can't imagine you flat-sharing," said Jim.

"And there you were all ready for me to move into yours! Do you reckon my landlady would keep my flat open in case it doesn't work out?"

Jim laughed. "Oh yeah, of course she will, nothing she'd like more than to have a flat standing empty and no rent coming in."

"Yeah, I see your point."

"Don't burn all your bridges Dave mate. Weigh up the pros and cons first. When do you have to let them know?"

"Oh, they are really fine about it. There is no rush. They said they didn't want to sell the place and would rather let it out to someone they knew than a complete stranger."

"Well, there you go then. Bide your time and think it through properly," said Jim. "Now, let me fill you in on what's been happening to me since we last spoke."

As they chatted, the Friday lunchtime crowd of regulars and early holidaymakers started to disperse. It was coming up to two-thirty when the barman called time.

"Well that was a cheap lunch," laughed Jim, as they walked towards the exit.

Dave punched his arm. "Didn't even get a second pint, where are you off to now?"

"I must just call in at the theatre and make sure everything is okay and then I am off home to catch up with Peter and Debbie. I am hoping they have managed to sort out some of their problems. If Karen was here she would have dealt with all of this, I am not sure I am best placed for the fatherly chat type of thing. In some ways it would have been easier with a son, not that I regret one moment having Debbie in my life, but you know what I mean?"

Dave nodded. "I understand your problem, but if there is one thing people admire about you mate it's your dedication to see something through."

The two shook hands and said their goodbyes and, as Dave headed towards home, Jim turned on his heels and headed for the theatre.

***

"Now Rita love you are okay about me taking old Haines out for drinks this evening aren't you?" said Ted, as he picked up some joke scripts to read.

Rita laughed out loud. "Oh Ted, if only I could be a fly on the wall. I told you I've got business to attend to this evening so you going out with old Lucinda will hardly spoil my plans. Just make sure you give her a good time. I hear the Coral Reef has an act on tonight, you could take her there."

"Be like going on a busman's holiday. I thought I'd take her to Divers and drop in on old Ruby. I haven't seen her since I came into town."

Rita smiled. "Old Ruby eh! Well if you do, give her my love. She can be a funny old thing at times but she is a bloody good barmaid and no mistake. You could also pop into the Theatre Tavern and see if your photo is still adorning their walls. I remember when you signed it."

Ted grinned happily. "There are some memories in this town and no mistake. I always enjoy playing Yarmouth."

"Great Yarmouth," Rita corrected. "If the locals hear you dropping the Great they'll have you lynched."

Ted settled down with his jokes, while Rita lay down on the bed. It was going to be a busy time for her and no mistake.

***

Maurice and the boys were already in full swing when Jim arrived, the dancers were going through a number and a very drunken-looking figure swayed at the top of a short staircase awaiting her cue. It was worse than Jim had imagined. Lorna began to walk down the staircase and promptly fell over.

"Cut!" shouted Maurice.

Jenny walked from the auditorium where she had been witnessing events and up on to the stage. Two of the girls were helping Lorna to her feet.

"Some very strong black coffee is needed here I think," said Jenny, surveying the situation. "How on earth do you intend to face a paying public when you're quite obviously pissed as a newt?"

It was the first time Jim had ever heard Jenny blaspheme and he couldn't help having a giggle to himself. Her usual plummy vowels sounded strange using language not normally associated with her.

Jenny turned to Maurice in the pit. "Do you think we should take a short break Maurice? I can't see this one being much use for at least half an hour."

Maurice laid his baton down. "Perhaps we could take the girls through the final number again. Don had a few concerns about it."

Jenny put her hand to her forehead and gazed at the floor for a moment, a favourite pose of hers when she was trying to take command of things. Her flowery chiffon top and black stirrup bottomed slacks were doing nothing for the brown sandals that she had on her feet. Her hair had been pulled back by a band that looked far too tight and gave her the expression of a woman who had been surprised by something. "I think you are right Mo." She clapped her hands and faced her troupe. Lorna, who was still being supported by Robin, was struggling to focus.

"Take Miss West End or whatever she is currently known as back to her dressing room and tell that chap Reuben or someone to sober her up. Gals, get changed into your finale costumes and be back on stage in fifteen minutes and we'll take it from there."

Jenny moved down into the auditorium and approached Maurice. "I have never in all my years ever seen such an exhibition from a professional before."

Maurice reached over and touched Jenny on the arm. "My dear, if you had played some of the clubs I have endured over the years you would have seen worse than that. I really can't understand Don's determination to let this charade go ahead. This show will go down in theatre history as the Titanic of all pre-season shows at this rate. This show would have been great without a headliner. I have said it before and I'll say it again, Don needs to make a decision and fast."

Jim moved down the centre isle of the theatre. "I wonder if I might have a quiet word with you both. Can you come along to the office, it won't take long?"

Maurice dismissed his boys and the two followed Jim, exchanging quizzical looks between themselves.

When they emerged from the office, both Maurice and Jenny knew what was expected of them.

Jim left the theatre having done all that had been agreed with Don. He called by the box office to say goodbye to Maud and headed back home to see how things had been progressing in his absence. He was relieved to find that Debbie and Peter were sitting together on the settee and not, as he had feared, at either sides of the room. He greeted Peter with a handshake and smiled at his daughter, who winked back and went off to the kitchen to organise a pot of tea and some scones she had made earlier, while Peter and Jim discussed the latest on the sporting front. It was going to be just like old times again.

***

It became clear that Lorna was not able to work any further that day and Maurice agreed to call time at three-thirty.

Robin poured her vodka in the dressing room and smiled. "Say old thing, you haven't half put away some of this stuff today."

Lorna half-smiled. "Need a little snifter now and again, it keeps the old Dutch courage up. You should try some; it does wonders for you to let your hair down now and again."

"I don't think they were much impressed with your performance," said Robin, his head indicating towards the stage area. "If you just focused on the songs, you were doing fine earlier. You do have a voice."

"They don't know a star when they see one," slurred Lorna.

A knock came on the door and, without waiting to be invited, Maurice walked in. "Mr Preston," he said, addressing Robin and ignoring the state Lorna was in, "you would be advised to take Miss Ashby home to sleep off whatever it is she has had to drink today. I think I can speak on behalf of the profession when I say that if she isn't stone-cold sober by tomorrow there is little chance she will be allowed through the stage door let alone on the stage."

"I will be escorting Miss Ashby to her hotel shortly," Robin replied, taken aback.

"I am very pleased to hear it. I understand that Jack will be locking the stage door in fifteen minutes. I bid you both a good afternoon."

Lorna giggled. "Who the hell does he think he is? I bid you both a good afternoon, sounds like some butler at one of those posh hotels."

"We had better make a move Lorna; I can find a cab to take us back to Gorleston."

Lorna downed the last of her vodka. "And we had better call in an off licence on the way."

Luckily they will all be closed, thought Robin to himself as he pulled Lorna to her feet and they headed unsteadily towards the door.

***

Lucinda Haines had gone to some length to make sure she was turned out to perfection for her evening on the town. Rita was quite taken aback that she had it in her; she had scrubbed up quite well, all things considered. She detected the faint whiff of Moonbeams, a perfume favoured by some older women, but it had not made its way into Rita's life, she much preferred a more subtle fragrance. Ted had put on his best bib and tucker and when he presented himself before Lucinda she considered herself to be a very fortunate woman indeed to have such a well-turned-out escort for the evening. Rita, who never failed to marvel at her husband's performances, waved them both off as they got into a cab to take them to Divers for an evening of, what Rita imagined, would be a hoot. She went back into the boarding house and set about putting her plan in some kind of order both on paper and in her mind. A chat with Don Stevens was a priority; things were changing more quickly than a Bluebell girl.

Chapter Eight   *"Reflections"*

" June Ashby – Mr Gerard is ready for you now," the sound
of a tinny tannoy announced. June gathered her coat and
handbag and headed for the audition room.

James Gerard and two others sat behind a long desk. He
greeted June as she entered and introduced his colleagues. As
she had been warned, Gerard was the epitome of a toad. She felt
his watery bulbous eyes burn through her clothing. He smiled,
revealing his unkempt teeth and wiped his brow with a greying
handkerchief.

"Miss Ashby," he breathed heavily, "what are you going to
give us today?"

"Titania's speech from A Midsummer Night's Dream."

"And for your song my dear?"

"Can't Help Singing, I have the score here," she replied,
approaching the table.

James Gerard took the score and handed it to the lady on his
right. "Miss Morton will accompany on the piano, but first dear
girl, Titania."

June took a central position and proceeded to capture the
spirit of the fairy queen addressing her entourage. Gerard
nodded his approval at the end of the speech and glanced
sideways to each of his companions. "Reminiscent of Anna
Neagle, so elegantly portrayed." A sly smile played round his
moist lips. "Do you dance Miss Ashby?"

June nodded. "I have studied ballet, tap and contemporary
dance with the Eve Ballard School in Kensington."

Miss Morton glanced over the top of her spectacles. "Eve
and I attended the same school as gals. You must remember,

James, she choreographed Moonlight in the Park a couple of years ago at The Mermaid."

"I know her name certainly, but the content of the show has passed me by."

The small, hunched gentleman, who sat to his left, waved a feminine hand upwards. "My dear fellow, Moonlight was one of the dreariest things I have ever sat through, a brave attempt at trying to make a musical out of nursery rhyme content. Ballard's choreography was magnificent given the dreadful material she had to work with. The show folded after a month and then toured the provinces for a few weeks, causing uproar as I recall; one local rag described it as 'Jack and Jill take a tumble that no vinegar and brown paper can fix'."

"Thank you for your input Vernon," Miss Morton replied. "Perhaps we should press on; there are several others to see."

James Gerard wiped his brow again. "Yes indeed Mary. Miss Ashby, perhaps we could hear the song now."

Vernon Vines shuffled the papers in front of him and, pen poised, sat attentively as Mary began the introduction to the number.

June, who did not win the part of Clara, was to encounter the threesome on many more occasions. James Gerard was a trusted producer of small productions and it seemed that wherever he went Mary and Vernon followed. After auditioning for a fourth time, June found herself in the dancing chorus of a musical based loosely on The Thirty Nine Steps with Vernon as choreographer. Vernon, who was in his mid-fifties, was a dapper little man who certainly knew his craft. Though regarded by some in the profession as a 'spiteful old queen', he took a shine to June and offered her private tuition for which he charged no fee. Within a few short months June was auditioning successfully for much bigger fry than James Gerard. She continued to see Vernon as often as her timetable would allow and he followed her success with the watchful eye of a caring parent. June needed an agent and she begged Vernon to step into the breach, but he declined the many offers she made. Unbeknown to June, Vernon had cancer and within four years of their partnership, was dead, leaving June with a void she felt she would never be able to fill.

It was setbacks like these that were to haunt her career. Whenever she found someone on whom she could depend, fate stepped in to deal her a blow. But, ever resourceful, June would pick herself up, dust herself off and, as the song went, start all over again.

As the parts became bigger it was her decision to make her sister Veronica her understudy. They shared the same strong bone structure of their mother and had sometimes been mistaken for each other, but there the similarity ended. Veronica was a weak carbon copy of the talented June, and Lorna, the other sibling in question, the least talented of the trio. June had always felt that Veronica would, given the chance, step in to take her place. So it was no surprise that she was later to learn that the wicked stepsister had done just that, but in a roundabout way. Using click-tracks of her original recordings to cover the fact that the singing voice would not match the powerful and recognisable tones of her own. Clever in its own way, but it was not up to the scrutiny of Moira Clarence. The one time sweetheart of the working men's clubs and cabaret circuit with an enviable ear, Rita had spotted the fraud.

June's high life and fame had long since eluded her and though there were happy memories on which to reflect, the more painful ones had a way of making themselves more vivid and real. Her lost child, the breakdown, the days she had spent through a haze of anti-depressants and counselling. Shutting herself away from the public gaze she had tried to map out a new life for herself leaving behind the insecurities of a life in the theatre.

Now here she was heading back to the world she had abandoned and a certain tingle she hadn't felt for many a year was evident once more.

***

Rita was very fortunate to track down James Gerard. Speaking to him on the telephone he filled her in on what he knew about June.

"In every sense of the word she was a professional. However, she was sadly let down by the support around her. Old Vernon Vines, now if he had lived he would have steered June in the right direction. As for the sisters, as I now recall, I was aware of their existence but I never really came in contact with either."

Rita busily scribbled notes for herself. "You would know June if you were to meet her?"

"Most certainly, though I suppose the years will have changed her slightly, but there is one feature that time would not have erased."

"What is that?" Rita asked excitedly.

"June has a birthmark on her right arm, I noticed it when she first auditioned for me. She was wearing a short-sleeved dress and it is how I recognised her from the hundreds that auditioned for us in those days. In my mind she was the actress with the birthmark. June later covered the mark with five and nine or wore long-sleeved outfits on stage. I remembered several girls in the same sort of way, there was one called Averill who had a nervous twitch and another who was pigeon-toed. Mary Morton and I often had a chat about these kinds of things; like me, Mary has a wonderful memory for trivia. She settled in Corton, not far from where you are now. I can give you her number if you like. She will be able to confirm my story."

Rita took down the number and added it to her list of things to do next. "You have been a great help James."

"Are you going to tell me what this is all about?" he asked. "I have to say I find all of this rather intriguing."

Rita gathered her thoughts and began to relate the tale, keeping a watchful eye on the clock. There was much still to be done.

"Well I'll be blowed," James blubbered when Rita had reached the end of her story, "and June is on her way to see you? I must say I am very tempted to drive down to Great Yarmouth myself, it wouldn't take too long from here. Monday you say."

Rita gasped excitedly. "That would be marvellous if you could. I am sure June would be delighted to see you and it would help me no end. And if I could get Mary to join us that would be the icing on the cake."

"You'll find Mary a game old girl, that's if you are lucky enough to find her at home. She is forever gallivanting about visiting old friends and taking herself off on trips, that's when she isn't organising shows and music festivals."

The deal was settled, James would drive down to Great Yarmouth and, as luck would have it, Rita did find Mary at home and after a conversation that lasted for nearly an hour Mary agreed to join the party at Mrs Haines' boarding house.

Monday 5th May

June Ashby gazed out of the window as the train pulled away from Ipswich station, Norwich was less than an hour away now. Her flight to Heathrow had been a pleasant one, but travelling across London in a cab to Liverpool Street less so. The traffic had been particularly heavy and although the cab driver had used his knowledge to navigate the quickest route he knew, luck had not been on their side. Numerous roadworks and hold-ups stumped their every turn. The gloomy, unkempt railway station had hit June with memories of her past life. People were milling about and the cries of "paper" filled the grimy air from news vendors keen to move their supply as quickly as possible. She purchased her ticket to Norwich after joining a queue that seemed would take for ever to shift.

There was time to kill before the next departure so she decided to have a cup of tea in the café. The tea was a dark dirge of colour and the teacake she purchased would have been better named a rock cake as it was so stale. She found a table that clearly had not been wiped clean for some time, but as it was the only free space to be had she sat herself down. The stewed tea hit the back of her throat like thick tar. She had forgotten how bad English catering could be, but the alternative was instant coffee. However, after the fresh aroma of the French coffee she was accustomed to she didn't want to risk the disappointment.

The teacake proved unappetising and after one mouthful she pushed the thick white tea plate away and went to purchase a couple of packets of the biscuits on offer. The choice was hardly inspiring, three digestives, three custard creams or three Bourbons in cellophane packs. She plumped for two packets of digestives and went back to her beverage.

Gazing around at the people sitting at the tables she became aware that she might be considered to be overdressed. The Paris fashions, it seemed, had not travelled across the Channel to London. She foraged in her handbag for her packet of French cigarettes and her gold-plated lighter, a gift from an admirer way back. It was inscribed with the initials JA and on the reverse bore the inscription from Sacha with love. The acrid smoke from the Gitane attracted quizzical looks from other passengers, but June, oblivious to their stares, continued to enjoy her second cigarette of the day. It was a vice that she was careful to control, limiting herself to four or five a day; it was one of her sole pleasures. She pondered on whether she should risk a cup of instant coffee, but settled for another cup of tea, which was surprisingly very fresh this time round. Obviously the last brew had completed its three-hour marathon in the urn and had been replenished. She finished her cigarette and looked up at the large clock on the wall opposite. She picked up her suitcase and headed back onto the concourse, stopping off at the news-stand to purchase a copy of Woman's Own. She headed towards platform nine and boarded the first class compartment. Settling into a window seat she noticed a lady opposite who was applying her lipstick. Not wishing to engage in conversation June opened the pages of her magazine and began to read an article on summer picnic baking. Yes, she was truly back in Blighty and no mistake.

At the sound of the whistle, the train pulled away and began its journey. Tiring of the magazine June decided to close her eyes and rest quietly, preparing for whatever ordeal may await her in Norfolk. She was awoken from her slumber by the cry of the ticket inspector.

"Thank you madam," he said, handing June back her now punched ticket. "Forgive me madam, but your face is familiar."

June smiled but remained silent.

The inspector rubbed his chin expectantly. "It will come to me." He exited the compartment with a further cry of, "Tickets please, have your tickets ready for inspection."

The lady opposite stood up and retrieved her case from the rack above and made towards the door as the train approached Diss.

"June Ashby," she said, turning back to look at June. "I'd know your face anywhere."

When June finally embarked onto the Norwich platform she looked about her for a porter. A voice startled her and she turned around. "Well I'll be dammed, Moira Clarence, you haven't changed a bit."

Rita smiled. "We have never really met, not properly, how did you remember?"

June smiled. "There are some faces you never forget. You were at the reception for one of my shows, come on you must remember."

"I have been at so many after show receptions. I saw you work once I think at the Savoy before you opened in South Pacific, it was a play."

"Seven for a Secret," said June, her mind travelling back in time. "I played the lover of the leading man, Gerald something or other. I was a last-minute replacement for the leading lady because she had been unwell. You were at the first night party, I remember one of the cast pointing you out to me. I had wanted to come over and say hello, but you know how these things go."

Rita nodded. "Well I'm just plain old Rita now. I've a car waiting outside the station, shall we, or would you like a cup of tea first?"

June shook her head. "I'll pass on the tea if you don't mind."

***

Lucinda Haines was in a state of great elation. Not only had she had a wonderful evening out with Ted, she now found herself preparing rooms for more guests, thanks to Rita. She was retelling her good fortune to anyone who would listen and this took her attention away from Ted who was mightily relieved. Lucinda Haines and a couple of gins were a force to be reckoned with and no mistake. Buying in some extra provisions she bumped into Freda and Muriel who she secretly referred to as the Dolly Sisters. Freda was deciding on what was the cheapest bacon to buy, while Muriel was toying over a gammon steak for her Barry's tea.

"I am telling you I have never been so busy this early on in the season," said Lucinda, handing over her money to Mrs Jary in the corner shop. Mrs Jary nodded and made busy with tinned produce that had just been delivered, not wishing to be drawn into the conversation with the trio.

"Well," said Freda, folding her arms and setting herself up for a good natter, "you take in theatricals and me and my Dick don't hold with them sort. They comes in at all times of the night and your front door is never your own."

"But they always pay up front," said Lucinda, looking at Freda as if she was dirt off the bottom of her shoe. "Not like your lot, who leave you with sand all over the carpet and bunk off without paying."

"Who's been talking?" said Freda, looking at Muriel with suspicion.

"Don't you look at me like that Freda Boggis, Lucinda has heard nothing from me!" said Muriel.

"No, my lot are very friendly and always willing to slip the odd complimentary when the house isn't too full," cut in Lucinda, preparing to take her leave before things turned nasty. "I'll bid you ladies good afternoon."

"She really gets right up my nose," said Freda. "Really thinks she's a cut above the rest of us with her 'theatricals'."

Muriel laughed. "She only does it to wind you up Freda, take no notice. I remember old Haines when she didn't have a farthing but, give her her due, she built up her own little business without any help from family."

Freda clicked her tongue. "Mrs Jary, I'll have a couple of tins of baked beans and a small loaf. Not the Heinz, the cheap ones will do, they can go without bacon."

"I didn't know you had any in," said Muriel.

"Arrived last night on the doorstep, wanted to stay for a couple of nights."

Muriel thought for a moment. "Have they got a blue van?"

"Parked out my front," said Freda, finding her purse.

"She's tall, blonde and he is a chubby little guy?"

"That's them."

"I'd cancel that order if I were you Freda Boggis, I saw them loading their suitcases and driving off just after nine-thirty this morning. If you used your front door more often you'd have noticed it for yourself."

Mrs Jary sighed and replaced the tins of beans on the shelf. "Just the gammon steak then Mrs Evans?"

"Thank you," said Muriel, smiling to herself and handing over a five pound note. "My Barry likes a bit of gammon, he's never been that keen on baked beans."

Freda Boggis huffed and hurried out of the shop.

***

As they settled in the back of the car, June removed her jacket to reveal a short-sleeved blouse and Rita duly noted the birthmark that James had mentioned. It was warm inside the car and Rita wound down the window slightly. Rita wasn't familiar with this particular driver but Andy, as he had introduced himself, had been chatty enough on their journey from Great Yarmouth. He drove a little too fast for Rita's liking and she felt herself pressing her foot to the floor on her imaginary brake on more than one occasion.

"Did you ever play Great Yarmouth?" asked Rita, as the car headed onto the Acle Straight. "I am thinking of the Little Theatre, they have a very good repertory company there every year. Though I hear there may be plans afoot to make it into a cinema."

"I hardly ever played seaside resorts, mainly Bath, Harrogate, Leicester, Manchester and the like. I played a week in Norwich once at the Theatre Royal. I was asked by a member of the company if I fancied a day out to Great Yarmouth and I declined. When I think back I appeared in some strange things, long before shows like South Pacific were offered."

"Do you miss the business?"

"I used to and I have had a lot of time to reflect on yesterday's glories."

Rita motioned to Andy to slow down a bit. "You must have been livid when you found out what your sisters were up to?"

June laughed. "Actually I wasn't. In a strange way it made me laugh. You have to admire their bravado. What does amaze me is the way others apparently have been taken in by their deception."

"I knew something wasn't right from the off," said Rita with conviction. "My Ted couldn't understand why the engagement was made in the first place. No disrespect, but the name June Ashby is not one you would associate with a summer season let alone a pre-season variety show."

June pondered for a moment. "But then someone wanting to make a comeback of sorts might just try a different route."

"But not in Great Yarmouth!"

"Well no, now you put it so strongly. If I had been preparing a comeback I would have approached one of my old contacts and done a deal to tour in a play, I wouldn't have chosen a variety show at the seaside."

"I have to say that you have taken all of this remarkably calmly," said Rita.

"There is no point in my getting worked up over it. But don't think for one moment I haven't considered the fun I'll have when I take to the stage and surprise my darling sisters. The look on Veronica's face will be reward enough for me, just make sure she is in the front row."

"So you are going to do it then?"

A wry smile played on June's lips as she looked Rita straight in the eye. "Just try and stop me."

Rita squeezed her hand. "I think I am going to enjoy this."

As the car approached Great Yarmouth, Rita instructed Andy to go over to Southtown first, explaining to June that there was someone she wanted her to meet first before going on to Mrs Haines'.

Jim opened the door. "Rita, what a nice surprise, please come inside. What a shame, Debbie and Peter have just gone out for a stroll."

"Jim, there is someone I would like you meet, I would like to introduce you to the real June Ashby."

Jim held out his hand in greeting. "You are the third June I've met."

June shook Jim's hand. "And hopefully the last, I can assure you I am the genuine article."

June followed Jim through to the living room as Rita asked Andy to call back for them in an hour.

Over a cup of tea, which June was delighted to savour, they discussed what had gone before and how they would proceed. Following the more recent revelations and the discovery by Rita of the real June Ashby, Don had taken the precautionary step of delaying the official opening of the show until Monday 12th May, which would give them all more time to get their plan in order. Derinda Daniels would open that evening, performing her own set for the whole of the second half; Derinda's own small band would accompany her, meaning less for Maurice and his boys to worry about. Ted Ricer with Brian and the Dean Sisters performing a shorter version of their acts would do the first half, with an opening routine from the dancers not planned for the original show. Maurice would do a short piano interlude on stage in the style of 'party pops' which was always popular with audiences who could sing along.

A meeting was planned to go ahead at Mrs Haines' the following afternoon. June nodded her agreement.

"I will pay a visit to Veronica and tell her of the change to the opening," said Rita. "It might be a problem keeping her out of the picture."

"We must cross that bridge when we come to it," said Jim.

"Perhaps I could offer to take her up to Hull with me on the pretence I have to collect some more material for Ted."

"But that would only be one day."

"Not if my car unexpectedly won't start and we have to stay in Hull for a couple of days while it is fixed."

"Does Mrs Haines know who I am?" asked June. "How will you introduce me?"

"Don't you worry about Lucinda old lover," said Rita, "she is so thrilled to think I have fixed up three extra bookings. I've told her you are all friends of mine from way back and are in town to see the show. I also mentioned that you, my dear, are rather shy, so she won't bother you. Besides, she is so wrapped up in my Ted I am wondering if I shouldn't start divorce proceedings. I'll ask Ted to keep her occupied as much as possible, he will hate me for it but will understand when he eventually learns the truth."

"So you haven't told him," said Jim.

"Least said soonest mended," said Rita. "Now, if I am not mistaken that was your bell Jim, I expect Andy is back to collect us."

They said their goodbyes and as Jim closed the door he wondered whether everything would go according to plan.

***

It was quite a hive of activity in the Haines household that evening. The expected guests duly arrived and Mrs Haines was so preoccupied with providing teas and snacks she barely had time to draw breath. It was a nostalgic moment for James, Mary and June and they recalled how they had all first met. Times had changed James from the unkempt person he used to be. He appeared to have smartened himself up and, if June wasn't mistaken, those were a set of white dentures gleaming back at her. Mary had changed from her dowdy outfits of yesterday and was wearing brightly-coloured trousers and a top that wouldn't have been out of place in the Carnaby Street of the early sixties.

Ted was totally baffled by everything and asked Rita who this other June was. Rita kissed her husband playfully. "Now Ted, you are to pretend that she isn't here. If old Haines refers to her, say her name is Julie and say she's an old friend of the

177

family. You are not to mention our visitors to anyone, all will be revealed in the fullness of time old lover."

"This has something to do with…" began Ted, but Rita stopped him short.

"Now old lover, no questions please. Tomorrow afternoon I would like you to take Mrs Haines out so that the meeting that is planned can go ahead without interruption."

"And aren't I to be part of this meeting?" Ted asked, looking quite hurt.

"Sorry Ted, but it is best you are kept out of this. Promise me you won't discuss this with another living soul."

Ted knew when he was beaten. "I promise."

"Now, I suggest you try and arrange a restaurant for this evening for our guests and get Anglia Taxis to pick us up. Try Avernida's in Regent Road; no, on second thoughts, book somewhere out Lowestoft way, the further we are out of town the better. Now, while you sort that out I am going to pay a visit to Veronica Bright."

***

"I am sorry but June is having a lie down," said Gwen, when she opened the door.

"It is imperative that I see her," said Rita, surprised by Gwen's presence. She pushed her way past Gwen and into the hallway. "The official opening of the show is being delayed until next Monday, some technical problems. A condensed version of the show will open with Derinda Daniels."

Gwen closed the front door, slightly puzzled by the news. "You had better go through to the lounge; I'll let June know you are here. I am sure she will be very intrigued about this turn of events as indeed I am."

After a few moments Veronica (June) came into the lounge leaning heavily on her stick. "Rita, what a surprise, I was just having a nap, I've been feeling a bit off colour." The voice was slightly slurred.

It was clear to Rita that the lady before her was not looking her best. Her eyes looked tired and her body language seemed all wrong. Rita expressed her regret.

"Gwen, I wonder if you could organise some tea and biscuits for Rita and me please."

Rita made herself comfortable on an armchair and Veronica sat in her chair near the window. "Now, what is all this nonsense about the show not opening for another week?"

Rita summoned up her acting abilities. "I believe bookings for the first few days aren't terribly good and there have been suggestions about making some changes. Even old Ted has to provide some new material, not to mention costumes. As this is a comeback of sorts for June everything needs to be perfect."

"Rather a lot of trouble for such a small production." There was suspicion in the reply.

"I have it on good authority that Don is organising lots of press coverage. He wants to ensure that June is back with a bang."

"First I've heard of it," said Gwen, carrying the tea tray into the room. "He never mentioned anything to me."

"I am only repeating what I have been told."

Gwen flashed a look at Veronica. "I'll see if the kettle has boiled."

"I was wondering," said Rita, "if you would like to come to Hull with me tomorrow. I have to pick up some more things for Ted and the company would be most welcome, it can be quite a lonely drive and I thought you might enjoy the outing."

Veronica considered for a moment. "That is thoughtful of you Rita. However, I think I ought to stay here and support my sister."

Rita was expecting this kind of response. "June will be absolutely fine. She has Robin at her side and now that all that nonsense of using click-tracks has been dropped I believe she is finding it much easier singing songs more familiar to her. I believe Robin plans to play for her, rather than using the full orchestra."

Veronica glanced out of the window for a moment. "Actually, a trip out might be just the thing I need. I have been cooped up in here too long. What time were you thinking of leaving?"

"About three-thirty."

"Oh, I thought you would want an early start, I am sure I could manage the morning."

"I have some business to attend to first and besides the roads tend to be clearer in the afternoon."

Gwen had been listening at the door and came in with the teapot. "I don't think it is a very good idea, you going out, you haven't been well."

"No one was asking you dear," snapped Veronica. "Besides, what harm can a trip in an automobile do me. Now, if you would make yourself scarce I would like to have a further chat with Rita."

Gwen bristled at the tone of Veronica's voice and, scowling at Rita, she left the room slamming the door behind her.

***

The news that the show had postponed the opening night had broken earlier that day and was soon being talked about around the town. The Eastern Daily Press led under the headline:

Show in Trouble?

Don Stevens has postponed the official opening of his pre-season show. In a statement given to the press last night he explained that the West End singing sensation June Ashby had been unwell, suffering with a throat infection. He had, however, secured the services of Derinda Daniels who would play performances until Saturday 10th May to allow Miss Ashby recovery time before her own appearance, now rescheduled for Monday. Miss Daniels is a well-loved vocalist and comes with her own musicians. She will play the entire second half. The first half will see the other members of the original company. Anyone wishing to change their tickets or have their money refunded should go to the theatre box office in person where the box office staff will be more than happy to help. Don Stevens continued, "I apologise for any disappointment this may have caused, but I can assure you that the show will go on and anyone wishing to see both Derinda Daniels and June Ashby and who book both the shows at the same time will be given a free programme and complimentary drink in the interval".

Bad publicity was something that Don Stevens could well do without and his decision to give the paying public a deal was a marketing ploy. A couple of other shows he had had in the pipeline had been hit by financial problems and had had to be cancelled leaving two other resorts without a pre-season attraction. Don hoped that if this show was a success he could repeat it in other resorts over the next few years. Variety acts were on the increase abroad, with several clubs looking for acts to fill their restaurant-come-cabaret venues. His old pal Jonathan had been on to him about the possibilities of sending acts on the cruise liners. It was important for Don to make as much money as he could over the next few years so he could retire as he had promised himself, before he got too old to enjoy the finer things of life.

***

Maud Bennett was not happy to hear about the postponed opening.

"Never been heard of," said Maud, getting into her stride to Barbara who had come in to help. "Postponing an opening indeed. The bookings were looking quite healthy. Though it has to be said, the advert in the Eastern Daily Press mentioning Derinda Daniels has stirred more interest. She even got a mention on the local radio. She is a very popular act. But now, of course, we will have some people wanting to exchange tickets for next Monday. I can't imagine how they are going to let people know about the change of programme, especially those expecting to attend an opening night party. I think the mayor was due to put in an appearance this evening. What a mess."

It was unusual for both box office windows to be open for an early season show, but now word was out about the change to the schedule all hell could break loose. However, a lot of people where happy to stay with their original performance and see Derinda Daniels but also wanted tickets for the following Monday night as well. Lilly came by the office and tapped on the door, the queue had now dispersed and she felt like a chat.

"I'll get off then," said Barbara, pulling on her coat. "The worst seems to be over."

Lilly settled herself on an available stool.

"Strange goings on here and no mistake," said Maud.

"You should see what's going on in the theatre," said Lilly. "That so-called top of the bill looks like she has a hangover. That chap she's got with her has been pumping her full of aspirin the best part of the morning. Jenny's gals are getting mighty fed up with all the stopping and starting and Maurice looks like he's about to throw in the towel."

"When I got that phone call from Jim yesterday you could have knocked me down with a feather. Postponed opening, I ask you, never in all my born days."

There was no doubt about it, Maud hadn't taken the news well and it had meant extra work for her, delaying her all-important knitting.

***

The Dean Sisters were seated in the stalls watching as Lorna went through her paces. "She is much better than she was," whispered Sue. "She seems to have perked her up having that bloke beside her."

"Lilly could do as well," said Jill, with a grin. "I've heard her in the mornings out front, fair gives the musicals a bashing.

Her Wouldn't It Be Lovely would give Julie Andrews a run for her money."

"At least they are not using click-track. That was a stupid idea," Dawn added. "We only use them in an emergency, otherwise it's us singing and not many people could do that while balancing on a ball."

"Come on you two, we had better go, we're supposed to on after this," said Jill, getting up. "That's if she ever finishes that song."

Just at that moment Don walked on to the stage. "Your attention folks if I may."

"Now what?" Jill sighed.

"With the exception of the Dean Sisters, Ted, Brian and the dancers who I would like to remain in the theatre, the rest of you may go. You will have read or heard that the official opening of this show has been delayed until Monday 12th. Derinda Daniels will be performing here tonight and for the rest of the week. June, I would like you and Robin to get off home and rest up in readiness for that opening. A full dress-rehearsal will take place on Monday afternoon."

"I don't understand, what is going on?" said Lorna, clinging to Robin's side.

Don looked her straight in the eye. "Get home and sort yourself out or your comeback will not happen."

***

Meanwhile the preparations for the new show were moving along at a cracking pace. Mystic Brian had resurrected a part of his act that hadn't been seen for a while so that he wouldn't be doing the same act when he opened with June Ashby. Likewise, the Dean Sisters had rehearsed a new number and added some tumbling to ensure everything looked fresh. Ted found some different jokes to tell and Jenny was using an opening number for the dancers that she had last used a few years before with the girls dressed as Follies Girls, head to toe in feathers. The feathers were beginning to moult a bit as they had been in storage for some time, but they should be okay for the Derinda Daniels show.

***

Amidst all the drama, Derinda Daniels opened at the Golden Sands Theatre that evening and the audience gave her a rousing welcome. Everything went as planned and Don heaved a sigh of relief when the curtain came down. He went backstage to thank Derinda personally, which she greatly appreciated. Jenny and the dancers had pulled it off with their opening routine, Brian's act went down a treat, Ted raised the roof with his jokes and the Dean Sisters brought gasps of surprise from the audience.

***

The meal in Lowestoft was a great success with everyone talking at once and recalling the old days. Rita had made an effort with a chiffon outfit she had purchased a few days before and was outshone only by the designer creation that the real June wore that sparkled as the light caught the delicate beading.

***

Ted found himself engaged in companionship with Lucinda Haines following his appearance in the show and treated her to a couple of games of bingo on the seafront and then a fish and chip supper out of newspaper before taking her for a nightcap in the Barking Smack. Spotted by Freda and Muriel, who were taking a constitutional, it wouldn't be long before the whole town was talking about Lucinda Haines and the company she was keeping.

Tuesday 6th May

Rehearsals for the real June would take place in the afternoons at a hall in Hopton and a full dress-rehearsal would take place for her on the Sunday afternoon at the theatre before opening on Monday. A plan to keep Lorna away from the theatre had been put in to action by Don earlier but it would require everyone's cooperation.

184

Don would ensure that he kept Gwen busy and would, if possible, pack her off back to London on the pretence that his wife was expected in Great Yarmouth. James and Mary offered their support and promised to help out where Lorna was concerned, if needed. They would pretend that they knew her from the old days. Robin, however, would be another problem. Jim thought he might be able to take him off for a drink somewhere, though personally he couldn't stand the man.

Throughout, June remained silent, but she felt the excitement building inside her. She had always thought she would never return to the business, but now she couldn't wait to stand in the spotlight again.

The party broke up and June was ferried to Hopton, with James and Mary in tow. The dancers and a pianist were ready to help her rehearse for her unexpected comeback.

Don caught up with Gwen back at the hotel. She was sitting in the lounge with a pot of coffee. As he approached her she looked up. "Look what the wind has blown in, what do you want?"

Don sat down opposite her. "I would like you to return to London Gwen, I need you there to look after things back at the office. I am going to be tied up here a bit longer than I had anticipated."

"That is the understatement of the year if what I have heard and read is anything to go by. What makes you think I want to go on working for you?"

"That, of course, is entirely up to you," said Don, and the tone of his voice suggested he wasn't bothered by the statement. "But if you want to be paid at the end of the month I suggest you get packed. Besides, Elsie will be arriving tomorrow and unless you want a showdown with her you had best make yourself scarce. Elsie will be assisting me while we go through this transitional period."

Gwen bristled at the news. "I suppose there is nothing to keep me here, now that the official show has been postponed. If I didn't know you better, I'd say you were up to something. Come on Don, spill the beans, what exactly is going on here? Why don't you just let the show go ahead as planned tonight, why bring in another artiste? June is doing okay now from what I've heard."

"There is nothing going on that need concern you. In fact here's the deal, I think you would be better served by looking for alternative employment."

Gwen watched Don as he stood up to take his leave. "I am sorry it has come to this Gwen, but it is probably best for all concerned."

Gwen sat staring into her coffee cup feeling totally used and betrayed.

Gathering her thoughts, she picked up her handbag and headed out of the hotel. Setting off in her car she arrived at Veronica's and let herself in. She found Veronica in the lounge putting some items into a small bag.

Veronica turned round startled. "Oh, it's you, you gave me a fright. I am just getting some things together for my trip out with Rita."

Gwen slumped herself down.

"What's eating you, cat got your tongue?"

"Don thinks I should look for another job – the old bastard has been stringing me along good and proper."

"But in effect that's what you've been doing too," Veronica said, easing herself into a chair with the aid of her stick. "You didn't really think he was going to leave his wife did you?"

"Why should she get money that by rights should be coming to me? I am the one that has been doing the work all these years."

"You speak as if you are expecting him to die any time soon."

"Well, with his kind of pressurised lifestyle it can't be too far off."

"You really are quite callous aren't you my dear?"

"It takes one to know one. I am going to make a drink, want a cup?"

"That would be very nice."

"Have you taken your medication this morning?"

Veronica nodded.

"Well, if you are set on going off with Rita for the day, you better make sure you have some with you. I'll get some from the bathroom."

Gwen put the kettle on and then headed upstairs; she opened the bathroom cabinet and emptied the contents into a small paper bag. Then from an envelope she had she tipped the contents into the bottle.

She ran down the stairs smiling.

"Pop these in your bag and don't forget what the doctor said, you must take them regularly and if you feel an attack coming on you should take two straight away. I'll get the tea."

Veronica looked out of the window and was pleased to see the sun shining. She was looking forward to going out for the day. It would be nice to be free of the house for a while and she had warmed to Rita. Many years before she had a friend just like Rita and when they weren't working they had taken themselves off to all kinds of places. Veronica missed the companionship and had once hoped she had found a new companion in Gwen, but Gwen had turned out to be similar to her, headstrong, cold and calculating.

Gwen returned with a tray and poured the tea. "I've made you a sandwich, thought you might want to take a tablet before the off. What time is Rita coming to collect you?"

"No specific time, she had some business to attend to this morning. She just told me to be ready." She sat quietly eating the ham sandwich as Gwen sipped her tea. When she had finished she swallowed a tablet from the bottle Gwen had given her.

"I have written a cheque for you Gwen, it isn't much, but it should be enough to tide you over until the other comes through. It's on the sideboard, don't forget to take it."

"Thanks," replied Gwen, "I won't. I think I'll go for a walk, I don't want to be around when Rita arrives."

"Why ever not, Rita is a very nice lady?"

"There is something about her that spooks me."

Veronica laughed. "You are a funny one and no mistake."

Gwen went over to the sideboard and picked up the cheque, it was for five hundred pounds. She noticed the chequebook lying nearby and picked it up too, slipping it into her jacket pocket unobserved by Veronica who was once again gazing out of the window. "Are you sure you've got everything you need, anything I can get you from upstairs?"

Veronica turned from the window. "No thanks my dear, I shall be back this evening, we are only doing a round trip."

Gwen picked up her handbag. "Well, I will leave you in peace. Have a safe trip, I am off for that walk."

Veronica picked up the bottle of tablets and took another two and sat herself down for a moment. It was turning into a very strange day.

Chapter Nine   *"The Masquerade"*

When Rita arrived to collect Veronica, she found her in a state of agitation. Veronica appeared somewhat breathless and was slumped in a chair. Rita had let herself in through the front door, which had been left open. Alarm bells rang in Rita's head.

"June, whatever is the matter?" said Rita, dropping her handbag to the floor and rushing to Veronica's side.

Veronica brushed away Rita's hand. "I'll be fine in a minute or two, I have just had a funny turn, it happens sometimes, nothing to worry about."

Rita fetched a glass of water. There were a few moments of silence between them and then Veronica said, "Well, I am ready to set off if you are."

"Are you sure you feel okay? I don't want you to be taken ill on the drive, it is quite a long way you know."

Veronica took her bag from the table. "I have my pills in here and besides, I can always take forty winks, the motion of a car often sends me to sleep."

Feeling slightly less alarmed, Rita picked up her own bag and the two of them headed outside where Rita had left her car running. Veronica locked the front door behind her and putting the key in her bag got into the front passenger seat.

"Mrs Haines has packed us two flasks of hot tea and some sandwiches and biscuits for the journey," Rita said, winding down her window. "We can always stop off at a café on the way if we want something more substantial."

Veronica patted Rita's hand. "I am sure we will be fine my dear, you seem to have thought of everything."

189

***

Gwen had taken herself along the seafront and sat down on a bench just outside the Wellington Pier and thought what she should do next. From her bag she took out the chequebook she had stolen and her expression darkened. She had picked up the joint chequebook that belonged to Veronica and Lorna and it required both their signatures in order to remove money from the account. She cursed as she dropped the book back into her bag and was taken by surprise when she heard the voice of Don from behind her.

"I thought you would have left town by now," he said, walking round the bench to face her.

"Don't worry, I will be leaving soon enough," she replied, not looking at him.

"I'm glad I found you, change of plan. If you return to the office you will find Elsie working there. She will be taking over until I can find a replacement for you. The keys you have will be of no use to you now as she is having the locks changed. I have asked her to have your salary made up and there will be a two hundred pound bonus. You see my dear, she is as keen to have you out of her life as I am to have you out of mine."

"You have thought of everything haven't you?" said Gwen, standing up and turning to go. "To think I used to be the thinking power behind your little empire."

Don laughed. "You thought you were, but believe me my dear I was always one step ahead of you."

Don watched as Gwen, swinging her bag over her shoulder, walked away. He saw something tumble from her bag and walked over to retrieve it, it was a chequebook. Don looked at the book and shook his head sadly. He put the item safely in his jacket pocket intending to return it to its rightful owner later in the week. He walked on to the Wellington Pier, mentally preparing himself for a meeting with the entertainments manager there in the hope of securing an end-of-season show for two weeks.

If the sea air seemed momentarily bracing, it felt as nothing to the coldness stabbing at Gwen's heart as she continued along the promenade. The people passing by enjoying the sights, sounds and smells of the seaside town barely registered with her. She had thought that everything had been planned to a fault, but it seemed that her plans were unravelling. She tried to think how it had all come about. She had covered her tracks carefully and never left anything to chance, but there had obviously been a flaw somewhere. For months she had been mentally working out how she could inherit a wealth of money that she knew had been so well hidden. But her constant investigating and turning up the correct papers stashed in old hat boxes had led her to the pot of gold. Now the pot had vanished and of the promised rainbow there was no sign. She now knew she had to move fast and get away before the rest of her plan was found out.

***

Jim caught up with Robin who had returned to the theatre to collect a few things Lorna had left behind.

"I don't know what has got in to her," Robin said sounding deflated. "I have never known her to hit the bottle quite this hard before."

"Look old mate, I have a plan and I will need your help to carry it out," said Jim, patting Robin on the shoulder. "I have made arrangements for you both to stay at a theatrical guest house in Norwich until you can both return for the opening. It will do you both good to go there and relax a little. Keep any kind of drink out of the way, visit the castle, do some shopping, but most of all keep an eye on things. I think you know what I mean."

Jim handed Robin a large envelope. "Everything is paid for and you will find the address of the guest house in here. Judy Allen will make you most welcome, she is an old pro from the music hall days. There is some spending money enclosed and a couple of complimentary tickets to see the play currently running at the Theatre Royal."

"Thanks Jim," Robin replied, taking the envelope, "that is very kind of you, I appreciate your help."

Jim grinned. "Just doing what is best all round mate, for the sake of this show. There are a lot of reputations riding on it, not least Lorna's."

"Oh yeah," said Lorna, appearing as if from nowhere, "there is nothing wrong with my reputation."

Robin exchanged a look with Jim and took Lorna by the arm. "We are going on a little trip together."

"I don't want to go on any little trip. I have a show to rehearse."

"Not today you don't," said Robin, taking firm control of the situation.

Jim smiled to himself, it had been easier than he thought and he just hoped it would work and that the pair didn't return unexpectedly. He walked backstage and down into the auditorium and found Lilly humming to herself as she cleaned the brass rail around the orchestra pit.

"Hello Lilly, did you ever think of going on the stage, you have the singing voice for it?"

Lilly stopped work and looked up. "Me, on the stage? My parents would have had kittens and what my late husband would have made of it I dread to think. No, I am just a cleaner me, but thanks for the compliment."

Jim smiled and made his way up the theatre aisle.

As he walked out on to the pier the bracing air had been replaced by a warm breeze gently blowing off the sea. The gulls were swooping and whooping and he could see one or two people taking a paddle in the cold waters of the North Sea. He lit a cigarette and inhaled deeply. Voices distracted his idle thoughts and he turned to see Robin pulling Lorna along the pier with bags swinging from side to side from her arms.

Dave sauntered up the pier waving at Jim. "Where are they off to?" he asked, inclining his head to the departing pair.

"Taking a break in Norwich to let the dust settle I hope," Jim said, pleased to see his old mate. "Things haven't been going too great here."

"You are telling me." Dave grinned, lighting up. "It's the talk of Palmer's coffee bar. I was in there earlier today and people were chatting about it. One old guy was very put out as he and his wife are going home tomorrow and will miss seeing June Ashby."

Jim nodded. "I do feel sorry for these people. It is probably their only break during the year and they look forward to seeing a show. I think it was a great mistake to make this twice nightly. To my mind there isn't enough business to warrant it this early in the season, though I do know bus loads from the villages are being brought in on some ticket deal that has been made with the coach companies."

Dave looked out towards the sea and took in the view. "I wonder why we put ourselves through this every year?"

"It's because we both love the job."

"Either that or we are barking mad."

And Jim concluded that his mate might well have a point.

***

Gwen caught up with Lorna and Robin as they were just getting into Robin's car.

"Where are you two off to, I thought you would be in the theatre?"

Robin explained the situation to Gwen as Lorna settled herself in the car. Gwen listened as Robin expressed his concern about Lorna.

Gwen opened her handbag. "I have just the solution," she said, handing him a bottle of pills. "These will keep her on the straight and narrow and calm her down a bit. Herbal things I use sometimes. A friend recommended them to me, they work like a dream. Three every couple of hours and all her problems will be over."

Robin thanked her and Gwen, smiling, waved as the car drove off.

Making her way back to Veronica's she headed for the spare room where she had hidden a locked suitcase. She took out the tweed two-piece suit, white blouse and court shoes. Going to the bathroom she removed her clothes and washed the makeup from her face. Then with artistry she applied a slightly darker foundation, false eyelashes, a pale eye shadow and pillar-box-red lipstick. She brushed her hair upwards and carefully pulled on the stocking wig cap and deftly put on the short, reddish-brown wig and combed it in to place. The slight greying at the temples which her friend Bruce had done for her at the salon was a stroke of genius. The set of top teeth which had been made for her by a theatrical dental practice in London gave her mouth a slightly protruding appearance. Her evening training classes as a professional makeup artist were coming in to their own. She had tried out a couple of disguises back in London and had even managed to fool Don one night in a public bar. Practising different voices had revealed her to be the perfect mimic and she could turn her talent to practically any given dialect in the country.

She discarded her stockings and pulled on the brown ribbed tights. Then, putting on the tweed outfit and court shoes, she looked at herself in the full-length mirror. She went to Veronica's bedroom and took one of her spare walking sticks. Returning to the mirror she practised leaning heavily on the stick and walked slowly up and down the room. The look wasn't quite right, she needed some extra accessories and Veronica's jewel case provided them in spades. A string of pearls and a pair of pearl-studded earrings would set the illusion off nicely. She looked at her manicured nails and quickly removed the pink nail polish. Brown leather gloves would hide the youthful hands so that her transformation to an elderly lady would be complete.

Moving quickly, she put her own discarded clothes and shoes into a carrier bag, intending to dump them in a bin. Into a weather-beaten handbag she placed a small wallet containing money she had accumulated from Veronica. Remembering the chequebook she went to look in the bag now in the carrier, but the book was missing. She must have dropped it and racked her brains to think where it might be. Looking at her watch she quickly cleared up any traces of her having been back in the house. The suitcase was quite heavy and she struggled getting it down the stairs and to the front door. Fortunately, the mini she had secretly purchased was parked only two streets away. She checked that she had the address of Rita and Ted's home in Hull and leaving the suitcase inside the front door went to get the car. Remembering she was an old lady, she walked slowly along leaning on the stick and taking her time. There were one or two people about, but no one she knew. She drove the car to the front of the house and put the suitcase in the boot. As she got back into the car and checked the mirror she saw that she had forgotten one other piece of her disguise, the spectacles. She opened the glove compartment and put them on. Smiling to herself and in a broad Scottish accent she uttered the words, "Oh Doctor Finlay, it's only Janet," and laughing she turned the ignition key and set off on her journey to Hull.

***

Marie Jenner busied herself in the shop and at last all the stock was displayed. She fell into the only chair she had and heaved a heavy sigh. Her thoughts returned to her daughter. She was worried in case anything had happened to her. Though Sara was a sensible girl and could look after herself, she had read so many things about girls going missing and dreadful things

195

happening to them. She wondered if she should involve the police.

A familiar voice invaded her thoughts and she saw Alf standing in the doorway.

"Thought you might be able to use a hand," he said, surveying the organised shelves.

"Just like a man to turn up when everything is done," said Marie, getting up. "You can take me home; I am in need of long hot soak and a cuppa."

"I'll drive if you like."

"Thanks Alf, that would be most welcome."

***

The traffic was proving to be slow. There seemed to be too many cars on the road that afternoon and Rita was finding her concentration lacking somewhat. She liked to set off and get to her destination with the minimum of fuss. Her companion had been relatively quiet. She had complained an hour into setting off of a mild chest pain and had taken some more of her medication when Rita had pulled into a lay-by for a drink from the flask. At this rate Rita wasn't going to need an excuse to keep Veronica out of the way, the traffic would see to that.

It was nearing seven o'clock when they finally arrived outside the house. Rita helped Veronica out of the car and then gathered a couple of shopping bags from the boot. They had pulled up at a shop on the way to buy milk and bread, with the idea of getting fish and chips for supper before setting off again to Great Yarmouth. While Veronica settled herself in the small lounge, Rita turned on the heating and set about making some coffee.

"I will go out for some fish and chips presently," she called out to Veronica as she carried a cup of coffee through to the lounge. Veronica appeared to have nodded off in the chair and Rita put the cup and saucer down on the table beside her.

She gave Veronica a light tap on the arm but there was no visible response. She tried again and Veronica's head flopped to one side. Rita leant nearer to her and could detect only a slight up and down movement of the chest. She tried to rouse Veronica by calling her name and tapping her hand. Then, remaining as calm as she could, Rita dialled 999.

Gwen had arrived half an hour after Rita and Veronica, just in time to see the ambulance pull up outside the house. She watched as the stretcher was carried into the back of the ambulance with Rita behind it. Gwen followed the ambulance with its siren blaring out, but she was unable to keep up with it as it darted in and out of the evening traffic. Slowing down she decided that there was really no rush and followed the signs to the general hospital. Finding a bay in the car park, she made her way to Emergency. She spotted Rita being spoken to by a nurse and decided to sit in the waiting area to see what would happen. There were a few people sitting around and she found a seat nearest to the drinks machine. Taking a hot chocolate she settled down and was surprised when Rita walked towards her looking decidedly grey. At first she thought that Rita had recognised her. Rita got herself a coffee from the machine and sat down in the vacant seat next to Gwen.

"Are you okay my dear?" said Gwen, turning to look at the worried Rita.

Rita who was normally in control of her emotions suddenly began to cry and told the Scottish lady about her friend who had suddenly collapsed.

Gwen listened and patted Rita's hand, "It happens to all of us as we get older."

Rita nodded and apologised for off-loading her worries. Just then a nurse came over and asked Rita to go with her and nodding thanks at her neighbour Rita followed the nurse.

Gwen decided that she would not wait any longer; it was obvious that Veronica would not be leaving the hospital that night, if at all. She drove off and booked herself in to a small hotel for the night under the name of Janet Cameron. A good night's sleep was what she needed and then, refreshed, she could return to the hospital the next day, a plan already in her organised mind.

Wednesday 7th May

After a long night at the hospital, Rita returned home early that morning in a taxi feeling drained and exhausted. Veronica had slipped into unconsciousness during the night and the doctors were of the opinion that the medication she was taking was not suitable for a woman in her delicate condition. Rita filled the kettle and made herself a hot drink and sank down into an armchair. She had been so concerned with the heavy traffic that she hadn't spotted the signs the day before that Veronica was not at all well, though her earlier observations should have alerted her. Her hands trembled as she put the cup to her lips and a horrid thought dawned on her, someone had tampered with the bottle of tablets she felt sure and that someone could only have been Gwen. She had witnessed Gwen giving Veronica medication on her visits and had also seen the array of bottles and potions in the bathroom back at the house in Great Yarmouth.

She pulled herself up and called Lucinda Haines to rouse Ted, she needed to act quickly.

Ted quickly washed and shaved and, draining the hot tea that Lucinda had brought to him, headed out in search of Don Stevens.

Lucinda's vivid imagination worked overtime, she hoped that Rita would not turn out to be a murderer if Veronica didn't make it. Who knows, she could be her next victim. Making eyes at a married man, whatever had she been thinking of?

***

The mood in the pier office was a sombre one. Don gave as many details as he could to the police and Jim said he would get

Rod, one of the backstage boys to drive up to Hull and collect Rita, who understandably was in no fit state to drive herself.

The whole company was assembled in the auditorium as Don, with Jim by his side, tried to explain to the company how Lorna Bright had been masquerading as June Ashby. The announcement was met with a certain amount of calm and it was left to Mystic Brian to stand up and say that he thought all along that something was amiss. The Dean Sisters nodded in agreement. It was Ted who stood up and asked that everyone remained quiet about this turn of events. It would be in the papers soon enough and this in turn would create its own questions and answers. Then it was the turn of the real June Ashby to walk on to the stage. Everyone fell silent as she spoke.

"Firstly, I would like to say hello to you all and in time I am sure you will learn how this rather crazy situation came to be. I would like to confirm to you that I shall be headlining this show from next Monday and I look forward very much to working with you fellow professionals. Can I just thank you all for rallying round the way you have and a big thanks to Miss Daniels for stepping in at the last minute, it really has helped us all out of a tight spot. As dear old Ethel Merman once sang Let's go on with the show."

A thunderous round of applause and cheering broke out throughout the auditorium and June felt she was on her way back to the business she had so long been away from.

Once things had settled down, preparations continued. The dancers were in fine step and their routines with June were winning comments from the rest of the cast. Mystic Brian's doves behaved themselves, the Dean Sisters rolled and sang on their glittering balls like never before and Ted, with an anxiety he hid well, told some of the best jokes of his career and had the orchestra falling about with laughter. When June came onto the stage, the company gathered holding their breath. Lilly, who had returned to do some last minute cleaning at the back of the theatre, folded her arms and watched. With very little rehearsal the words of long-forgotten songs from musicals had come back to June and she felt a slight tingle as the orchestra played in the opening bars. Maurice gave her an encouraging smile and a warm and melodic voice filled the theatre. When June sang Some Enchanted Evening, Ted felt a tear prick his eyes and he remembered back to the days when he and Rita had first met. Mystic Brian hummed along to himself and the Dean Sisters swayed in time to the melody. When June reached the end of her set, she was physically moved by the reception she received. Her hands trembled slightly as she took a long and deep bow and happy memories of opening nights danced through her mind.

Derinda Daniels, who sat in on the rehearsal, told Don to make sure that there were tickets for the Monday night for her and her band, she didn't want to miss June's return, and she had been as intrigued as everyone else by the unravelling tales she was hearing.

James and Mary greeted June in the wings, congratulating her warmly as they went with her back to her dressing room. Mary set about making a drink, while James sat in quiet thought as June sat down at the dressing table.

"It's like you have never been away," said James, with a smile, "it was just like old times."

June smiled. "I have no idea where it came from. The limited rehearsal time, I found myself almost swallowing the words and the power at first seemed sadly lacking. Even I was taken by surprise today, it must have been the orchestra playing from the pit and the warmth from the spotlight that made everything come together."

"June, it is so wonderful to see you back on form. I can't tell you how much I have longed for this moment. You were a star back then and you will be again."

"One step at a time James, but you know, I think I might just be willing to put my toe in the water one more time."

"That's my girl," said James happily, "that's my girl!"

Jenny popped her head round the door. "Hi June, just wanted you to know we are taking a break, but we would like to go through the routines in say an hour?"

June nodded. "That will be fine."

"Your costumes are being taken care of by a local lady we sometimes use; she will pop in later for some measurements. Some of the stock costumes will be okay for the group numbers, but Don wants you to have a couple of new gowns for your solo spot and the finale. Lots of feathers, sequins, you know the stuff."

"But will they be ready in time?"

Jenny winked. "Don't you worry, my mate Betty is very experienced with needle and thread and her good old treadle."

As Jenny disappeared June laughed. "Do people still use treadle machines?"

"If you don't mind me saying so," said Mary, entering with a tray of drinks and some biscuits, "treadles are far more reliable than those electric things they make these days. My old Gran still uses her treadle and she will be ninety-eight next month."

A few minutes later June found herself alone with Wally who had arrived earlier, but had stayed in the background. June had taken a sharp intake of breath when she first spotted him; he looked as handsome as she had remembered. The conversation was awkward, it had seemed better on the phone, the distance between them had made the conversations easier. They skirted around the issues that for years they had wanted to talk about. Now they were looking at each other and remembering; remembering the joy they had once shared and the pain that had ensued. Their lives could have been so different. Wally took June by the arm and led her out on to the pier. They walked silently together, allowing the sea air and the sound of the seaside to engulf them. Then suddenly they both stopped and turned to look at each other. Their eyes met and they both knew that the time had come to put the past behind them and with a gentle embrace they kissed.

***

Robin's call to the theatre office came in the middle of things and Don was called away from rehearsals to take it. He listened to Robin, noting the words carefully. After the week he had been having, nothing surprised him any more. He found Jim and reported the news. Jim was shocked by what he heard. Lorna was in the Norfolk and Norwich hospital after having her stomach pumped of the tablets that Robin had innocently given her. It was early days, but the doctors expected that Lorna would make a full recovery. It was also thought that she would be admitted to another ward later on to help her with her drink dependency.

***

When Jim arrived home later that day, he found Debbie and Peter watching a hospital drama on the television. How apt, he thought, recalling the moments of the last few hours, and went to pour himself a large brandy left over from Christmas.

***

After a late breakfast, Gwen in her guise of Janet returned to the hospital and enquired at reception where she might find Veronica. She explained that she had been in the night before when her friend had been taken in. Gwen was asked to take a seat and was shortly approached by the Sister. The Sister explained that it was out of visiting hours but she could allow Gwen to visit Veronica for ten minutes and no longer. She showed Gwen into a private room.

Gwen looked at the Veronica who was hooked up to a drip; she looked tired and drawn, but peaceful. Checking that no one was nearby, Gwen approached the bedside. She took one of the extra pillows at the bottom of the bed and held it over Veronica's face. "Goodbye my dear," she said. When she felt quite sure she had smothered her, Gwen replaced the pillow and left the room.

She thanked the receptionist and said she would be back to visit again later.

A nurse came into the room and checked the chart at the bedside and gently lifted Veronica's head to a more comfortable position and as she did so Veronica opened her eyes and blinked.

Gwen returned to her car and retrieved the suitcase from the boot then returning to the hospital she went to the toilets located on the ground floor next to the snack bar. Locking herself in a cubicle she quickly removed her disguise, only to replace it with another one. This time a slightly longer brown wig and lighter makeup gave her a more youthful look. She changed her tweed for a black trouser suit and pumps. A pair of tortoise shell glasses and a headscarf completed the transformation. Quickly closing her suitcase she left the cubicle and checked her appearance in the mirrors over the sink area. She decided to adopt a light, lilting Irish accent and went out to test it on the receptionist first, asking where she might find a payphone. It worked perfectly, the same receptionist whom she had spoken to earlier did not recognise her as the Scottish lady she had spoken to before and pointed towards the telephone.

Gwen called the theatre management office and asked where she might be able to locate Lorna Bright as she had some flowers to deliver. The office assistant who answered asked her to hold while she checked. A few moments later she explained that Lorna was in the Norfolk and Norwich hospital. Gwen replaced the receiver and planned her next move. First she must drive to Norwich, go to Sanderson's who supplied professional workwear and obtain a nurse's outfit for her impersonation of a caring Irish nurse.

***

Rita arrived safely back at the boarding house and thanked Rod for coming to collect her from Hull. Worry and lack of sleep had drained her. She still felt much shaken, but on the return journey had had time to reflect on the events that had unfolded. She had given a statement to the police expressing her fears and they were satisfied with her report. They had checked her details and knew where they could contact her.

Lucinda made a light snack and left Rita and Ted to their own devices, not wishing to pry any further. Putting on her light evening coat and hat she took herself out to the town and ventured into Divers where, lo and behold, she found Muriel and Freda huddled in a corner putting the world to rights over a schooner of port apiece.

Lucinda ordered herself a large brandy and went to find herself a table away from the gossiping pair; she really was in no mood for their chatter.

"As bold as brass she was," said Freda, "as if butter wouldn't melt."

Lucinda looked their way and caught their eye, she raised her glass and nodded to them both and, with a gulp, downed the brandy in one.

"Did you see that?" asked Muriel, looking at Freda knowingly. "We all know where she picked up drinking habits like that from, brazen hussy!"

Lucinda savoured the moment and ordered another large brandy and a bag of crisps in the comfort that at least her guests paid their bills before leaving!

***

"Oh Ted me old lover," said Rita, pushing her plate of half-eaten food to one side, "I felt so awful finding her like that. I am getting quite fond of the old fake. I wished I had realised things weren't right in the car, but the traffic was so busy and I was worried we wouldn't reach Hull until all hours. I feel bad about leaving her on her own at the hospital; I really think I should go back."

Ted reached out and took her hand. "It's not your fault my dear and as soon as there is any further news on her progress the hospital will be in touch. If you have to go back then you will not go on your own. Now that we have had news on Lorna, it seems that Gwen may be behind all of this. Don Stevens must have been out of his mind getting involved with the likes of her."

"Ted old lover, as well you know, when you get infatuated by someone you don't always see what lies beneath."

Ted stood up. "Come on, grab your coat, I think we are both in need of a constitutional."

Rita smiled in agreement.

The seafront was quite busy. The night air was reasonably warm; some of the amusement arcades were doing a good business and there were signs of life as they walked on to the jetty. A couple of men were fishing and one or two couples were enjoying the sea view. Ted and Rita stood in silence and let the events of the past hours flow over them. Taking her hand in his Ted led Rita off the jetty and they continued to walk on in silence each enjoying the other's company.

Rita's mind drifted back to the old lady back in Hull, but a reassuring touch on her arm from Ted brought her back to the here and now.

When they returned to Mrs Haines' some two hours later, they found Lucinda dancing around the lounge with records blaring, a bottle of stout in one hand and a cigarette in the other one. They looked at each other in disbelief and burst out laughing.

"Come on in and join the party," said Lucinda, kicking up her legs to a rousing Dean Martin recording. "I am letting it all hang out."

Rita, observing the fall of Lucinda's blouse, couldn't have agreed more while Ted tried to avert his eyes from the spectacle before him.

***

Dave handed Dan a cup of cocoa. "We are behaving like an old married couple aren't we, look at us. You have the night off and here we are getting cosy for the evening."

Dan smiled. "Nothing wrong with getting cosy."

"Do you think it is all happening a bit too fast?"

Dan shook his head. "No I don't. Don't you feel comfortable with me?"

"Oh yes," replied Dave, "very comfortable. I think I am going to tell Jim about us. I have been thinking about it. I did think I would approach the subject through his daughter Debbie, but it would be better coming from me first-hand."

Dan thought for a moment. "Any idea what his reaction might be?"

"Not really," said Dave, "but we have been such good mates all these years, I don't think the news will rock our friendship. I must choose my moment."

Dan took Dave's hand and squeezed it but wondered if, only days after meeting, this was the best course of action. He hoped that Dave's confidence in his friend paid off.

***

June was trying to relax with a glass of gin and tonic in her room, but her thoughts took her back to what had become the eventual end of her career. How many nights had passed since the realisation that things were not as they had seemed had set in? The company in her last show didn't seem to be pulling together and silly mistakes were being made. Audiences were picking up on the unrest and were becoming increasingly fidgety, some not returning after the interval. Having missed several preview performances June had lost the thread of what her profession demanded, namely perfection and dedication.

Stupidly, as she now recalled, she had allowed a stage door Johnny to wine and dine her to the extent that nothing else in her world seemed to matter. Failing to turn up for much needed rehearsals to cut down the running time meant her understudy had had her work cut out. Once at the top of her profession, the cracks were beginning to widen and June knew in her heart that she either had to get out or face the consequences of being at the hands of her critics. It was a difficult decision to make, but then she found out she was pregnant. She had known in her heart that Wally was the father. Wally was a kind and caring man whom she had deep feelings for, but after her encounter with a couple of stage door Johnnies she had shied away from becoming too attached. She told Wally about the pregnancy and, gallant as always, he had offered to marry her. But marriage was the last thing on her mind. She felt she needed to get her career back on track but now, with a baby on the way, that seemed an unrealistic goal.

After one particularly stressful performance when everything seemed to be going wrong she had felt unwell and had severe stomach cramps. Getting out of the theatre as quickly as she could and ignoring the autograph hunters at the stage door she had hailed a cab. It was the cab driver who had carried June into the Casualty Department, not knowing where else to take her. Two hours later she had lost the baby and it was then that she decided she could not return to the theatre, she needed to get away. Wally had pleaded with her to reconsider, but her mind had been made up. Stories of her sudden departure from the show appeared on the front pages over the following week, the cab driver came forward and told his side of things and became the hero of the hour. The rest was, as they say, 'history'. The real June Ashby was never heard of again.

June drained her glass and was tempted to pour another but, glancing at the clock, she thought her bed would be the best place for her. As she settled back on her pillow she had a vivid picture in her mind of her and Wally and what might have been.

It was then that she heard a gentle tap on her door. She opened it and came face to face with Rita.

Rita told her story between sobs and tears. When she mentioned that Lorna was also in hospital, June was visibly shaken. In her own way June was hoping that she could mend bridges with the pair. Whilst it was unkind of them both to try to masquerade as her over the years, something about this had made June smile. She knew that the sisters had had some talent between them and pulling off the impersonation stunt must have put them both to the test. They had probably suffered enough at the hands of each other and there would be no need for June to take further action.

June comforted Rita. "You mustn't worry about a thing. I am sure they are both going to pull through. It just might take some time. We must look on the bright side. I will try and visit them as soon as I can."

Rita wiped her eyes and blew her nose. "They don't know about you yet. Oh my goodness, what a muddle. What a bloody mess."

"I thought you might have gone along to see Ted perform tonight. I have to say I was very much impressed with the show when I crept in for a peep last night."

"I couldn't face going to the theatre tonight," said Rita. "Ted doesn't need me there in this state."

"Let me get you a drink," said June, getting up, "I think you are in need of one."

Thursday 8th May

The next morning the police were at Mrs Haines' to question Rita. Ted insisted on being present.

"Do you remember seeing an elderly Scottish lady?" was the question from the WPC.

"See her, I spoke to her. She comforted me shortly after Veronica was admitted, she was very kind."

"That ties in with the story from the Sister on duty and the receptionist. The lady came back the following morning and asked to see Veronica, she mentioned you by name, giving her own as Janet Cameron."

"Doctor Finlay's Casebook," said Ted.

The WPC looked puzzled. "Sorry, I don't follow."

"Janet is the housekeeper to Doctor Finlay and Doctor Cameron in the television series. I bet that was no Janet Cameron at the hospital."

Rita grabbed Ted's arm. "Oh my God Ted, do you think it could have been Gwen?"

Ted nodded as the WPC made some notes. "What makes you say that?" she asked, writing furiously.

"Well, when I think back to it, there was something familiar about her. Some of her words didn't quite sound Scottish and the way she quickly attached herself to me. People don't do that, at least not in this country, they don't put themselves forward. I know it sounds stupid but she appeared to be a very well-dressed lady, but the bag and shoes were way off the mark, they looked brand new."

"You are very observant," said the WPC.

"That's my Rita; even in a crisis she never misses a trick."

"But why did she go back to the hospital?" Rita asked. "If Veronica was okay, it doesn't make sense."

"Maybe she went back with the intention of getting rid of Veronica once and for all," said Ted, looking at the WPC for some kind of explanation.

The WPC nodded. "We believe an attempt may have been made on her life. The nurse who tended her shortly after our visitor departed said that a spare pillow was lying at the side of the bed. Veronica could not have moved it herself as they are kept on the foot cage at the end of the bed. Veronica has spoken and said she had felt a pressure on her face, but had managed to turn her head slightly. In her panic Gwen may not have applied as much pressure as she thought. Veronica, who had been sedated, had remained relatively still during the attempt and this Gwen may have thought she had suffocated her."

Rita felt worried. "If she finds out where Lorna is, oh my goodness…"

"We are already on to that. Lorna will be guarded round the clock and is being moved to Great Yarmouth General this evening. Veronica will be moved from Hull to the Norfolk and Norwich hospital for the time being and then to Great Yarmouth so that the sisters can be kept together for their own safety."

"Why not move Veronica to Great Yarmouth now? asked Rita.

"Transport problems among other things, besides they have both been through a lot and things need to be done at a gentle pace. I must ask you both that you do not speak about this beyond this room. We intend to catch our lady visitor red-handed if possible."

The WPC thanked Rita for her time and said she would be in touch when there was any more news. Mrs Haines came in with a tray of tea, it had been a very unusual start to the day and that was putting it mildly.

***

Gwen found the members of staff at Sanderson's to be most helpful. With her lilting Irish accent two members of staff were keen to help the nurse out.

"I can't believe it," said Gwen, trying on the white shoes. "I arrived here yesterday, unpacked my suitcase and had forgotten my uniform, how could I have been so stupid. I can hardly report for duty at the Norfolk dressed inappropriately."

The two assistants murmured their concerns and set about finding the correct attire for Gwen to try on. They were used to dealing with nurses from the hospital, often a young nurse would come through the doors saying that she had ruined her uniform in the wash and looked desperate for help. It was true of many other professions that Sanderson's carried stocks for. As long as there was money to pay for the goods, or an account to charge, Sanderson's were there to help. Gwen handed over the cash, thanked the two young ladies for their help and left the shop. One down and one to go, she thought to herself.

Chapter Ten *"Defining Decisions"*

Friday 9th May

The three Dean Sisters had decided to relax a little and had taken off to the beach with a couple of rugs and three bottles of Corona. The sun was out and only a gentle sea breeze made it cooler than it might have been. After a morning practising their rolling, it was nice to kick off their shoes, push their aching feet into the sand and watch the world go by.

Jill opened some greaseproof paper and handed round the potted meat sandwiches she had made.

Dawn bit into hers and gave a groan, "Now I know why they call them sandwiches, this one has got grit in it."

"That will be the crab paste, they are always a bit gritty," said Sue, happily munching on hers. "Did anyone remember to bring a flask of tea?"

"Just you hold on a minute," said Jill, "I can't do everything at once."

The three finished their lunch in silence and then Jill handed round plastic cups of the brew she had prepared in the Thermos.

"My mum always said that a hot drink on a warm day was more refreshing than drinking a cold one," said Sue, slurping hers noisily.

"Your mum said you should never trust a man in brown suede shoes, but that never stopped you dating that Eddie Seabrook. What a creep he turned out to be," Dawn added, as her friend cringed.

"Don't bring him up," said Jill, coming to the rescue. "We all agreed never to mention him again; he was bad news and no mistake. Now let it drop."

Sue nodded her thanks to Jill and got to her feet. "Anyone fancy an ice cream?"

Two hands shot up and Sue set off to the kiosk at the end of the pier.

"You should know better, bringing up that Eddie bloke," said Jill, looking at Dawn who had laid herself down on the sand.

"Sorry, I wasn't thinking. He just came into my mind at that moment and it sort of came out."

"She will never be able to have children you know," said Jill, putting away the flask and cups into her wicker basket, "and Sue would make a brilliant mum."

Dawn nodded. "Yeah, you're right she would. If I ever see that Eddie geezer again I'll string him up."

Sue arrived back with the ice creams with a young gentleman in tow. She handed her friends their cones and introduced her companion.

"This is Joseph Carlio from the circus along the way."

Joseph beamed a smile at Jill and Dawn. He was neatly dressed in tight trousers and a gaily coloured, open-necked shirt. His dark curly hair was neatly brushed and he had a rugged look about him. His twinkling blue eyes were only outshone by his dazzling white teeth. He spoke with a slight accent that was easy on the ear and one which captured his audience.

He explained that he had been allowed to watch some of the rehearsals from the back of the theatre and was much impressed by the girls' act. He was on the lookout for new talent to join his father's group of acts and wondered if the girls would be interested.

Joseph was part of an aerial act and would be spending the summer season at the Hippodrome in Billy Russell's summer circus.

The girls listened making mental notes of what was being offered. They were invited to meet the Carlio family any time over the next week when Joseph's father would be in town overseeing the rigging of the family act. As Joseph bid farewell the three girls watched him walk away over the golden sands.

Sue was the first to speak. "You could have knocked me down with a feather when he approached me at the kiosk. He obviously recognised me, even without the blonde wig."

"It wouldn't hurt to check it out," said Dawn. "We haven't much lined-up after the end of September, though I am not sure about travelling with a circus."

"I wonder if the rest of the family are as good looking as him?" said Jill, finishing her cone. "He was very easy on the eye."

"Well, we best go along and introduce ourselves one afternoon," said Sue. "That way we can check out the other brothers, there may be two others just like him."

Jill smiled to herself; it was good to see a little bit of the old Sue showing itself.

Dawn got up from the sand and brushed herself down. "Come on you two, before we have to go back to rehearsals let's walk up the beach to the Wellington Pier and then come back along the promenade."

They set off in silence, each lost in their own thoughts; Joseph had given them all something to think about.

***

Jim was enjoying a cigarette and watched the three sisters as they walked across the sands. They seemed to be a nice trio and had certainly added a bit of sparkle to the company. He was suddenly aware of his name being called and turned to see Debbie and Peter walking towards him arm in arm smiling.

"What brings you two up here?" Jim greeted them warmly.

"Well, it was a lovely day and we have some news for you that wouldn't wait until you came home," said Debbie, looking at Peter for support.

"Come on then out with it."

It was Peter who spoke. "Jim, I am really sorry but I have to get back to Huddersfield. I phoned in to get some extra leave, but the plant is particularly busy at the moment and they can't spare me. We would have both liked to stay for the official opening of the show but it just isn't possible."

"Sorry Dad but I am going to go home with Peter, I hope you will understand."

Jim smiled, though his heart felt heavy. It was obvious that whatever problems the pair had had were now sorted out and he was thankful for that. He had seen too many young couples split at the first sign of trouble and he was glad that Debbie and Peter weren't going down that route.

"Of course I understand. When were you thinking of setting off?"

"In the next hour or so," said Debbie, trying her best to break the blow gently because she knew how her father was feeling. "I have made a shepherd's pie and put some vegetables in a saucepan for you for when you get home. The pie is in the fridge, you only need to warm it through for half an hour."

Practical, just like her mother, Jim thought, and not for the first time. "You have time for a coffee with your old dad before you go don't you?"

Debbie and Peter smiled. "Of course we do Dad."

"Come on then, we can sit in the Green Room."

***

Wally and June walked along holding hands not saying anything. It was as if the hands of time had turned back to all those years ago when they had first started courting.

"Penny for your thoughts," said Wally, squeezing June's hand. "You've been very quiet."

"I have made a decision Wally and it concerns both of us. Let's have a seat and I will explain."

They sat down on a bench and June turned and looked at Wally. "I want to do this show, but once the run is over that will be that. Show business and I are through. It isn't about me any more, I have seen the new talent that has been coming through and I am no longer a part of all of that. I don't want to be the artiste people book as a curio. I don't want to make guest appearances in musicals as a grand duchess. When I gave up the business it was for a reason, deep down I knew that I had had enough. I had to sacrifice a lot and I don't want to have to do it again. We have found each other once more and I would like to see where that leads us without something getting in the way that would spoil it. If it hadn't been for Veronica and her mad scheme I would never have been put in this position. I am only doing it to fulfil a contract, one that I wasn't responsible for, but I can't see the likes of Ted Ricer, Mystic Brian and the gang let down over a mere formality."

Wally smiled. "You have really thought this through haven't you? What will you tell Don Stevens, I am sure that even now he is making plans for the future that involve you?"

"Don is a survivor. I will speak to him and tell him my decision. You never know, he might just be able to salvage something from this masquerade. Lorna, given the right coaching, could probably make something of herself as long as Veronica didn't have a hand in it. I know I should hate the pair of them for what they have done, but I can't help laughing. Did they really think that trying to pass Lorna off as me would work?"

Wally laughed. "You amaze me. You walk into all of this - how did you put it? - masquerade and you haven't an ounce of malice in you. Most people would want to see those two swing for what they have done to you and your reputation."

"My reputation hasn't been damaged, at least not yet. The papers will have a field day if they ever get hold of this lot."

"Which is why measures have been put in place to prevent that happening," said Wally reassuringly. "When you open on Monday evening Joe Public will be none the wiser. Of course the company know, but they aren't going to snitch on you and on that I have their word."

"What have you been up to Wally?" said June questioningly.

"Don and I have had several conversations and I was able to act fast, with some help from old friends of mine in London. While you have been busy, everyone has been interviewed, right down to the cleaner. They are a pretty special crowd once you get to know them. Jim put a word in with the staff; he says in all the years they have worked together, they have never unwittingly spoken of what goes on behind the scenes, as gossipy as some may first appear."

"I am truly amazed," said June, "and most grateful. Thank you Wally, thank you for everything."

"I have another piece of news for you, Lorna is to be moved to a private clinic at the Great Yarmouth General. She is not as bad as they first thought. Veronica, although shaken, is on the mend and will join Lorna shortly."

"Oh that is good news, I must let Rita know, she has been so anxious."

"No need," said Wally, "it has all been taken care of."

June reflected on what she had just heard and felt that she could now begin to look forward to a new beginning.

***

Lilly got very excited. She had been reading an article in Woman's Realm about authors and how they got published. It was quite by chance that she had purchased the magazine as she usually only entertained The Weekly News above her normal daily read. Her neighbour had given her a bundle of magazines the week previous which she thought would come in handy for the hospital and Lilly had spotted in a copy of Women's Realm the forthcoming article on story writing and had promptly gone out and purchased the latest issue. The article listed several publishing house addresses and, taking the bull by the horns,

Lilly put pen to paper and took a chance by writing to The Duchy Publishing House and asked how she might go about submitting a story to them. She stuck the stamp on the envelope and went down the road to post it, feeling elated that she had taken an initial step. She returned home and re-read the article several times. It covered several angles from short-story writing to the more accomplished novel and a few lines on writing verse for greetings cards. She crossed her fingers that she would receive a reply to her enquiry in the not too distant future.

***

Gwen, dressed in her nurse's uniform and with a small black shoulder bag swinging, walked determinedly into the Norfolk and Norwich hospital and headed for one of the wards. She encountered a Sister who was just leaving her desk.

"I am terribly sorry to trouble you, I appear to have lost myself," said Gwen in her best Irish accent. "I am looking for a patient by the name of Lorna Bright. I have been sent by the agency."

The Sister eyed her curiously. "I thought you weren't one of our nurses, you are not wearing a name badge."

Gwen blushed. "Sorry Sister, I am Nurse O'Rourke, Wendy O'Rourke."

The Sister sat herself behind her desk. "Indeed. Have a seat and I will check our records. Bright you say, when was she admitted and what for?"

"A couple of days ago, suspected suicide," said Gwen, thinking on her feet. "At least that's the information I was given."

The Sister made a phone call, eyeing Gwen as she did so. She spoke quietly and quickly and Gwen could not hear what was being said above the noise of a tea trolley that was doing the rounds.

"Nurse O'Rourke, you will find Miss Bright in the Quanta's ward, the private section on the third floor. Take the lift at the end of the corridor."

Gwen thanked the Sister and retreated back down the ward and out of the door.

The Sister dialled. "She is on the way up now, as nervous as a bunch of turkeys at Christmas. You can't miss her; the wig is a dead giveaway, not to mention the Mary O'Hara accent."

Gwen wasn't sure why, but she suddenly felt uneasy. She pressed the button for the lift and waited. She was aware of two nurses coming up behind her who were chatting away about how well they had done in their latest exams.

Gwen stepped into the lift followed by the two nurses who were now at giggling point. Gwen gave them a steely glance and the two quietened down.

"Which floor?" asked Gwen in a rather gruff voice.

One of the nurses muttered, "Three please."

Gwen pressed buttons two and three. When the lift arrived on the second floor she got out and marched down the corridor. Looking back to see if the other two were behind her, she was relieved to see that she wasn't being followed. She approached a cleaner who was polishing the floor and asked for directions to the staircase.

Slightly out of breath she arrived on the third floor and looked for a signpost that would direct her to Quanta's ward. She found it without too much trouble and addressed a young Butterfly nurse as to where she would find the private room of Miss Bright. The nurse, who was obviously new, stuttered a reply and pointed towards two doors further down the ward.

Gwen walked sedately down the row of beds observing the nursing staff going about their business. She reached room 4b and knocked.

"Hello Gwen dear. How lovely of you to drop by, I have been expecting you."

Gwen froze as she entered the room, there sitting up in bed as large as life was Veronica.

***

When Jim arrived at the pier there was a large queue at the box office. He saw Mystic Brian and waved. "Bit of a crowd here this morning isn't there, what's brought that on I wonder?"

"June Ashby has been on the wireless; they have been playing her old recordings and plugging the show. That's what has brought this lot out. Old Maud is having a fine old time in there on her own, you best get hold of Barbara and see if she can come and give her a hand before the old girl blows a gasket."

Jim laughed and patted Brian on the shoulder. "I'll get on to it right away."

"Hi Jim got a minute?"

Jim turned and saw Dave walking towards him. Jim smiled, pleased to see his old mate. "Sure, but you'll have to walk along with me I have a call to make. Have you seen that queue at the box office?"

Dave grinned. "They have been playing that June Ashby on the wireless and mentioning the show a few times. It seems to have done wonders."

"I agree," said Jim, "someone has obviously been putting the publicity machine into overdrive."

They reached the stage door and Don was just coming out. "Morning Jim, seen those queues, isn't it wonderful? Old Wally got in touch with an old mate of his they did a short interview with June over the blower and, hey presto, she has been heard all over the county."

"I'm just going to phone Barbara to see if she can come in and give Maud a hand."

"All in hand my boy, she is on her way," said Don, looking happier than he had looked since he had landed in the resort. He waved and continued on down the pier with a definite spring in his step.

"Now there is something you don't see every day," said Jim, with a chuckle, "Don Stevens in jovial mood, long may it last. Now let's find ourselves a cuppa and a smoke and you can tell me what it is that's on your mind."

Dave followed Jim through the stage door and bid hello to Jack who was looking slightly dazed by all the comings and goings he had seen that morning. Things were afoot and no mistake.

The Green Room was empty and the only noise to be heard, apart from June doing some warm-up exercises, was the tapping of the dancers trying out a new routine on stage.

Dave felt a nervous pang in his stomach. "I don't know how to tell you this Jim; we have known each for so many years."

Jim nodded. "That we have Dave and we have never had any secrets from each other. I have been watching you and I get the feeling you have got itchy feet and want to move on. Are you thinking of giving up your job?"

Dave shook his head. "I don't know why you would think that. I sometimes get fed up with the work, but it's the same with whatever game you are in, it passes. I've wanted to tell you something for some time, but the time never seemed to be right."

"And now it is," said Jim, offering Dave a cigarette.

"You know, you and Karen..."

"God Dave, you haven't got cancer, please mate not that," said Jim, beginning to quake inside at the thought.

"No Jim, nothing as bad as that. I mean when you and Karen got together we all became a big family. She became part of us; it didn't make any difference to our friendship did it?"

"No mate it didn't," said Jim, feeling slightly relieved that the conversation wasn't going where he had worried it might be.

"Well, I am not like you were with Karen. I am different."

"You can say that again. You have never wanted to settle down."

"But I think I want to settle down now."

Jim took a long draw on his cigarette and thought for a moment. "Go on."

"Jim I'm queer, I'm homosexual, a bender, whatever way you want to put it."

"So?" said Jim. "What do you want, a round of applause? I'm not Karen you know."

Dave was stunned. "You mean you don't mind? You aren't ashamed of me?"

Jim put out his hand to Dave. "Why would I be ashamed of you? You are my best friend and always will be. You have always been there through the good and the bad times. Just because you fancy other men doesn't make you any less of a mate in my eyes."

Dave had never felt such relief.

"If you think that means you and I can't go out for our usual pint then think again. Boyfriend or no boyfriend, no one is going to come between us," Jim continued. "It's that Dan isn't it? I saw the looks he gave you when we went in the bar that lunchtime."

"You mean you knew?"

"I had a good idea. Karen and I had talked about it once. She was going to ask you about it, but I said it was best left alone. If there was anything to tell, you would do it in your own good time."

"I can't tell you how relieved I am," said Dave. "I was so afraid it would ruin our friendship."

"Now if my Karen were still here she would offer you some advice so consider this to be from her. There is no harm in you and Dan getting to know each other, but you can't just rush into these things. And for goodness sake, do not move in together. Leave things as they are for the time being and then later on, when you are both certain that this is what you want, take it from there."

"Thanks mate," said Dave, "you make a lot of sense. I must admit things seem to have been moving a bit fast and it has really only been a matter of days."

"So put the brakes on. Don't confuse 'falling in love' with 'infatuation'. Karen said that's what happens in a lot of these kinds of relationships."

"Excuse me." It was the voice of Mystic Brian. "Have either of you seen Lottie, only she seems to have gone missing?"

"Brian."

"Yes Jim."

"Fuck off!"

Chapter Eleven *"The Book of Revelations"*

D an was relieved to hear Dave's news. He had been expecting the worst. Dave was full of it when the two of them sat down together. He explained everything that he and Jim had talked about and Dan agreed that it would be best for them to slow things down a bit before moving in together. Dan was to go with Dave to the opening night of the show and to the party afterwards. It was all set. They discussed how the news might leak out to others, but decided they would cross that bridge when they came to it.

***

Maud and Barbara had been rushed off their feet, tickets were flying out of the box office. There had been party bookings and it looked like the following day would be even busier as June Ashby was to appear on Look East that evening. Don Stevens was rubbing his hands together and the company were walking round with permanent smiles on their faces, even Mystic Brian's doves were behaving themselves at last. Jenny Benjamin had worked in two more routines and the costumes had been borrowed from a local group. The front page of the Eastern Daily Press showed a lovely photograph of June and all the company and the few paragraphs written about it stated that this would be June's last ever performances. Palmers Department Store, Woolsey and Woolsey, the Carr and Carr record shops and Arnolds Department Store had ordered in large quantities of June's vinyl recordings.

June had agreed to do a signing session in Palmers on the Saturday following the opening. The departmental buyer was gearing herself and her staff up for an onslaught on the Saturday morning with the management expecting a high footfall, with extra sales as people made their way through the store to the basement. A part of the main window of the store had been specially commissioned with a large photograph of June and several smaller ones depicting her many musical appearances. The Great Yarmouth Mercury would have a whole page devoted to the show and its stars. It was going to be free publicity that Don Stevens had only ever dreamt of.

Don had given another interview to the Eastern Daily Press admitting it had been professional suicide putting on a pre-season show twice nightly, but as it had turned out the gamble was paying off. Although the summer season shows did well in general, most houses ran with a seventy-five percent capacity, with the odd exception when a particularly well-known star was topping the bill, thanks to television coverage.

The company as a whole felt genuinely blessed and there was the promise of work to follow. The Dean Sisters were about to secure a contract to appear in a circus show and Mystic Brian had received several enquiries but mainly on the keeping of doves, which seemed to have captured the public's imagination when several photographs of him and his girls had appeared in the press.

Derinda Daniels congratulated Don and June and said it had been a pleasure to stand-in while things were getting sorted out. The publicity hadn't done her any harm either and her future bookings around the country were secured.

***

Freda and Muriel had been reading the articles with great interest and were looking forward more than ever to the opening night. Muriel had treated herself to a new frock, whilst Freda had dug out an old faithful and added a few sequins that had been knocking about in her sewing basket. The old faithful could have done with dry cleaning as there was a certain odour about it, but Freda wasn't going to incur any more expense than she had to and sprayed it with some lavender cologne that had been sitting on her dressing table for some years. She had also found an old sparkly brooch of her mother's and thought it would complete the look. The old faithful was a dusty-pink colour with chiffon overskirt and she matched it up some old pink satin shoes from her long ago dancing class days. Back then she had fancied herself as a bit of a Ginger Rogers, though it was later commented by a few unkind acquaintances that Roy Rogers was nearer the mark.

She gave Muriel a sneak preview one afternoon when they were having an afternoon cup of tea. When Freda entered the sitting room in all her splendour it was all Muriel could do to stop choking on a slice of angel cake. She tried to find the right words to say to her friend, but all she could visualise was Bette Davis in Whatever Happened to Baby Jane.

"What do you think?" said Freda, doing a twirl. "I think my mother's old brooch sets it off a treat."

A firelighter would set it off better, thought Muriel, as she swallowed hard. "Yes it does add a certain something. What's that smell Freda, you're not having problems with the drains again are you?"

Freda didn't notice any smell and shook her head. "Not that I know of love," she replied innocently.

Muriel got up from her chair and moved closer to Freda. The full power of the odour from the pink creation mixed with the smell of worn-out lavender hit her nostrils and she had to take a step or two back.

"Freda I'm surprised you don't treat yourself to a new outfit. I spotted some lovely gowns reduced in Arnolds that would suit you a treat."

Freda eyed her friend. She knew Muriel of old, something was on her mind but she was obviously having trouble getting the words out. "You don't like it, do you?"

"Put it this way Freda, it's a tad old-fashioned. Lovely in its day I'm sure, but this party promises to be something a bit special and it would be nice if you and I as the leading landladies of the town were captured in our best light. We might even get our photographs in the Mercury."

Freda thought for a moment. Put like that maybe Muriel was right, she did deserve to treat herself. Making her mind up there and then she went and changed out of the outfit, grabbed some money she had had hidden in her bottom drawer and insisted that Muriel accompany her up town to see what they could find.

Saturday 10th May

Rita walked into the private room in the Great Yarmouth General and found Veronica sitting in a chair looking out of the window; she turned as she heard Rita enter.

"Rita my dear, how lovely to see you. I only arrived here just before lunch, I feel like a gypsy, I haven't travelled so much in years. Would you care for a cup of tea? I can get one of the nurses to rustle up something; they have been very kind to me."

Rita greeted Veronica with a kiss on the cheek and sat herself down opposite.

"I am so pleased to see you up and about, I have been quite concerned. Ever since that night in Hull I have worried whether you would pull through. It is good to see you looking so well."

Veronica nodded with a smile. "It would take more than an encounter with Gwen to knock the stuffing out of this old broad."

"How is Lorna?"

"Much improved and on the mend," said Veronica. "I fear Gwen had a bigger hand in her downfall than was first realised."

Rita settled herself into the chair and let Veronica tell her story.

"Gwen and I go way back," she began. "We were lovers. Gwen was the person I trusted, but to my disappointment that turned rather sour. It was she who put me up to the idea of putting Lorna on the stage. Getting more involved with Don Stevens was all part of that plan, but what she didn't allow for was the fact that she would fall in love with him. I knew that Gwen was more than interested in money and she very sneakily began to bleed me dry. It was Lorna who spotted discrepancies in the accounts we kept. Gwen was earning good money with Don and I know he slipped her the odd bonus when business was particularly good. But, as with all money-mad people, Gwen got greedy. She had mastered signing my name on cheques and was covering her tracks pretty well until she started getting careless. I tackled her about it and at first she played dumb, then she started messing about with my medication, switching tablets. Oh yes Rita, I knew about that, you look surprised."

"But if you knew, why take the medication on the day we left for Hull?"

"That was a careless mistake on my part. When Gwen had given me a bottle of pills to take with me that day I had marked it with a pen so I wouldn't mislead myself. However, I was very tired and really I should have noticed the signs and rather than go with you in the car, I should have stayed at home with my feet up. It was through my lack of concentration that I took the wrong tablets.

Gwen had been doing a similar thing with Lorna. She was leaving bottles of vodka around that Lorna was drinking at an alarming rate, due to her nerves and insecurities. I put Lorna under that unnecessary strain, trying to deceive those around us that Lorna was indeed June Ashby."

"Was Robin in anyway involved in any of this?"

Veronica shook her head. "Oh no, not at all my dear. But he became a useful smokescreen for Gwen. She was always feeding Robin advice on how to handle Lorna. Robin was only here at

Lorna's request; though the boy is very fond of Lorna, Gwen used that to her own end."

At that moment a nurse came into the room to check Veronica's blood pressure and temperature. Rita used this moment to go along to get them both some tea and biscuits. When she returned she found Veronica looking at some papers. She accepted the tea with grateful thanks.

"When did you first suspect Gwen was up to no good?"

"A few months before we came here; firstly, she wasn't coming home every night. She was spending more and more time with Don out of hours. When challenged she said it was all part of the master plan, the one that would make us rich."

"But surely you didn't think you would get away with the pretence, someone would eventually cotton on that Lorna wasn't June?"

"The way you did Rita or would you prefer me to call you Moira?"

"Moira Clarence is long gone. Anyone who tried the same scam you tried to pull off with that name would have had me and Ted on to it right away. I chose the name because I knew it would stand out. My great grandmother was a Moira and her husband's name was Clarence, I just put them together. If my agent had had his way I might have been known as Fifi Lamar."

Veronica laughed. "I don't think Fifi would have suited you at all." She paused for a moment, talking was tiring when you weren't feeling well. "The fact was that June was safely tucked away in France; this façade was only meant to happen here in Great Yarmouth. The idea was that Lorna would eventually be revealed as a fraud, but a very talented one and the news story it would have created was to have led to other things."

"So you never meant for it to go on indefinitely?" asked Rita curiously.

"Never!" Veronica replied, sipping her tea. "It was to be stepping stone for Lorna, unfortunately she turned out to be less than capable."

"What will happen if June decides to prosecute, she could you know?"

"I think I know June pretty well and, although to my shame I have pulled an unforgivable stunt, I don't think June would want to pursue the matter. It would drag up too many things from the old days. There have been some painful memories for all of us all along the way."

There was a long silence before Veronica spoke again. "If June did decide to take matters further, I would have no quarrel putting my hands up. I am as guilty as Gwen, perhaps more so for being so foolish as to believe it could work out favourably."

Rita thought for a moment about something that Wally had said on the telephone that day, "Veronica Bright is a dangerous lady; take very good care when you are around her Rita." And yet Rita didn't feel that danger, but something nagging at the back of her mind told her she needed to check on Lorna, who was housed just along the corridor.

A voice from the doorway made them both turn their heads. June was standing there with a bunch of flowers and a smile on her lips. "We have a lot to talk about Veronica and I have an idea that might just appeal to you."

Rita made her farewells and left the two alone. She knocked on Lorna's door and went in. Robin was busy with a crossword.

"Hello you two, I am sorry to burst in, but I thought I would see how you were."

Lorna looked at Rita and smiled. "Rita isn't it?"

Rita smiled. "I brought you some chocolate."

Robin looked up and acknowledged Rita and then returned to his puzzle.

"Lorna," Rita began, "I am slightly concerned for your safety. I have reason to believe that Veronica may wish to harm you. Gwen has tried and failed and I think Veronica may attempt something."

Robin put down his book and was now fully attuned to what was being said.

"Why would Veronica want to hurt me?" said Lorna. "The truth is out there now that the real June is back. Robin told me."

Rita looked at Robin. "Who told you?"

"Jim did when I phoned the theatre. He has kept me up to date on the goings on and besides it has been on the radio."

"Yes of course," said Rita. "Have either of you spoken to the police since you were moved here? Has anything been said about Gwen?"

They both shook their heads. A sudden fear struck Rita's heart; Gwen must still be out there somewhere. She said a hasty goodbye and left the hospital without another word.

Rita made her way down the road and on to the police station. The clerk at the desk listened to her story and asked her to take a seat.

Some fifteen minutes later WPC Helen Waterhouse invited Rita to join her in the interview room.

"You are here about the Ashby/Bright case. The file is still open; no arrests have been made as yet. When questioned, Veronica Bright said Gwen had not shown up at the Norfolk and Norwich. Yet one of the Sisters on duty that day had alerted our WPCs that a woman fitting her description had asked where she might find Lorna Bright. When our WPCs eventually turned up at the room, Veronica was quite alone and seemed relatively relaxed."

"You said when they eventually turned up at the room, what did you mean by that?"

WPC Waterhouse looked at the notes. "It appears the WPCs in question got trapped in a service lift at the back of the hospital, not wishing to use the ones meant for visitors."

A thought was troubling Rita – Veronica is a dangerous lady, Wally had said. "So Veronica could have done away with Gwen and nobody would have been any the wiser," said Rita, beginning to become slightly alarmed.

"Hang on there you are going too fast, what makes you think Veronica would harm Gwen?"

"Something that was said to me about Veronica the other day, that she was a dangerous woman. I know it doesn't make any sense, but I can't help feeling there is some truth in that statement. You haven't found Gwen yet have you?"

"And if she was a dangerous woman, as you surmise, Veronica must have concealed the body, but where exactly?"

Rita sighed heavily. "The room was a private one, like the one she is in now in at the General, and it has its own bathroom. She could have hidden the body until the coast was clear. Do you know if the room was searched?"

WPC Waterhouse had a troubled look on her face. There was nothing in the report to suggest it and, in fact, when she had spoken to one of the WPCs she had said that after checking Veronica was okay they then searched the hospital in case Gwen had been spotted. They had reported back to Veronica that all appeared to be well and they let her know that arrangements would be made to move her to Great Yarmouth.

Rita watched WPC Waterhouse's face in disbelief. "They didn't search the room did they? I know Veronica didn't come to Great Yarmouth until late this morning. A phone call was made to my landlady asking that I go and see Veronica at my earliest convenience. That gave her ample time to hide the body. I bet if you make a search of the hospital, somewhere you will find the body of Gwen."

WPC Waterhouse looked up from her notes. "Have you ever considered a career with the police? We could do with people like you on the force."

***

Back at the hospital June's conversation with Veronica had reached its conclusion and she said goodbye and left. Veronica went to the bedside drawer and took out the syringe and checked it. She concealed it in her bathrobe pocket and made her way along the corridor to Lorna's room.

She found her sister lying on the bed, Robin in his chair with his crossword.

"Oh, hi Veronica," he said, looking up. "The nurse has just given Lorna something to relax her; she is sleeping, so perhaps you would like to come back later."

"I am not feeling so good; I will wait a while if you don't mind."

Veronica sat herself down on the vacant chair. "Just had a visit from June, she has a marvellous idea for a film, all about our life, me, her and Lorna. She thinks if we had the right script our story could be told on the big screen. Our parts would have to be played by actresses of course, I wonder who would play me, or you for that matter?"

Robin looked slightly surprised. "Me! Why me?"

"Well, you would be part of the story wouldn't you?" replied Veronica, coughing slightly. "Oh I am so dry I could murder a nice cup of tea."

Robin laid down his book. "I'll go and get one if you like. I could do with stretching my legs."

"That would be wonderful. I'll just sit here and enjoy the quiet; perhaps you could bring a slice of cake back if they have some."

When Veronica was quite sure that Robin had left, she took the syringe from her pocket and looked at Lorna's face. She made an approach to Lorna, but was caught off guard when Lorna moved. Veronica looked at the syringe again and then, as tears began to run down her cheeks, she dropped it into the wastepaper basket. Sobbing she sat on the bed and held Lorna's hand, memories came flooding back of the better times they had

had together and instead of the bitterness she once felt, she now felt love and compassion. "I'm so sorry for even thinking it. I'm so sorry for all the pain I've put you through. Please, please forgive me."

***

June had decided to leave Lorna for another day. She had had mixed feelings about meeting her sisters again, but her conversation with Veronica had lain to rest one or two ghosts. She was due to meet Wally back at the theatre and then they would go out for a meal, she didn't want to be late.

When Robin returned with the tea and cake, Veronica appeared to be much brighter. They chatted for a while and then Veronica made her way back to her room.

Sunday 11th May

The following morning, with Rita and Wally by her side, WPC Helen Waterhouse broke the news to June that Veronica had been arrested and charged with the murder of Gwen. Gwen's body had been discovered by the cleaning staff in a laundry basket in the basement of the hospital. Veronica, it seemed, had taken the arrest calmly, no doubt helped by popping pills. Rita's fears had been realised.

There was no way that the story could now be kept out of the press, though every stop would be taken to ensure that June Ashby wasn't the main focus of the case. If the name of Veronica Bright was used there need be no connection made to June. Wally was all in favour of calling off June's opening night, but June had decided the show must go on. Rita was blaming herself for not realising sooner the wisdom of Wally's words and Wally was kicking himself for not following his hunch.

The news was kept from Lorna, though Robin had been told. His mind went back to Veronica's visit the day before. It had been the first time she had come into the room to see Lorna. He remembered how he had found her sitting on the bed holding

Lorna's hand. A thought came into his head but, looking at the now relaxed Lorna who had sat up in bed,, he dismissed the thought and went back to his crossword.

***

Rita broke the news about Gwen to Don, who broke down in front of her. She held his hand and as gently as she could, told him all she knew. After a couple of large brandies at the theatre bar, Don pulled himself together. He thanked Rita for being the one to tell him, he would have hated to have heard it from anyone else. He went back into the auditorium as if nothing was wrong and called the company together.

Earlier, his wife had been on the telephone intent on coming down to the resort. Don had stalled her, explaining it wasn't a good time. Thank goodness he had. There was no way he could deal with his wife in the light of what he had just been told. Later, on hearing the news, he had taken the photograph of Gwen from his wallet and torn it in to tiny pieces. He needed all traces of her to be removed from his life now. His wife Elsie would learn of Gwen's death soon enough.

The following day would see the official opening of the show, but the day could be marred by the headlines the local community would wake up to.

Chapter Twelve
"Another Opening, Another Show!"

Monday 12th May 1969.

The headlines in the Eastern Daily Press were not of murder, but the concern for the welfare of seals that were coming up on shore from Scroby Sands. There was also an article about a new attraction for the Pleasure Beach funfair and a whole page dedicated to Billy Russell's Circus at the Hippodrome, who would continue the circus tradition of the town with new and exciting acts.

Tucked away on page eight was a small paragraph, it read:

A woman has been arrested for the suspected murder of a woman whose body was found at the Norfolk and Norwich hospital by laundry staff. The Police have refused to name either of the women until a further investigation has been carried out.

Several people were heaving a sigh of relief. It meant that the planned opening night would not be overshadowed. June was slightly concerned, it was inevitable that sooner or later the full story would emerge and to that end she had to get her story in place. Wally said he would help her and would make an approach to a local solicitor he had heard good reports of from Jim.

With Rita at her side, June decided to pay a visit to see Lorna. Permission had been granted by the ward sister and Rita would be there to support June when she told Lorna the news concerning Veronica.

Lorna was sitting up in bed when they arrived and Robin made himself busy organising some tea and coffee. At first the conversation between June and Lorna was strained, each eyeing the other up, looking for a crack in the armour.

When eventually June told her what had happened to Veronica, Lorna was remarkably calm. Robin was witness to the conversation and Lorna looked at him as the story was told.

"I knew about it," said Lorna, taking Robin's hand for comfort. "Veronica told me what she had done."

June looked at Rita, startled. "I don't understand, you mean she confessed it all to you?"

Lorna nodded. "She came to visit me, she thought I was asleep, but I only pretended to be. I didn't know what I was going to say to her. You see I had let her down, I was supposed to be you, but I couldn't manage it. I have never been a great singer but I had enough of a voice to get by, but Veronica kept pushing me and pushing me."

Her voice faltered and she took a deep breath before continuing. "Veronica told me she had got rid of Gwen once and for all and that she was sorry for the way she had treated me. There was lots of other stuff too. Then Robin came back and she stopped. But I knew what she meant. She and Gwen had been lovers once, but Gwen went off with that Don Stevens and Veronica couldn't bear the competition. She hated rejection and I know she had been subject to rejection more than once in her life. Gwen was her last chance of happiness."

June was visibly moved by the story and squeezed Rita's hand. "I am sorry we all lost touch, things could have been so different for all of us."

"I know what we did was wrong," said Lorna, looking at June, "pretending to be you. Stupid really, but Veronica wasn't thinking straight. I was too weak to stand up to her and Gwen. My big weakness was alcohol and Gwen knew it. I would often find bottles hidden about my room. She was the one who supplied me with uppers and downers, pills to make me sleep, pills to give me energy, pills to relax me."

"She bullied you," said Robin finding his voice. "She deserves to rot in prison for what she did to you."

Lorna shook her head. "No Robin, she needs help, like we all do from time to time. One thing is for certain, if being in prison doesn't kill her, the cancer will."

"This is going to be tough on all you," said Rita. "And until the police charge her it's going to be difficult to second-guess what to do."

June moved to the bedside and took Lorna's hand. "Whatever the outcome we will do this as a family, together. We have to put past events behind us."

"That's very magnanimous of you after all that has happened," said Robin.

"Not at all," replied June. "First we must get this one well again. I will see to it that you have the best care available. My adviser, Wally, will take care of the details, you are to worry about nothing."

Rita looked at her watch. "I am sorry to butt in, but there is a dress-rehearsal in half an hour and it wouldn't do to keep Don waiting, today of all days."

June kissed Lorna on the cheek and shook hands with Robin and promised to visit again and tell Lorna all about the opening night.

When they had left Lorna got out of bed and walked over to Robin. "Oh I do hope things are going to straighten themselves out," she said, looking at him.

Robin hugged her. "I think things are going to be okay from now on, you heard what your sister said."

"Funny, but I have never really thought of her as my sister. We hardly know each other."

"Give it time," said Robin, "give it time."

***

Jim was just about to leave for the theatre when the phone rang, it was Debbie.

"Hi Dad, just wanted to wish everyone good luck for this evening."

"Thanks Debs, I will pass on your message to the company. How is Peter?"

"Oh, he is fine. He is just trying to get his head round the fact that in the not too distant future he will be a dad."

Jim nearly dropped the receiver in shock. "You are pregnant, Debs why didn't you tell me before?"

"I had to have everything confirmed and it was the reason I came down to see you. Peter had thought it was too soon to start a family when I told him. I left him to think things through and now I think he's quite pleased, in fact I would say he is over the moon."

"And so am I," said Jim happily. "If only your mother were here, she would be delighted."

"But she is here Dad and she always will be and if it's a girl I am going to name her after her grandmother."

Jim was lost for words and swallowed hard afraid of embarrassing himself.

"Dad, it's okay to feel upset, it's okay to cry."

And as Jim had concluded on more than one occasion, Debs was just like her mother and that would always be a great comfort to him until the day he died.

***

Lilly called by the box office on her way from the theatre. She had been putting the finishing touches to the place ready for the opening. Maud had just finished dealing with another large queue and was hoping that Barbara wouldn't be late as she was in need of a break.

"You should see that lot back there," said Lilly, making herself at home and inclining her head to the theatre, "running around like headless chickens. Brian's doves have been flying about the place; put me in mind of that Hitchcock film. What was it called, it had birds in it?"

"The Birds," replied Maud, laughing at her friend.

"I'm looking forward to this evening," said Lilly. "I can't wait to put on my new outfit; it will be one in the eye for Freda."

"Talking of Freda," said Maud, getting into her stride, "Muriel was telling me that she went out and bought a new frock. Apparently she had planned on coming in her pink chiffon which Muriel said made her look like Barbara Cartland. She said the smell was something awful."

Lilly laughed. "I remember that frock; she used to wear it down the Floral Hall years ago. Back then, of course, she wasn't a bad dancer. Surprised she could still get in it with all that weight she has put on."

"Muriel said it was something of a snug fit."

"I'd put money on it," said Lilly, with a grin.

Jim came bounding into the box office and nearly had Lilly off her stool.

"By the heck Jim you are looking very pleased with yourself," said Maud, "won the pools?"

"I am going to be a granddad."

Maud flung her arms round her friend and hugged him. "I am so happy for you, is Debs okay?"

"Blooming I think the expression is."

"I best get knitting," said Lilly, "though I don't get much time these days."

"Hark at her," said Maud, "anyone would think she was writing her memoirs."

Sometimes fact could be stranger than fiction.

***

Don Stevens felt as if someone had put lead in his shoes as he made his way down the auditorium. He was doing his best to muster what little energy he had. He had gone over things in his mind a million times, had he done the right thing calling a halt with Gwen? If he hadn't would she still be alive now? He was brought to his senses by the sound of Maurice and his boys getting into the orchestra pit.

Maurice waved. "Hello Don, all ready for the big night?"

Don waved back. "As I'll ever be. I just hope the troops are up to it."

"I think they will be. There is a certain buzz back there that I haven't seen in a while. I think everything will go very smoothly."

Don sat himself down in the fifth row. "I hope you are right Maurice, I really do."

Backstage the Dean Sisters were making last minute adjustments to one of their routines, Brian was getting his doves to focus, and Ted was running through a couple of new gags he had heard in the pub. The dancers were doing their limbering-up, while Jenny fussed about making sure all the costumes were in order and were not in need of any last minute repair.

Rita was helping June into her opening-number gown as Jim knocked on the dressing room door.

"All ready for the off ladies?"

June smiled. "I think we are."

Rita made a slight adjustment to the wig June was wearing and smiled at her new friend. "You look every inch the leading lady."

June laughed. "Let's hope the audience will think so tonight."

Jim walked on to the stage and put his thumbs up at Don. "We are ready to begin when you are Don."

Don gave the signal to Jim, the lights lowered in the auditorium and a spotlight hit Maurice as he conducted his boys through the overture.

***

That evening the town and its finest turned out to see the show at the end of the pier. Women in fur stoles and high-heeled shoes walked sedately towards the theatre on the arm of their husbands. Lilly and Maud spent a pleasant hour and half in one of the restaurants on Regent Road before making their way.

Ahead of them they could see Muriel and Barry Evans with Freda and Dick Boggis trailing behind. Coming across Marine Parade Maud spotted Dave with a young man in tow; she waved and received one in return from both of them.

The front-of-house crew, in their black and white attire, were showing people to their seats and complimentary programmes were being handed out to the VIPs, others were parting with a shilling to secure theirs.

Some were making the most of the balmy May air and enjoying looking at the sea before taking their seats.

Don Stevens, flanked by Jim, stood proudly at the main door and watched the crowd enter. Derinda Daniels arrived and gave Don a hug; she was followed by the boys from her band. Never in his wildest dreams had he ever imagined such a good turnout. The box office news was excellent for the short run and there were only a few seats remaining for some of the first-house performances.

Three members of the press were the last to arrive and were ushered to their seats by Don himself. He then took up his position looking at the empty seat beside him with some regret. This is where Gwen would have sat. Then he saw Rita coming along the row and she sat beside him.

"Thought you might need some company," she whispered, having anticipated this.

Don patted her arm gratefully and, feeling his emotions getting the better of him, he busied himself with his programme, though it was clear to Rita he wasn't reading a word.

Finally the lights dimmed, Maurice turned to face the audience and with a swish of his baton the orchestra played the overture.

People began tapping their feet to the familiar tunes and, turning to each other smiling, nodded their appreciation.

The curtain rose gently and The Jenny Benjamin Dancers were high-kicking in salute to The Tiller Girls. As they exited high-kicking into the wings, Ted came bounding down the staircase at the back of the impressive set and went into a two-minute quick-fire routine. He then asked the audience to put their hands together to welcome back the star of the West End theatre "June Ashby".

June appeared at the top of the staircase in a sparkling purple gown trimmed with ostrich feather and shimmied down the staircase to the opening bars of a song that had been specially written for her only two days ago by Wally.

The words she sang were these...

Once upon a time the spotlight beckoned me

And then one day the magic faded, the spotlight let me be.

Doors were closing one by one, shattered dreams upon the floor.

Songs unsung, a life undone, for me there was no more.

Then once more a footlight beckoned

To give me another chance

To sing the songs of yesteryear

And again for you I'd dance.

Memories fill my cluttered mind

Of all the dreams I'd left behind.

But when the curtain falls again

It will be time for me to part.

A final goodbye to my theatre world

I'm leaving now with a happy heart.

When the song had finished it was met with silence. Don felt his hands sweat with anticipation and then thunderous applause rang through the theatre and a smiling June acknowledged her public.

The spotlight faded and June left the stage to get ready for her next number.

Now it was the turn of Mystic Brian and his beloved doves. Don cried with laughter, he had never seen Brian in such good form. He hoped Brian had held enough back for his second appearance later in the show.

Ted made another brief appearance and introduced "The fabulous Dean Sisters" direct from their successful appearance on Opportunity Knocks.

They were a great favourite with the crowd; this first part of the act was performed without the rolling balls, which would appear in the second half of the show. The girls showed off their juggling and fire-eating skills, a new routine that had been added to great effect.

The dancers bounded on to the stage in a soldier routine and then June appeared once more to sing songs from a couple of her West End musicals, leaving South Pacific to last when the dancers rejoined her in grass skirts.

Another quick-fire routine from Ted followed and the first half closed with June recalling songs by Ethel Merman.

At the back of the auditorium with Robin beside her, Lorna had watched. "You see I could never have done that. Isn't she brilliant?"

Robin pattered her arm gently and said nothing.

Don and Rita went backstage as the audience busied themselves with interval drinks and ices. There was certainly excitement in the dressing rooms as the whole company were engulfed in their success.

June was close to tears when Rita spoke to her. "I didn't think I could pull it off, really I didn't."

Rita turned to Wally. "Those words you wrote for that opening song were wonderful. I didn't realise you had a hidden talent."

Wally smiled his thanks. "It was just something I rattled off quickly."

"Bloody brilliant," was all Don could say to each of the company as he walked up to them. He was totally knocked out by what he had seen and words, for once, were failing him.

The two-minute bell sounded and the audience began returning to their seats. Don was so excited that he forgot himself and kissed a surprised Rita just as she had popped a chocolate in her mouth.

The prelude over, the dancers filled the stage in their Red Indian routine which, with the painted backdrop, was surprisingly good. Brian and his doves made their second appearance and were as funny if not funnier than their first time.

Ted now did his longer routine and had the audience in the palm of his hand. Sometimes the old jokes went down the best, even Don laughed.

The Dean Sisters now rolled on to the stage in bejewelled leotards and headdresses. The audience was spellbound as the girls, singing Puppet on a String, rolled the glitter balls around the stage apron and then onto the three-tiered steel construction, juggling as they did so. The audience's cries for more said it all as the tabs closed.

The voice of Jim was then heard over the sound system as he announced the star of the show "June Ashby".

Once more, in a stunning gown, June walked on to the stage and in the solo spotlight sang the songs she thought she would never sing again.

A total blackout on the stage followed and then the stage lit up for the finale. Len Smith of Rex Studios had certainly kept his best set for last. A gold-pillared staircase swept in a curve from stage right and jewelled curtains were swathed above, giving a Busby Berkeley feel to the finale. The dancers in feathered headdresses high-kicked their way on to the stage and then the walk-down of the artists began. First Brian in his white tuxedo and then the Dean Sisters in matching purple and black satin dresses with matching gloves, followed by Ted in his Sunday finest and finally, in yet another wonderful creation, June Ashby was met with rapturous applause as the audience rose to their feet to give them all a standing ovation.

"I think they liked it," said Rita, clapping hard and turning to Don who was looking pleased with himself.

He smiled at Rita. "Let's hope the press vultures think so too."

The invited guests made their way to the bar for the after-show party; the three personnel from the press made a hasty retreat to get back to their offices to do their piece for the following day's papers.

Glasses of champagne and sweet sherry were handed out as people entered the lounge, whilst the more discerning headed to the bar for a pint of bitter and a gin and tonic.

Rita hugged Ted as he came to her through the sea of bodies. "Ted you were on top form, I have never seen you so good."

"Thanks Reet, that means a lot."

Mystic Brian was receiving pats on the back as he walked through the lines of guests and the Dean Sisters were greeted with murmurs of, "wonderful", and "well done". But the focus of attention was on June. When she entered the bar on the arm of Wally, she was met with applause and cheers.

Maurice and Jennie came in with the orchestra members and dancers and were met with equal rapture from the gathering.

Outside the theatre in earshot of the goings-on Robin held Lorna close to him, he could only imagine the sadness she was feeling at that moment. Now he had to get her back to the hospital and to the care of the people he hoped would finally put her demons to rest.

Lucinda Haines, who had also been invited along to the party, went over to Rita and Ted to thank them for a wonderful evening. Ted, while winking at Rita, took the rose from his buttonhole and gave it to Lucinda. "For a darling of a landlady and thank you for all you have done for me and my lady wife."

If Ted had given her a twenty pound note she couldn't have been happier.

"Did you see that," said Freda, nudging Muriel and managing to spill half a gin and tonic down her frock, "brazen that's what I call it, and in front of his wife too."

The band who had been hired for the party struck up and several people began to dance.

"If I died tonight I would die a happy man," said Ted to Rita, as Lucinda went in search of another drink.

"Well don't do that old lover; there are a few more shows to knock out here first."

"Here, here," said Don, as he squeezed his way between them. "A wonderful evening, here's to many more."

Dan and Dave enjoyed watching everyone else enjoy themselves. Dave was delighted when Jim told him the news concerning Debbie and Dan offered his congratulations.

"Look, if you two aren't doing anything one Sunday, come over to lunch, I do a mean roast beef and Yorkshire pudding."

"Thanks mate we'd love to," said Dave.

"I'll get some more drinks in," said Dan, "and leave you two to catch up."

"Thanks again Jim, that invitation means a lot."

"Don't be daft," said Jim, knocking back his beer. "If Dan is be part of the family, best get him geared-up. Told Debs about you two and she said that if Dan passes muster she may well ask you both to be godparents."

"Now whose rushing things?" said Dave, with a grin.

It was Brian who went over to June and whispered in her ear, "Someone wants to see you in the manager's office, Jack asked me to tell you."

June looked puzzled, thanked Brian and made her way through the party and back into the auditorium.

"I wonder where June is going?" asked Ted. "Hey Brian, where is June off to?"

"Manager's office, I think the police are here."

Rita squeezed Ted's arm. "You keep things going I'll go after her, I think this requires a woman's touch."

Rita caught up with June.

"Oh Rita, whatever is all this about, will you come with me?"

Rita recognised the face of WPC Helen Waterhouse, who was accompanied by a male officer.

"Miss Ashby I am sorry to break up the party, please take a seat."

"What has happened, is Lorna okay?"

WPC Waterhouse cleared her throat. "I am sorry to inform you that Veronica Bright has been found dead in her cell. We have every reason to believe she had a heart attack. The police medic did the best he could but…"

June nodded. "I see. What happens now?"

"The case against her will be dropped of course. The police need take no further action. I am sorry to bring this news tonight of all nights, really I am."

Rita took June's hand. "Perhaps it is for the best love. Imagine what you would have gone through. Veronica wasn't in her right mind. I'm sorry old love."

"You will need to come down to the station at some point and collect Veronica's personal effects. There are a few items of jewellery, some money, her clothes, of course, and some medication."

Rita looked at the WPC. "Did Veronica have access to her medication?"

"I believe so. We understood it was the medication she needed to take on a regular basis. Are you thinking that perhaps she took an overdose, if so the autopsy will reveal the fact?"

"I don't think she would have taken an overdose," said Rita, "that isn't the impression I had of her when I spoke with her last. I wondered if she might have by mistake taken the wrong medication."

"Sorry, I don't follow," said the WPC, making some notes.

Rita explained about the medication switches that Gwen had made and that it was possible in her state of mind that Veronica may have taken the wrong ones.

"I am sure all of this will be made clear to us in due course. With regard to Gwen Taylor, a close relative has been contacted and she will be taking care of things."

"Gwen had a sister?"

"No, it is a cousin, her details were found in her car."

It put to rest Rita's theory that there might be two Gwen's on the prowl. What with all the Junes she had encountered over the last week or so, anything seemed possible.

"I will go with you to the station tomorrow," said Rita, squeezing June's arm. "Best to get things sorted out as quickly as possible." June nodded her thanks.

June left the office, she needed some time alone now, and the party could go on without her. She walked along the pier to the back of the theatre, her mind all over the place. She had just enjoyed one of the happiest moments of her life and also one of the saddest. She had struggled to understand why Veronica had acted in the way she had and how Lorna had become the centre of her crazy plans. She still knew nothing of the working of the human mind and could only think that Gwen Taylor was behind a lot more than had been revealed. It mattered to her that Lorna should find some peace and something she was cut out for. Maybe the stage wasn't the right place, but she had proved herself as an actress. Why, everyone had been convinced she was the real June Ashby, until she attempted to sing. Perhaps acting would be good for her, or a position with a theatrical agency. She would discuss the possibilities with Wally. She wanted to do her best by Lorna; once she knew she was settled she could begin to remap her own life. Perhaps she could write a book based on her life in the theatre. One thing was for sure, if anyone were to write about what had happened in Great Yarmouth in such a short space of time, no one would believe it.

Rita thanked WPC Waterhouse and showed her and her accompanying officer out of the theatre. As she returned to re-enter the theatre Rita's eye caught the advertising poster. "Summer Frolics, you can say that again," she hissed under her breath.

Chapter Thirteen   *"More Tea Vicar?"*

Tuesday 13th May

Several people with hangovers opened their Great Yarmouth Mercury the following morning to be greeted with a front page photograph of June Ashby and the company of Summer Frolics. Inside the Mercury critic had lavished praise upon the show and had stated it was a shame it wasn't playing the full summer season. As promised, there was a full-page spread advertising the appearance of June on Saturday at Palmers. A similar article and smaller advertisement were carried in the Eastern Daily Press and a couple of the national papers including The Express were featuring the news of June Ashby's comeback in a spectacular show at the seaside resort.

Mrs Haines took great delight in reading the articles out to Ted and Rita at breakfast. Lucinda was featured in one of the party photographs in the Mercury and was threatening to have copies made and put into frames.

When June saw the papers, she did her best to muster up some delight, but her heart was telling a different story. Once again she was experiencing the gut-wrenching feeling she had so many years before. The show must go on and when she headed out to the theatre later she would have to ensure that the smile was firmly in place.

Freda and Muriel were disappointed they had not appeared in any photographs despite their efforts to do otherwise. It seemed that they were always in the wrong place at the wrong time.

Elsie Stevens had seen the article in The Express and had phoned Don to congratulate him. It was then he decided to tell her about what had been happening. Elsie listened and caught the hesitation in her husband's voice and, biting her tongue, decided to leave well alone until another day.

***

Before going to the police station, Rita and June went along to see Lorna to break the news about Veronica. It was written all over Lorna's face that this was going to be another hurdle to overcome in her already troubled life.

June signed for Veronica's belongings and took them away in a couple of bags. When they were sitting in the car, and with June's say so, Rita checked the bottles of medication and sure enough she found the rogue tablets in a marked bottle. There was no way of knowing whether Veronica had unwittingly taken any of them and if she had they had most certainly contributed to her heart failure.

To take their minds of the situation Rita drove out of town to Wroxham Broads where she knew that Roy's of Wroxham did some wonderful elevenses.

They settled themselves down and talked about the opening night and the splash it had made in the papers. The subject then slowly turned to making funeral arrangements for Veronica and Rita reassured June that with the help of Wally, she and he could manage everything. June must concern herself with her performances and her appearance the following day in Palmers.

"Ted has a wonderful wife in you Rita. I have been hearing the stories of how you follow him up and down the country."

"Stories!" exclaimed Rita. "With Ted they go hand in hand and not all confined to the stage I'm afraid. He has been a good husband despite his indiscretions from time to time, but I wouldn't have him any other way."

"He is very lucky to have you."

"And I think he knows it. Watching him last night was a revelation. He does so many shows and cabarets that they all become one and the same, but last night I saw the spark of the old Ted and it warmed my heart. Now I am getting sentimental."

They finished their coffees and pastries and headed back to the car. The ducks were waddling across the road to the Broads and for the first time that morning June laughed, reminded of the ducks back at her home in France.

They drove back to Great Yarmouth and once they had unloaded the car of the meagre possessions they got themselves ready to have lunch at The Star Hotel where, at Don's expense, the company were expected.

Don raised his glass to the gathered throng. "A toast to you all. Thank you from the bottom of my heart for last night. I would like to wish you continued success for our short time here in Great Yarmouth."

Everyone drank to that.

As the meal was coming to a close, Don received a tap on the shoulder. He turned round and to his surprise there stood Elsie. He was delighted to see her.

"Attention everyone, I would like you to meet the person so often heard of but never seen, my wife Elsie."

Cheers went up from the company as Don and Elsie made their way to the bar for a chat.

It had been a hectic twenty-four hours and with a show looming at 6.10 most of the company decided to go and have a lie down.

Ted and Rita decided to stroll back to the boarding house, needing the fresh air to clear their heads. Jim headed for the butchers to order a good joint of beef for the weekend, while the Dean Sisters walked back to the caravan park to put their feet up and revel in their success. They had received a congratulatory telegram from Hughie Green earlier that day.

***

That evening Don and Elsie stood at the entrance to the theatre and watched as the first-house audience began to enter.

At 6.10 on the dot the overture struck up, the curtain rose and the show that had captured the critics' hearts the night before was off to a flying start. The performance kept to schedule and the curtain came down shortly after 8.20. The first audience left by all the available exits, ushered by the theatre staff, and once the doors were secured shut the second audience began to enter.

***

Elsie had seen many of Don's variety shows, but even she was surprised at the sheer slickness and professionalism of the performances that pounded the pier stage. Over the years her husband had taken some knocks, lost hard-earned money and at times had almost given up the art he loved so much. This show was the icing on the cake and it was Elsie's hope that there would now be a turnaround in her husband's fortunes.

***

After the second house, an exhausted company made their way to the bar for a quick drink and some headed for their digs. June, on the arm of Wally, began to think of her appearance at Palmers the following day. So many things had happened in the short space of time that she had been in the town, that it was hard to keep a track on time. There were things to organise and a funeral to attend, but for now she would try to bask in the glory that for the moment belonged to her. But in her heart of hearts she knew it could never be as it once was all those years ago. This show was only hers to borrow.

Saturday 17th May

June was greeted at Palmers reception by the Managing Director and he then introduced her to Jean Kerr. They took tea in the board room and chatted generally before June was led by Jean to the basement department that housed words and music. A crowd had already begun to gather clutching their programmes of the show they had seen the night before and several more were holding the record sleeves of the vinyl discs they intended to purchase and obtain the signature of this West End star. Wally had stayed in the background accompanied by Rita. Other members of the company had stayed away not wishing to distract the attention away from June. Cameras flashed as June posed for photographs with fans, some who had been lucky enough to see her in London. She signed her autograph so many times with messages of dedication that she soon lost count. The tills rang to the sound of sales and the whole thing was deemed an enormous success.

June was whisked away in a waiting car by Rita and Wally and they headed off to have a much deserved rest at Mrs Haines'. June felt elated by the experience and recalled similar appearances she had done in her West End heyday. Wally brought the reminiscences to a halt and gently conveyed to June that she needed to go and lie down.

***

The Dean Sisters had been along to the Hippodrome to meet with the father of Joseph Carlio who had seen the early show the night before and had been very much impressed with their act. He decided there and then to offer them a contract to appear with his family at the Manchester Christmas Circus and then from there a possible tour overseas. Joseph suggested that singing should not feature in the act at all, but that he could work on some extra balancing routines with the girls that could be incorporated in the overall act. The girls were excited by the prospect, but wanted to take the contract away to allow Don Stevens to give it the once over. This was agreed and a meeting was arranged for the following week to iron out any problems.

Since Opportunity Knocks the girls had had no sole agent and they wondered if Don would want to take them on to his books. They needed someone to look out for them.

When they approached Don later that day he was flattered by their request but, after giving it his due consideration, he turned it down on the grounds that he would not be able to look after them while they were overseas. However, there was one glimmer of hope, he might be able to put them in touch with someone who could help them. He said the contract they were being offered was a sound one and the Manchester trial didn't make them bound to a European tour; it was just a stepping stone to it if they wanted it. Feeling much happier about things the three girls decided they would sign the contract when they had their meeting. It would be make or break, but in show business there was always an element of risk.

***

Don had been visited by the theatre manager of the Wellington Pier who had been very impressed with the show. He told Don that he would be happy for the show to have a two week end-of-season showing at the Wellington with or without the leading lady. A large conference party was expected in at the Carlton in September and with a few late visitors to the resort and some well-placed advertising the show could prove to be a sell-out. Don would discuss this with the company, emphasising that it would play once a night. Elsie was pleased and knew that this offer would not be the last Don would receive; the success of the show was being talked about in other resorts.

Tuesday 20th May

Veronica's funeral was a quiet affair. Rita and Ted accompanied June, Wally, Lorna and Robin to the small church in Lound where arrangements had been made for a private service and burial. Lorna, who was heavily sedated, leaned on Robin's arm as the service led by the local vicar went through its various stages. The sun shone brightly as the coffin was lowered into the ground. June threw a handful of earth on the coffin and Lorna, who was visibly upset by the whole process, threw a single white rose.

Wally thanked the vicar on behalf of the group and then escorted the party to the waiting cars. Wally took June's hand and in silence they journeyed back to Great Yarmouth.

***

"Well me old lover," said Rita, "I am glad that is over. It is so sad to think how things have turned out. Lorna must be feeling awful, and as for June…"

Ted pattered his wife's arm. "My dear, we cannot do anything about the dead, but we can help the living."

"Yes you are right, of course. I just wish I had seen the signs earlier."

"Stop fretting Rita. No one was expecting you to spot all the signs; after all, you are not Miss Marple."

But just at that moment Rita wished she had been.

***

At Wally's suggestion, June and he moved into the Star Hotel, which gave them both the space they needed. They had sent Lucinda a large bouquet of flowers and a beautifully wrapped box of chocolates with a card of thanks and asked that she be present at the closing night of the show and to stay for drinks afterwards. Lucinda smiled to herself happily; that would be another one in the eye for the dolly sisters and no mistake.

James Gerard bid farewell to return to his London home followed by Mary who returned to Corton and promised to keep in touch and that she would come back for the final performance.

Wally and June spent their time during the day getting to know each other again. They visited nearby villages and explored the pretty surrounding countryside and small public houses off the beaten track. June insisted on going back to Veronica's grave several times, she felt there were things that had been left unsaid and only in the silence of the graveyard could she begin to find inner peace through quiet prayer.

Lorna had been receiving expert care paid for by June and was progressing steadily, it was hoped that by the end of the month she would be able to return to her London home with Robin by her side. Any future plans June had in mind for her could wait their turn. It was more important that Lorna returned to full health first.

***

The audiences continued to enjoy Summer Frolics and Maud and Barbara had their work cut out turning people away at the box office. Bookings were now coming in thick and fast for the main summer attraction and any chance for a quick brew with colleagues were few and far between.

***

It was a rather surprised Freda and Muriel who accepted an invitation to take afternoon tea with Lucinda. Lucinda had never been one to entertain at home, unless, of course, the guests were of the paying kind.

Freda had made an effort to look her best and not to be upstaged by Muriel who looked as if she had just walked out of Palmers fashion window.

The two were greeted by a smiling Lucinda, who was wearing a rather bright blue skirt and blouse with a necklace just touching the collar line. Her feet, normally encased in some comfortable house slippers, were adorned in some rather smart court shoes and to her credit she had even made an effort with her hair, which was done up into a rather fetching bun.

She escorted the two landladies into the lounge where she had laid a small table with a fine tiered display of assorted cakes and fancies, courtesy of Matthews Bakery. The large bouquet from June and Wally was unmistakably placed so as to catch the eye of anyone who entered the room. The large box of chocolates, wrapped with a rather splendid red ribbon, was laid at the side of the vase with the thank you card visible for all to see.

Lucinda excused herself while she went to make a pot of tea, leaving Muriel and Freda to survey the setting.

"Fancy man's flowers," said Freda, looking enviously at the arrangement, "and with him and his wife under the same roof. There is no shame to that woman."

Muriel, used to her friend's ranting, wasn't so sure. "It could be her birthday."

Freda huffed and sat herself down. "It could be Christmas, but it ain't!"

"Freda Boggis you are one jealous cat at times. I think it's nice that Lucinda has been given some flowers, it shows appreciation."

"And chocolates too!" exclaimed Freda. "Flowers and chocolates spells fancy man, you mark my words."

"I am sure you have received flowers in your time from happy holiday guests and your husband?"

Freda thought for a moment. "The last time Dick gave me flowers was when he nicked some out of Doris Smith's garden on his way home from the Legion. Never even put them in paper, bulbs and all there were. I got him to confess, of course. I bumped into old Doris one day at the market and there she was telling me that some louts had stolen flowers from her beds in the dead of the night. I shall never forget that woman's face. I can't stand daffodils."

Just then Lucinda returned with the tea tray.

"Now ladies," she said, as she handed them tea plates and then proffered the cake stand. "Please help yourself and I will pour."

Freda helped herself to a jam puff. "Is it a special occasion?" she asked, as Lucinda poured the tea.

"One doesn't need a special occasion to have tea with friends. I just thought it would be a nice start to what I hope will be a busy summer season for us all. We rarely get the chance to have a little chat."

Muriel took a bite of her cream slice and smiled. "You are right Lucinda, once we get the visitors in it's all hands to the pump."

Lucinda handed them both their tea and sat herself down.

Freda could contain her curiosity no longer. "I was admiring your flowers when we came in, that's why I thought it might be your birthday."

Lucinda shook her head. "That is months off yet. No they are a thank you from Miss Ashby and her companion for an enjoyable stay here, the chocolates too. Maybe when we have finished our tea we could sample one or two."

Muriel smiled to herself. She knew it, not so much a chance to chat as a chance to swank. Lucinda Haines was priceless and no mistake. And with that she helped herself to another cake; she meant to have her money's worth.

***

Lilly had returned home after a particularly long day cleaning at the theatre and hospital and found a letter awaiting her from Duchy Publishing House; they requested that Lilly send them the first four chapters of her story for their consideration. In a state of excitement Lilly had retrieved her manuscript and removing the first four chapters from the folder headed back to the hospital. She was very friendly with Gerry, one of the porters, and it was he she approached to do her a favour. Gerry smiled at his friend and agreed to photocopy the handwritten notes Lilly was clutching to her chest.

An hour later Gerry handed Lilly the copying and with the promise of a couple of drinks one night in the Growler, she headed home. On her way she purchased a large manila envelope and some rather fancy writing paper she had spotted. It cost a few pennies more than she wanted to part with, but first impressions were important.

Once back home she wrote a letter in her neatest handwriting and placed the letter with the copied chapters into the envelope and addressed it for posting first thing in the morning. She smiled happily to herself and set about making herself a pot of tea and a toasted teacake. She felt she deserved it. Now all she had to do was wait and see what Duchy Publishing House made of her efforts.

Chapter Fourteen *"The Winds of Change"*

Thursday 22nd May

Dave popped in to see Marie. She had just finished serving a customer and smiled when she saw him.

"Any news on Sara?" he asked. "I don't mean to pry but I know how worried you have been."

"Haven't heard a thing," said Marie. "Alf says no news is good news."

"Have you tried calling any of her friends?"

"Sara didn't have a lot of friends and those she did have were mainly from the rock factory. I did wonder if she had met a young man, but it seems unlikely. One girl who Alf knows there said Sara never mentioned boys as such."

"I hope you hear some news soon. I'll look in again when I am passing if you don't mind."

"Mind? I welcome the distraction Dave, you really are one of the kindest men I have met in a long time."

***

Jenny Benjamin had been doing a lot of thinking since her chats with Don Stevens. She had come to realise that Don was probably right; at the age of fifty-seven she had become very staid in her work. The world back in the 1920s had been a very different place and although her schooling had been thorough and she had come from parents who tried to make the best of this only child, their hope of her ever making something of herself had been dashed when Jenny had shown an interest in the dance. Reluctantly her parents had let her join the Miss Mabel School of Dance in Caister. And it was there that Jenny had learned of Miss Bluebell, Miss Mabel having been an admirer of the work that Margaret Kelly had done in launching the famous Bluebells Girls in 1912. She could spot talent a mile off and she recognised something in the young Jenny that filled her with great hope. And so it was that after arduous auditions in London and Paris in 1932, at the age of twenty Jenny Benjamin became a Bluebell. She measured up to all the requirements being just over five feet ten inches and having firm breasts, long legs and a well-formed derrière.

Jenny was excellent at ballet and tap and showed a unique flair for all that Margaret 'Miss Bluebell' Kelly required of her girls. She had shown little interest in men, though they had shown a keen interest in her and she had often been the recipient of large floral bouquets and chocolates, much to the envy of some of her colleagues.

Jenny had been a happy Bluebell; she worked hard and adored the twice nightly performances at the Lido on the Champs Elysées. But when she reached the age of 26, she decided to return home to Great Yarmouth and set up her own dancing school and troupe in the safe knowledge that all she had learned under the watchful eye of Miss Bluebell would not go to waste. As with all her girls, Miss Bluebell took a great interest in her protégée and Jenny would write the odd letter informing her of her progress, though the outbreak of the Second World War would bring its own difficulties on both sides of the Channel.

Undeterred by the battles around her, Jenny Benjamin soldiered on and provided entertainment to some of the troops.

Her parents became proud of their daughter and ploughed money into her dancing school, and when they were both killed in a tragic car accident Jenny found she had inherited a wealth well beyond the needs of her well-tailored life. So the money had helped to provide scholarships for young girls to attend theatre schools and when she thought she had found that special talent, Jenny would arrange to have the lucky girl audition for Miss Bluebell.

The Tiller Girls came along in the sixties and Jenny watched as they became a great feature of the variety era. She incorporated some of the Tiller Girl routines she had seen with her own girls, but the dance groups like the Gojos and The Young Generation who came along later left her cold and she could never quite grasp that her own girls were beginning to look slightly dated.

Jenny had accumulated a comfortable bank balance and although she knew she didn't have to work herself quite so hard getting her girls into summer and pantomime seasons, the calling of the theatre had never left her.

Jenny had to make a difficult decision. Was it time to move over and allow young talent to take the reins and for her to take a back seat? In order to do this she had to find someone whom she could trust with her legacy to take her dance school forward. She had two people in mind, both had been dancers of hers and both still trod the boards in local amateur productions. So a visit to see Doreen Turner and Jill Sanderson might just be the solution to her dilemma.

A phone call secured a meeting with Doreen and Jill who were both curious to hear what Jenny had to say. There had been rumours that Jenny was having a hard time and they wanted to know if these rumours were founded. They had great respect for Jenny, she had taught them well, but even they had realised their tutor was somewhat behind the times. They all met in Palmers coffee shop and Jenny, who had had time to do some groundwork, laid out her proposals to the two.

"I have long regarded you both in high esteem," Jenny began, "and I was wondering how you would both feel about the possibility of taking over my dance troupe?"

Jill and Doreen looked at each other and smiled.

"You would, of course, earn a small salary and I would remain in the position of guardian to my plan until such times as I signed over the dancing school completely. I have no family to speak of and I would hate all the long hard slog to go to waste, I would like the Benjamin name to live on after I have gone. I think you could both breathe new life into the school and add some of the sparkle it has sadly been lacking these last few years. There are bookings lined up for the rest of the year and so a quick decision would be welcome. I could have contracts drawn up in a matter of weeks. I just wanted to get your feelings on this idea of mine."

"It would be a great honour to carry on your work," said Jill, "But I would need to consult my husband first. If Doreen is in agreement I am sure we would work very well together."

Doreen nodded. "It is a most interesting proposal Jenny. Unlike Jill I don't have a family to consider, but if you are sure of what you would be giving away I would like to give it a try. I could give up my part-time job at Arnolds and do something that would give me a great deal of pleasure."

Jenny smiled. "I wouldn't be giving it away, I would be entrusting it to two great dancers and, if I may call you such, colleagues. Perhaps you would like me to leave you both so you can discuss it in private. You know where to find me and if you could let me know your final decision within the next few days I would be most grateful."

Both Doreen and Jill thanked Jenny and watched as she walked away from them with a certain spring in her gait.

When Jenny arrived at the theatre later that afternoon she went and talked with Don and told him what she had done. Don was impressed.

"It means that you will still be in control, but have the input of new ideas from two people you can trust."

Jenny smiled. "I did a lot of thinking and a lot of soul-searching and I know I have made the right decision. And I am almost certain that the answer I will receive from Jill and Doreen will be a positive one. Though I did spring it on them rather."

Don touched Jenny's arm. "It was a brave decision and, as you say, the right one. I have had to look at my work schedule and some time ago I decided I needed to scale it down. However, the sudden success of this show has had offers coming in thick and fast. Unfortunately, June Ashby has been making decisions of her own and it is unlikely I will be able to persuade her to change her mind and continue with the business."

"I am sure if you tried a little harder the old Stevens charm would do its stuff. Perhaps she would consider it as a short term option. It seems a shame that after all the interest from the media she is going to settle for a farewell from a theatre pier in Great Yarmouth. A West End season would do the job so much better."

"I think it is the media's attention that is worrying her. So far it has been possible to keep any connection with her sisters away from her, but if the story ever got out, it would cause all kinds of problems."

Jenny nodded in agreement. "And then there is the connection that can be made to Gwen. The media would have a field day with that lot and no mistake."

Don looked around him. "Who would have thought that such an innocent looking theatre and a lovable seaside resort would be the basis for such a thing?"

"Yes it is certainly more akin to an Agatha Christie," said Jenny with feeling.

***

Lilly, who had been doing some last bits of cleaning at the back of the auditorium, had been making mental notes of the conversation she had just heard. It would make a great basis for her next novel. She intended to make some notes when she got home. Excited by the prospect she gathered her cleaning materials together and headed for the rear exit.

Don, disturbed by the noise, turned and watched her go. He hadn't realised there had been anyone else in the auditorium and wondered how much of the conversation Lilly had heard. Perhaps he would have a quiet word with her.

Lilly made her way down the pier just as the Dean Sisters were making their way along to the theatre. They waved at her and Lilly smiled in return.

I wonder what stories those three could tell, she thought to herself. Maybe I ought to have a little chat with them sometime.

Maud was just leaving the box office. "Hello Lilly, fancy some company?"

Lilly was always pleased to see her friend. "We could treat ourselves to a knickerbocker glory in Vettessies."

"Lilly Brockett, anyone would think you had come into a lot of money."

Lilly smiled to herself. She was itching to tell someone about her book offer, but didn't wish to tempt fate.

Maud linked her arm, it was nice to see Lilly so happy of late. She had no idea why this was but she was very pleased to see her old friend in such fine fettle.

Vettessies was quite busy, but they managed to find a table. Maud ordered two ham sandwiches, a pot of tea and two knickerbocker glories to follow.

"I was just off to see my sister. She has got some notion about moving in with me permanently and leaving the flat above the shop empty."

"But I thought you two didn't get on under the same roof for too long?" Lilly questioned, as she made herself comfortable.

"The problem is Enid gets lonely. I don't mind being on my own but she gets fed up with her own company and as we are both getting older it would make sense for us both to move in together."

"But it would leave the shop vulnerable with no one living there," said Lilly, moving her bag from the table to make way for Gino who was bringing their order to them.

"We could let out the flat I suppose; it would make a nice home for a couple."

"What you really need in there is a man to keep an eye on things."

Maud agreed. "It would have to be someone we knew, I wouldn't want it going to just anyone. I will have a word with Enid tonight and see what she makes of the situation. I could even have the house made over, so we had our own living areas, that way we wouldn't always be under each other's feet."

"Perhaps old Jim could give you a hand and Dave too. They are a dab hand at the old carpentry."

"Now there's a thought," said Maud, pleased with Lilly's suggestion. "It might be the solution I need."

Lilly set to with her sandwich while Maud poured the tea.

"Everything okay ladies?" asked Gino, as he passed by. "You are both looking very beautiful today, you make my heart sing."

Maud looked up at Gino. "And that's enough of your Italian flannel you old Romeo, Gina will have your guts for garters."

Gino chuckled and moved on.

Lilly had blushed, it had been a long time since anyone had called her beautiful and she meant to savour every moment of it and she knew deep down that Maud was tickled pink too.

Saturday 24th May

Any hopes that the story surrounding the body of Gwen found at the Norfolk and Norwich Hospital and its connection to the late Veronica Bright had been put to bed were dashed when Mrs Haines handed Rita a copy of one of the national papers as she and Ted were enjoying a leisurely breakfast. An old photograph of Veronica headed the piece on the inside page and as Rita read the story out loud, June Ashby's name had not escaped the reporter's pen. Lucinda Haines had read the piece earlier and after delivering the paper to Rita and Ted had dashed out to the local newsagents to see if any other papers had covered the story. Joe Darby the newsagent was surprised to see Lucinda taking such an interest in the nationals and commented as much.

"I see that star at the pier has made the front of the Eastern Daily Press this morning," he said, looking at Lucinda as she looked through every daily she could find.

"You had better let me take a copy of that," she said, fumbling for her purse in her housecoat pocket. She had even forgotten to change her fluffy mules which looked somewhat out of place away from the kitchen. "You didn't happen to spot any other mention of it in other papers did you Joe?"

"Funnily enough I did look through them all this morning but the Sketch and the Eastern were the only two. No mention in the Mercury."

"It says here in the Eastern," Joe continued, as he looked through the article, "that there is another sister, or step-sister by the name of Lorna. They all sound like head cases to me."

Lucinda snatched up a copy of the Eastern Daily Press and laid the exact money on the counter. "They are not all head cases as you put it. I happen to know that June Ashby is a very nice lady."

"Been staying with you has she?"

"That's for me to know Joe Darby," said Lucinda, folding the paper and putting it under her arm.

"Well you had better watch out," said Joe, lighting his ninth cigarette of the morning, "there will be reporters all over the place once word is out."

Lucinda nodded her head at Joe and headed for the door. "Thanks for the warning I'm sure."

"That's okay Lucinda, if it all gets out of hand you let me know and I'll come round and protect you."

"I can well do without your protection Joe Darby; you need to keep your mind on your wife and kids."

And knowing exactly what that comment meant, Joe Darby blushed and gave a nervous cough.

"What were the chances of this not getting out?" said Ted, buttering another piece of toast. "It was bound to. Someone just doesn't get murdered and no one says anything. The police had a duty to release a story, the hospital staff were hardly going to keep it quiet for ever, and you know how gossip starts."

"I feel sorry for June. She has been enjoying such good publicity with the show and things seem to be coming together for her. Have you noticed the way she looks at Wally when they are together?"

"You are just an old romantic," said Ted, eying his wife with a smile. "Do you think we should go over to the Star Hotel and speak to June?"

Just then Lucinda came into the dining room. "It has made the front page of the Eastern Daily Press, but none of the other nationals has mentioned it. Joe round at the shop thinks it will be headline news in the Mercury next week and no mistake."

Rita looked at the paper. "The local press will have a field day with this lot."

"Look on the bright side," said Ted, thinking aloud. "June will be able to tell them very little, apart from the history of the family. She wasn't in on the goings-on with this Gwen character. Don Stevens could well find himself the centre of attention for a while and I wouldn't want to be in his shoes for all the tea in China."

Rita looked at her husband and realised how many narrow escapes they had had with stories leaking out about their somewhat unconventional partnership that would have kept the papers in stories for months.

Lucinda made a fresh pot of tea. Then the doorbell rang and before Rita could get to the door to answer it, Lucinda had let in a rather white-faced June Ashby supported by Wally.

"We saw the paper this morning, a member of staff pushed it under my door." June sank down into the nearest chair and Lucinda went to get some more tea and toast for her unexpected guests. "This means all the old stuff is going to come to the surface and I am going to have to relive some very painful memories. And what about Lorna? This could really tip her over the edge."

Rita watched as June began to sob; Wally did his best to comfort her, but she wouldn't be comforted.

It was going to be a very long day and it was going to take more than tea and toast to get through it. What they needed was a plan and Rita decided to take the matter in hand herself and get things on an even keel as best she could.

"Look, I have some ideas that just might see you through this. Firstly, we have to keep June away from the public gaze as best we can." Rita began scribbling something on a piece of paper she had taken from her bag.

"But June has a show to do tonight," said Wally. "How are we going to get her onto the pier without attracting attention?"

"I've thought about that", said Rita. "We disguise her, pop her in a wheelchair and wheel her down the pier. The reporters can't interview her while she is on stage."

"They could get backstage," said Ted. "I can't see Jack the doorman putting up much of a stand against a determined reporter."

"We can get Jim to help out and rope in that nice friend of his, Dave," Rita replied, warming to her theme.

"But we have to get June out of the theatre again afterwards," said Ted. "What do you intend doing, lowering her into a boat through the trapdoor beneath the theatre?"

Rita frowned. "Now there's a thought."

"Don't even go there."

June blew her nose loudly into her handkerchief and looked up at them all. Lucinda, poised with the teapot in one hand and toast rack in the other, waited to hear what was going to be said before she interrupted the proceedings.

"We need to get June and Lorna away from Great Yarmouth, and today if possible," said Wally with some conviction.

"That would leave the show without a star. The audiences will turn away in droves," said Ted, drumming his fingers on the table in some agitation, he was out of cigarettes and was desperate for a smoke. "And it being a Saturday night too!"

Rita looked at the gathered throng and thought for a moment. "The show needn't be without a star. We can create a whole new range of publicity; Moira Clarence could make an unexpected return to the stage."

The room went silent as they all looked at each other. Lucinda, who was beside herself with the excitement of it all, dropped the toast rack. "I thought she was dead," she stuttered, nearly dropping the teapot as well.

"Oh no," said Ted, with the biggest grin he could muster, "she is right here beside me."

"I will go and speak with Don," said Rita, getting up, "and see what he has to say on the subject. You, my dear, must remain here if that's okay with you Lucinda?"

Lucinda nodded.

"Wally, you must go to the Star and retrieve your luggage. Ted, you must get on the phone to Jim and arrange for Lorna and Robin to be bought here as quickly as possible. Lucinda, will you be a love and look after everyone. It is imperative that this plan is executed speedily. June, Wally, Lorna and Robin must leave here today and unseen. If there are any reporters it will be my guess they will go to the theatre first. No one knows where June has been staying, not that in a town of this size it would take much detecting to find out. Now, you all know what you have to do."

They all nodded in grateful acknowledgement of Rita's plan. As she headed out of the door Ted smiled in admiration. "I knew old Reet would know what to do. She's always good in a crisis."

***

Rita interrupted Don and his wife at breakfast and asked if she could speak to him privately. They retired to the bedroom and Rita began to reveal her plan. Don listened in amazement; he had heard one of the staff at the hotel talking about the article, but as yet hadn't read it for himself.

"You are quite incredible," said Don, patting Rita's arm. "I can't believe you have come up with this plan on your own and so quickly."

"Believe me Don, when you have been married as long as I have you need to think on your feet. How will you handle the press?"

"I will have to tell Elsie of course," said Don. "I just hope my affair with Gwen won't come out, though there is no reason that it should. Although Elsie does know all about it she would be the one who would suffer. Look, I am very grateful for you resurrecting Moira Clarence, but what will you perform, what will you sing?"

"Let me worry about that Don. I will get Maurice and the boys together and run through a few favourites of mine. I am sure Jenny will be able to come up with some choreography to lighten the mood. What you have to do is get on to the local radio when we have got June and co safely out of the town. You can tell them that due to personal reasons you have had to replace the star and have been fortunate to secure the talents of Moira Clarence. I am not unknown in these quarters and with a few well-chosen quotes, which I will give you, the publicity will generate a new interest in Summer Frolics and hopefully move some of the attention away from what people have been reading this morning over the breakfast table. By tomorrow the newspapers will be chip wrappings. If you speak to the press by eleven this morning there is every chance that it will make the local evening paper tonight. Who knows, it may also trigger interest with the local television station. You could give them a call; it will help stir things up. The key element has to be that we make so much of the fact that Moira Clarence is making a big comeback that it detracts from the other matter."

"I have nothing but admiration for you my dear," said Don with great feeling. "It's people like you that helped this country win the war."

Rita stood up ready to take her leave. "Then we must get the troops into active service and quickly, there is no time to lose."

It was only just eight-thirty when Rita headed back to Mrs Haines'. Wally had gone to the hotel to carry out his allotted task. Ted had been on the phone to Jim who had swung into action and was then heading off to collect Lorna and Robin. June had eaten some breakfast, with Lucinda keeping a watchful eye on her, and once she had finished she began to make her own plans on how best to leave the town.

Half an hour later, Jim turned up at the house with a rather tired Lorna and somewhat bewildered Robin in tow.

Wally returned with the luggage and June then set about changing and covering her own hair with a wig from her wardrobe.

It was decided that Jim would drive them all to Norwich where a car would be hired to return them to London where they would make plans for their trip over to France.

Lorna was looking particularly fragile and a concerned Robin had expressed his fears. But with speed being of the essence there was no time to waste and the plan was notched up a gear as they all said hasty goodbyes to Rita, Ted and Lucinda.

***

Maurice was somewhat surprised to get a call from Rita, but agreed to assemble the boys at the theatre. The thought of hearing Moira Clarence sing filled him with some delight; Jenny Benjamin was equally excited as she gathered together her girls for some changes to their now well-rehearsed routines.

***

Jim wished them all a safe journey as he waved off the four from Norwich and headed back to Great Yarmouth. When he arrived at the pier the box office seemed to be under some kind of siege from photographers and a couple of reporters. An Anglia Television van had just pulled up on Marine Parade and it was obvious that the media had sprung into action. Maud was being asked questions she had no way of answering and Jim quickly intervened. He explained that a press release by Mr Don Stevens could be expected shortly and asked them to be patient. Maud wanted some kind of explanation, but Jim felt unable to give her one at that moment. He decided that the fewer people who knew what was going on the better.

He walked into the theatre and discovered Rita in full vocal power on the stage. Maurice and his boys were easily able to play for her without any score as they had done this consistently in the clubs they had played over the years when singers had turned up without any proper music to speak of. It had been agreed that Rita would sing some of the show tunes June had performed but add in a few of her own favourites.

Jenny had been busy with the dancers below the stage and had come up with an interesting, if not entirely new, routine that would accompany Rita on her opening number. The rest of the routines they had used with June would remain the same, with Rita coming in if and when she felt able. Jenny couldn't remember ever feeling so intrigued by all that was going on around her following the revelation she had read in the paper that morning.

Meanwhile, back at the box office things had calmed down. The reporters had given up trying to get anything out of Maud, who obviously knew nothing about what was going on. It wasn't

278

until Barbara showed up clutching the local paper that Maud was even aware of what had unfolded earlier. She suspected that Jim knew more than he would let on, but realised he must have his reasons.

By twelve noon the reporters were buzzing with the news that June Ashby had disappeared leaving Moira Clarence to carry on in the pre-season seaside show. Don had given a full report to the local press office and then headed towards the pier where he was eagerly interviewed by the crew from Anglia Television. He made little of the June Ashby side of the story saying he had learned she had withdrawn from the show late the night before, but that he had been very fortunate to be able to engage the talent of Moira Clarence who had agreed to come out of retirement to help an old friend out of a fix. He promised that Moira would be available to give an interview within the hour; he just needed to go and put the wheels in motion.

Maud and Barbara who had overheard much of the conversation were very animated by the rolling news and it prompted Barbara to break open a box of chocolates she had intended to take to a friend she was visiting later that day. Such things didn't happen often and Maud intended to take advantage of the situation and eat all of her favourite centres.

Don enquired how the rehearsal was going when Maurice had laid down his baton.

"Don, if the rehearsals had been like this with the original star of the show (he meant Lorna) I fear that none of what we are privy to now would ever have come to light. Moira, Rita is a revelation; she has taken command of this show and needs little or no help from me. Jenny cannot believe that a routine she put together only minutes ago is now planted in Rita's head and that she knows all the steps. This is how professionals work and we have one in Rita and no mistake."

Don thanked his old pal and went to speak to Rita. He thanked her again for what she was doing and then briefed her about what she could say to the eager press boys who waited without.

Donning an outfit she had found backstage and with the help of some carefully hidden safety pins, Moira Clarence presented herself to the reporters. A proud Ted looked on from a distance and Jim smiled at him.

"She really is the business isn't she?" he said to Ted. "The way she is managing to handle them all and she is taking no prisoners. They certainly have their work cut out interviewing her."

"That is one of the things about Rita," said Ted, wiping an escaping tear. "She has always been the power behind me and gave up her own stardom to concentrate on my career."

"She obviously loves you very much."

"I have never for once doubted that Jim. I only wish I had been the husband she had wanted me to be. I have let her down."

"I am sure she doesn't think that," said Jim reassuringly. "She worships the ground you walk on."

"And right now I worship her," replied Ted. "What man wouldn't be proud to have Rita as their wife?" And silently Jim acknowledged what the old trouper had said.

***

The local evening paper led with a big article on the return of Moira Clarence and a photograph taken earlier that day. A few lines were given over to June Ashby, but the main theme of the story was that the local theatre had given rise to the return of another old favourite. Moira was seen on Anglia Television that evening and the presenters, one of whom remembered Moira in her heyday, had nothing but praise to bestow upon who he described as the darling of the entertainment world.

Queues had again formed at the box office, even people who had seen the show previously with June Ashby, were eager to see Moira Clarence. Unsold tickets for the first house quickly began to sell out.

***

That evening when the curtain went up on Summer Frolics, a whole new generation was introduced to the talented Moira Clarence. Ted stood proudly in the wings as his wife went through her routine before the finale. He applauded loudly with the audience and hugged her as she came towards him to exit the stage. By the reception she had received, Rita was in no doubt that Moira Clarence was well and truly back.

Elsie and Don Stevens watched from the back of the auditorium with smiles on their faces as the audience on both houses that night rose to their feet when Moira took her final bows.

In the theatre bar afterwards, people were asking Moira for her autograph and she happily posed for photographs with those fortunate to have cameras with them.

***

Lilly had shown up at the second house being keen to see what all the fuss was about. She was itching to call on Freda and Muriel the following morning and tell them exactly what they had missed. Green with envy wouldn't come into it!

Chapter Fifteen   *"Moving On"*

The excitement of that night settled down and the company continued to play out their short run.

Maud took Jim to one side and broached the subject of the possibility of her sister moving in with her.

"The thing is, I don't want to leave the flat over the shop empty. I would feel happier if I had someone in there I could trust."

Jim considered his reply carefully. "How would you feel about Dave and his friend Dan moving in, I happen to know that they are looking for somewhere?"

"That may be okay for the interim, but what happens when this Dan fellow leaves after the season?"

"I don't think he is likely to do that, not unless Dave goes with him."

Maud put down her mug of coffee. "Are you saying what I think you are saying young Jim?"

Jim smiled. "Do you have a problem with it?"

"Not especially. I just thought our Dave would settle down one day with a girl."

"Well, he is settling down," replied Jim, "only with another bloke. And whilst I warned him about the problems of moving in together too soon, I have seen the way they are together and I think it will work out for them both."

"As long as he's happy with the arrangement, it is no skin off my nose. I am sure me and Enid would be very happy for them to occupy the flat once I have got the house sorted out to our liking."

"And that's where me and Dave come in," said Jim, taking the bull by the horns. "I am sure we can do some work on the place for you, so you both have your own living spaces."

"You are a darling Jim," said Maud, with a big smile. "I didn't know how I was going to ask you."

Jim hugged Maud. "You should know me better than that and just come out with it. Me and Dave will be more than happy to help and I am sure Dan will chip in too once he hears the news on the flat."

"That's grand," said Maud gratefully. "I will fill our Enid in on the details later today; she will be as relieved as I am to have our little problem solved."

"I am going to go off and have a word with Dave," said Jim, taking his leave. "We need to draw up some kind of plan between us."

"Perhaps you should engage the services of Rita, she seems to be full of them," said Maud, with a laugh.

"You may be right," said Jim and waved goodbye.

Jim found Dave walking down Wellington Pier enjoying the sea air.

"What an old darling," said Dave, when Jim told him the news. "Of course I will help you sort out Maud's house and I know I can speak for Dan when I say that he will lend a hand too between his shifts at the pub."

"Things going on okay between you two then?" Jim enquired.

"It is early days, but yes, so far so good," Dave answered happily, offering Jim a cigarette. "How long do you think it will take us to sort out Maud's place?"

"Keen to move into the flat are you?"

"Quite the opposite really," said Dave, looking out to sea. "I want Dan and me to get to know each other better first."

"Look, it is going to take the best part of our spare time throughout the season to get Maud's house to rights, so you are looking at the end of September beginning of October at the earliest. We also need to get someone in to do any kind of plumbing. I can turn my hand to most things but with a house of that sort, I wouldn't want to chance it."

"Perfect," said Dave, turning away from the view to face his friend and smiling. "That will give us plenty of time."

"It is good to see you not letting your heart rule your head."

"I need to be sensible; it is a big step for me to settle down with someone I care about. I want to get it right."

Jim smiled at Dave and patted him on the shoulder. "You are doing the right thing and I wish you every luck and happiness with it."

"That means a lot mate, thank you."

***

Lilly's hand trembled as she picked up the envelope from the mat. She recognised the bold heading; it was the Duchy Publishing House. She went into the kitchen and poured herself another cup of tea and sat down. She stared at the envelope for what seemed like an age then, following a gulp of tea, she gingerly picked up the envelope and carefully opened it. The paper was of high quality, Lilly was impressed by the feel of the parchment-like sheet she held in her hand which had been neatly folded. She opened out the sheet and another piece of paper fell on to the table. Ignoring it she read the typed missive.

It thanked her for sending her manuscript, which had greatly interested the publishing house. She was to be assured that it would be returned to her safely once another editor had read it. Following his recommendation Lilly would then be asked to submit the completed story within six months with a view to her book being published. There would also be a meeting with one of the editors to explore possibilities of further stories. A cheque had been enclosed as a goodwill gesture and retainer; a contract would be drawn up and sent under separate cover, which Lilly was advised to take to a solicitor for verification. Lilly read the letter several times and looked in disbelief at the cheque that had fluttered on to the table. She went upstairs and retrieved her manuscript and sat on the bed clutching it. As she gazed at the photograph of her late husband a silent tear rolled down her cheek and the realisation swept over her that her life would never be the same again.

For some time Lilly had been busy with her story, in fact only a few days before the letter had arrived she had completed it. She had taken the manuscript to Norwich where she had had two copies made at the Jarrolds stationery store. Over a period of time she had been putting aside money to cover the cost of the photocopying which was not cheap. She could have got it copied in Great Yarmouth, but as she knew many of the staff that worked in the various stationery outlets, she was wary of her secret being found out. On her trip to Norwich she was alarmed when she heard the voices of Freda and Muriel who were on one of their monthly trips to the city to do some shopping and treat themselves to a steak at the Berni Inn.

"Hello Lilly, where are you off to? Not often we see you on the train," said Muriel, sitting opposite her, while Freda huffed and puffed her way along the aisle. Freda was mumbling to herself that the train was too hot and was it necessary to have the heating on at this time of the year? it had long been the opinion of Muriel that her friend had been going through the change of life and not, it seemed, for the first time.

Lilly clutched her bag tightly and looked up and smiled. "I thought I would have a day out for a change. I don't get out of town very much, my work puts paid to that."

Muriel, noticing what appeared to be a heavy load that Lilly was holding, wondered what on earth she was carrying. "Brought a packed lunch with you?" she asked, as Freda heaved herself into the seat beside her, causing Muriel to shift nearer the window in case she got squashed more than she thought acceptable.

Lilly blushed. "No, I will probably have some chips on the market."

Muriel was about to reply when the ticket inspector approached them and with the distraction Freda caused finding her ticket, the moment passed and the conversation turned to the problems Freda had been having with her water supply, her veracious veins and the price of butter.

Lilly listened in silence and slipped her bag quietly to the floor out of sight and hoped that neither of her travelling companions would mention it again.

"Why don't you have lunch with us," offered Muriel, when Freda had come to the end of her monologue which, if she was honest with herself, had given her a headache. That was the problem with Freda, once she had started talking she never came up for air. She had been the same as a young girl and, though quite fair of face in those days, she had chewed the ears of many a prospective boyfriend and had them running in the other direction. Many a time she had been asked to leave a cinema because she was disturbing the other members of the audience. The poor young men who had been with her on various occasions had never dared show their face at the Empire cinema again. Over the years that followed, several young men who had been acquainted with Freda had signed up for the Army, much to the surprise of the parents. "I always thought our David wanted to be a fishermen like his dad," one had said at the time, whilst another mother was so upset that her Tommy was off to join the services she had taken to the drink.

"Thanks for asking," said Lilly, "but I don't suppose I will be long in Norwich and I don't have money to spare for steaks and the like."

Muriel felt a pang of sorrow for Lilly whom she knew had had a hard life. "I can treat you if you like. I had a win at bingo the other night."

"You kept that quiet," said Freda, popping a cherry Tune in her mouth. "I didn't think you were that keen on the game."

Muriel ignored the comment and smiled at Lilly.

"It's very kind of you," Lilly replied, "but I don't like to interfere with your plans and I have to get back as I have some things that need doing."

Muriel nodded and said no more, but turned to Freda who was now sucking loudly on her boiled sweet and making a noise you would normally associate with a kitchen sink. Sometimes she felt that her friend Freda let the side down completely.

Lilly left the pair at Norwich station and walked slowly up the incline past the imposing castle on the hill to the city centre. The bag was heavy, but she didn't want to take a bus with her friends as it might mean her getting caught up with them for the rest of the day. Jarrolds was quite busy when she stepped inside and she had to wait patiently to be served. Ever aware that Freda and Muriel might just walk in the door, she fidgeted nervously and kept turning to look behind her in case they suddenly appeared. The young male assistant suggested that Lilly leave the package for copying and call back in an hour when he would have it ready for her. She paid a small deposit and went out of the store. It was too early for chips, so she decided to go and look around C&A, who she knew had a sale on, where she might just find herself a bargain in the separates department. It was hardly cold outside, but like so many stores C&A had their heating on full pelt. Lilly undid her coat and made her way up the stairs to the ladies section. She found several blouses she liked but, even in the sale, she knew her money would not stretch that far, well not today at any rate. She was approached by a couple of sales assistants willing to help show her the garments on display and encouraging her to try them on. That was the trouble with shopping by yourself; you were seen as an easy target. Lilly mooched about for another half an hour, picking things up and admiring some of the newer fashions that had made their way into the store. What young people wore these days she would never have got away with in her young days! But Lilly was philosophical, you had to move with the times and let youngsters have their freedom. Yes, they could be rowdy at times with their motor scooters up and down Marine Parade at weekends, but on the whole they were a good bunch, just growing up and experiencing the world. Being a teenager was neither being an adolescent nor an adult, it was an awkward age. She knew friends who had found their offspring to be quite alien, always staying out late, getting into trouble at school or, as seemed the norm these days, girls coming home pregnant. Not like when Lilly was young, she had always been told by her mother, "Keep your hand on your halfpenny and only have a light kiss on the cheek."

She left the store and took herself across the road and went into a small coffee shop. She hadn't had a hot drink since breakfast and felt it would help to kill some more time before she went back to Jarrolds. She ordered a pot of tea for one, resisted the temptation of a scone and butter and found a table near the window where she could watch the world go by. Being a Wednesday the city was quite busy with people doing their market shopping. It was certainly better than waiting until Saturday when, like the market in Great Yarmouth, the place would be heaving with people. Mothers and those big Swallow prams were the worst, why they felt it necessary to drag the poor mites out to a busy environment rather than take them to a park was beyond Lilly's comprehension.

She drained her second cup of tea and then, thanking the lady at the counter, made her way back to Jarrolds. She was relieved to find the shop wasn't as busy now and that the young man who had attended her earlier was still behind the counter. He gave Lilly a friendly smile and retrieved the now heavier package for Lilly to put in her shopping bag. As Lilly parted with, to her way of thinking, the large amount of money she thanked the young man for his help and headed for the door. Perhaps a bag of chips would be about right now, it was nearly twelve-thirty and if she hurried she would be in time for the train back home at one-thirty-five, mission completed, well almost. All she had to do now was save enough money to post the manuscript and await her fate.

As she headed down Castle Hill she allowed her mind to wander, thinking what it might be like to become an author. Should she use her own name? Would Lilly Brockett look right on the front cover of a book? But then, as the name had seen her through most of her life, she hardly felt it right to call herself anything else. What would be the point? No one would know who it was and she wanted them to know, she wanted the likes of the Muriels and Fredas of this world to know that she, Lilly Brockett, had made her mark and she secretly couldn't help wondering what the response was going to be. She could imagine the look on Freda's face and even though the product of her labours was weighing heavily in her hand it was that thought alone that kept her spirits up as she proudly marched ahead to Thorpe station.

Meanwhile, in the Berni Inn, Freda and Muriel were enjoying steak, chips and mushrooms and pushed the boat out and had a gin and tonic apiece.

"Lilly seemed in a rush this morning," said Freda, taking another sip of her gin. "Not like her to come over to Norwich. She usually shops in town or goes over to Caister to see that friend of hers from school, Mary something or other. I never did like her, all front and no substance."

Muriel frowned. "Lilly is as entitled to come over to Norwich as anyone else, just because she doesn't go round broadcasting the fact."

Muriel very nearly choked when Freda agreed with her. It must be the gin and in that event Muriel must order another, it may make Freda stump up for afternoon tea later and that would be a first in anyone's book.

Lilly completed her journey into Great Yarmouth and reflected on her busy day. She had made much progress with her story and she felt very proud of herself, to think that she, Lilly Brocket, was an author. She popped into Matthews on the way home and purchased two fresh cream cakes and a meat pie. She felt she deserved a little treat and as they occurred so infrequently she intended to push the boat out. She might even break open that bottle of sherry someone had given her for Christmas, and with that thought in mind she set off down the road with a smile on her face.

Chapter Sixteen
"The Writing's on the Wall"

Rita took the phone call with great interest. She had been waiting to hear whether or not June and company had arrived safely in France.

June explained that the ferry crossing had been rough on the day they had travelled and that Lorna had been quite ill. They could have flown, but Lorna had expressed a fear of flying. But now they were all safely in June's chateau and a doctor had been called in to administer to Lorna needs; things seemed to be improving for the girl. There were no firm plans for the future and exactly what Lorna and Robin would do in the long term could not be decided upon until Lorna was back to full health. Wally was going to return to London for a few days and tie up some loose ends. June was delighted to hear about Rita's triumphant return as Moira and wished her all the best for the future. She again thanked her for all the help she had been and promised she would drop a line or two from time to time and catch up on any news.

Rita retold the conversation to Ted and an interested Lucinda and then she prepared herself for a sea air walk in readiness for the shows that evening. Ted noticed a new vigour in his wife, her cheeks glowed and her natural love of life came into its own once more. It was good to see her looking so radiantly happy as she set out for the promenade with the dark glasses shielding her eyes from the sunshine and, she thought, from the general public out to spot the star of the end-of-the pier show.

***

Jenny had just finished a meeting with Doreen and Jill in an attempt to move things on now that her own mind was firmly made up. With Doreen's and Jill's agreement, Jenny had been on to her solicitor to get the ball rolling. She spotted Rita heading down the promenade and caught up with her. The two exchanged pleasantries and then Jenny told Rita about her plans for the dancing school. Rita was pleased for her. It was just what was needed, it would mean that Jenny Benjamin's name would live on long after she was gone and all that hard work wouldn't have been for nothing.

As they reached the Wellington Pier Jenny suggested that they go into the Merrivale Model Village, which had just opened its gates for business. It was lovely to view the miniaturised village again and take in the beautiful landscaped garden with its running railway and trickling water features.

Rita enjoyed being in the company of Jenny and after all the drama that had gone before it was nice to get back to some kind of normality. At the end of their tour they entered the small café and sat down for a coffee and a slice of cake. Their talk turned back to show business.

"You must find it strange treading the boards again after so long," Jenny ventured.

"Funnily enough I found it rather easier than I expected. It must be all those years of travelling round the country with Ted and watching the various acts he has worked with. When I left the business all those years ago I never expected to return to it. I have never had a yearning to do so. However, when I stumbled across this show and I knew things were not as they should be, a little voice inside my head kept telling me I should get back in the routine again and the little voice was right. For years I have looked after Ted's needs and his act, it feels quite nice to be looking after something for myself for a change."

"And you have looked after it well. I watched you on that stage. If only all artistes were as easy to work with as you were. You picked up that routine in a matter of moments."

"You are a good teacher Jenny," said Rita. "I have watched how you work with your girls before. You do know your stuff and you do it very well indeed and against some very trying odds."

"Thank you," said Jenny, rather taken aback. She wasn't often given such compliments but she knew that coming from Rita it was given truthfully.

"Old Don is keen to get me on his books," said Rita, finishing her coffee. "And I am seriously considering it. I have agreed to do the show at the end of the season and Ted is arranging for me to do a couple of appearances during the season with some of his contacts. My future could be quite different now."

Just then they were interrupted by an elderly gentleman. "Moira Clarence, I wonder if you would do me the great honour of signing your autograph in my programme. My wife and I saw you last night and you were wonderful."

Rita smiled. "Of course I will." She signed the programme with love and best wishes and the gentleman bowed and went on his way happily.

"So much for the dark glasses," said Rita with feeling.

"You will have to get used to that sort of thing," said Jenny, with a smile.

"And I think I am going to rather enjoy the attention. It is just a shame that they are all likely to be as old as or older than me."

"You never know your luck; you might catch the attention of a young man one day."

Rita laughed. "With a guide dog of course!"

With a chuckle from Jenny they finished their snack and went back onto the promenade to continue their walk.

***

Dan was thrilled to hear the news Dave had for him when he dropped into the bar for a quick lunchtime beverage.

"Jim has suggested we three get together with Maud one afternoon and work out some kind of plan for what is needed for the house. It will mean us having to fit it in on days off and the like, but providing we work as a team we should be able to do most of it ourselves. I have seen the flat above the shop when I went there some time back and it will be just right for the two of us. Jim said Maud took the news about us surprisingly well, not even a raised eyebrow."

"I am sure she probably knows more about these things than she lets on to you and Jim. I have worked with plenty of women, it is their natural intuition. It took Stella all of three days to work me out."

Dave ordered another pint and turned his attention to the season ahead. He filled Dan in on a few more details that would help him to know what to expect.

Dan left Dave to his pint as he served a group that had just come in from a coach tour. They seemed a lively lot and Dan entered into a little light-hearted banter with them. He soon had them chuckling away with his northern humour. Dave finished his drink, waved goodbye and set off back to work for one last look at the proceedings. He had left two of his workmates painting the dressing room doors and he hoped they would be finished by his return. He popped in to say hello to Marie Jenner who was busying herself in her gift shop. They parted after a few pleasantries and not for the first time did Dave wish there was something he could do to help the lady.

***

The Dean Sisters, Mystic Brian, the dancers and orchestra had agreed to do the show at the end of the season. The Dean Sisters envisaged new contract would not happen until later in the year, which suited them all well. It meant they had time to get used to the idea of joining a circus.

***

Don Stevens was pleased that Summer Frolics had turned out so well and he was already planning a show for next season with Moira Clarence topping the bill if he could agree the relevant terms with the lady. He knew Ted would be only too happy to work with his wife in summer season having registered the sheer delight in the theatre bar after that first night. Rita was certainly taking her role seriously and he saw none of the problems he had experienced when he had first walked in on Lorna (the supposed June Ashby) that first day. He had thought he could see his world crashing in around him, but Moira Clarence had restored his faith in the ever-insecure world of show business. His earlier thoughts of retiring from the business now seemed a million miles away and he knew that, as long as he paced himself and did as the doctor ordered, he had a good few years left in him yet.

***

It was the final day of Summer Frolics and the company were feeling rather sad. They were all enjoying lunch together and trying to make as much of this final curtain as could be mustered. Mystic Brian was in unusually fine form and kept everyone entertained at some rather quiet moments. Rita reminded them all that they would all be back together at the end of the season and they could have a big party then. A few smiles were exchanged and then Don called time on the proceedings and went to have a private word with the theatre management about putting on a small party in the bar after the final curtain that evening.

As Don approached the pier he was stopped in his tracks by a young man eager to speak with him. The young man flashed a press card at him and Don knew he was going to have to tread carefully.

297

"What can you tell me about June Ashby, do you know where she has gone?"

Don cleared his throat. "If I knew where she was I would tell her to get her arse back here pronto, I have a show to put on here and she was being paid handsomely to appear in it."

"How do you feel about the murder of your secretary Gwen Taylor?" said the young man, warming to his theme and making notes on his pad.

Just then the voice of Elsie intruded into the conversation. "My husband is naturally distressed that his trusted secretary has so tragically died. Now young man, sorry I don't know your name, but any further information you require can be discussed with our solicitor, you will find the details on this business card." Elsie handed the reporter the card. "Now if you will excuse us, my husband has a show to oversee. Goodbye."

Elsie took Don by the arm and an astounded reporter, pen still poised, watched as his hope for a good story walked quickly away.

Don heaved a sigh as they walked into the theatre. "Elsie you were brilliant. Thank you for coming to my rescue."

Elsie smiled at her husband. "We have to stick together for both our sakes. Brian Jarvis will deal with all press enquiries from now on. I engaged his services a few days ago when I could see where this might be going."

Don sighed again. For the second time in only a short time, two strong women had taken command of his ship and he was eternally grateful to them both.

***

Lilly, Muriel, Freda and Maud had all got front row seats for the last performance and although Maud had pleaded with Enid to join them, the request had fallen on deaf ears. Enid wasn't one for theatres, preferring the sanctuary of Coronation Street. Besides, she had heard on the grapevine that one of Mystic Brian's doves was called Enid and it didn't sit well with her at all.

Lilly was secretly pleased that Barry and Dick would not be coming along, they always, to her mind, lowered the tone of things and with Freda in tow it was pretty low to begin with. All had promised to wear their best outfits and Muriel hoped that Freda would not let the side down with one of her creations of yesteryear.

***

Rita had taken a thirty minute nap after her exhilarating walk with Jenny. Jenny had really opened up to Rita on their jaunt and revealed some of the history that helped to fill in the missing pieces. Rita was as frank about her own life. It must have been something in the air that day that had bought about these confessions. All Rita knew was that it was healthy to get things off her chest and she rather thought her companion had felt the same way. "Confession is good for the soul," her father had once told her and he had been proven right!

When Rita got up she found Ted having a heart-to-heart with Lucinda in the lounge.

"I was just trying to entice our friend here to come along tonight and see our last performance," said Ted, as Rita entered the room with a smile.

"Yes Lucinda, you must come along," Rita said, sitting herself down.

"I would like to," Lucinda replied, "but I have some business I need to attend to and I am expecting some new arrivals after you leave tomorrow. My season starts proper then and I need to make sure the rooms are in good order. Besides, I will be able to join you all when you return at the end of the season."

"Well, if you can make it, it would be lovely to see you; we will leave a ticket in your name at the box office."

Lucinda thanked them both and went off singing to the kitchen to prepare a light repast for them all. She had got some Battenberg in special.

***

Jim waved to Dave as he walked onto the pier; his friend was just heading across to Regent Road, no doubt off to see young Dan. It was good to see his mate looking so chipper. As he entered the stage door he could hear Maurice talking to his boys and the sound of Jenny's dancers going through a tap routine on the stage above. It was like a first night all over again. He reflected that this experience had certainly been an eye-opener. It was only the month of May and yet he had encountered three Junes to date and not one of them anything like the other. It was a funny old world.

***

Dave settled himself in for a night in Henry's bar and watched Dan and Stella busily serving the customers; landlord Ken was, as usual, nowhere to be seen. When business had died down a little Stella had a word with Dave. "Not seeing the closing show at the pier then?"

"No, I thought I would give it a miss."

"Dan seems to be settling in okay. He's a good worker and Ken is very pleased with him."

"That's good to know," said Dave. "You always need a good barman in these places, especially during the season."

"There is talk that he may be taken on permanent at the end of the season. We get pretty busy in here at nights, especially the latter part of the week. Last year it was just me and Ken most nights and he doesn't do a hand's turn if he can help it. Changes a few barrels and leaves me to it. Ruby used to do an odd night here and there, but she seems to have settled in at Divers full-time now."

"Where's old Ken tonight then?"

"Where do you think?" said Stella, passing a damp cloth over the bar surface. "Out with some floozy he met last week, probably treating her to a hotdog and onions and a pint of best somewhere."

Dave laughed. "Put another in there Stella and take one for yourself."

"Thanks Dave, don't mind if I do."

***

The curtain fell on the final performance of Summer Frolics and for the first time in the whole of his working life Don shed a few tears. This show had been a roller coaster ride from the start and he had never been sure that it would ever amount to anything. But he had to agree with his wife that they had witnessed one of his biggest successes ever and it was on track to happen again.

The company gave each other hugs and kisses and enjoyed the food and drink that had been laid on for them by a very grateful Don.

Ted hugged Rita and whispered in her ear, "Moira Clarence you are the best."

He then gave her a single red rose and received a cheer from the onlookers, among whom were Lilly, Maud, Freda and Muriel.

Freda had a fur stole around her shoulders, though the evening was very warm. Muriel wasn't at all sure it was a fox fur as the head didn't look quite right. It looked more like a weasel than a fox and it gave off a strange aroma which, mixed with the perfume her friend was wearing, made one think that the drains were definitely playing up again. Several of the people in the second row had been heard to comment on the smell, but Freda seemed unaware of anyone else's concerns.

Freda was wearing a pink frock she had picked up on the market two seasons ago. The design was of large flowers and wouldn't have looked out of place at a fifties tea dance. A string of beads hung loosely round her neck and her shoes were black patent leather, not matching with anything she was wearing, least of all the fur stole. Her bra appeared to have given up the

301

struggle causing her large breasts to hang nearer her stomach than was usual.

Lilly, on the other hand, was dressed in a smart grey two-piece with matching shoes, her hair neatly arranged and a wafting smell of rose petals surrounding her.

Maud was in a rather nice trouser suit with a crisp white frilled blouse, a string of pearls and flat-heeled shoes. Muriel had gone completely overboard and was dressed in a long evening frock with long evening gloves and a feather boa and looked like she was just about to announce the winning team on Come Dancing. The open-toed shoes were a striking red and she was having problems balancing on the stick-thin heels.

Lucinda, who had been unable to attend the show, turned up with a bouquet of flowers for Rita. Freda and Muriel nearly choked on their cheese and pineapple.

"Well I have never seen her give anyone as much as a daisy chain," said Freda, drawing in her breath sharply.

"For him no doubt," said Muriel accusingly.

Maud who grew tired of these two and their gossip turned on both of them.

"I hear that the Am Drams are doing Macbeth this autumn, there would be two handmade parts in it for you both, and they audition quite soon."

Muriel gave Maud a steely look. Freda hadn't a clue what Maud had been talking about, but Lilly had and she burst out laughing much to the annoyance of Muriel and the delight of Maud. Lilly's reading of the classics certainly enabled her to steal a march on Freda.

It was an evening of laughter and tears and people generally enjoying the evening. The throng began to depart shortly after twelve-thirty.

The following day after breakfast Ted and Rita packed their things into the back of their car and thanked Lucinda for everything. They had rebooked a room with her for the end of the season when they returned. The boarding house wasn't up to their standard, but they had made good ground with old Spitfire and an understanding landlady was one to treasure. Lucinda was sorry to see them go as, unlike most of the guests she had stay with her over the years, she had grown very fond of and attached to them both.

It was a busy day at the theatre too with the sets of Summer Frolics being taken away and the ones for the summer show being set up.

***

Dan had settled into his work at Henry's where he found the job and the people to his liking. The season would be a busy one, but he was well-prepared to enter the fray and do his bit. If he survived the next two months he had been promised a rise in his hourly rate, something that Stella wholeheartedly agreed he deserved. He was a breath of fresh air to work with and didn't take advantage like so many she had worked with before.

***

And so the real summer season of 1969 was launched. All the ice cream parlours, coffee houses and amusements were fully open. The Pleasure Beach funfair held an open day with free rides for the first hour. The loud music from the switchbacks could be heard blaring out across the park. Screams from the revellers on the roller coaster could be heard above the din and the sound of horses hooves up and down the parade intermingled with the general hubbub of the holidaymakers. At night the golden mile took on a new look with flashing lights beaming out from the arcades and the coloured lights on the fairground rides lighting the night sky with some spectacle.

The bucket and spade sales took off and families headed for the sands to enjoy a fun day sunbathing, paddling and playing the many beach games they all loved.

***

Once the summer shows had settled into their routines, Dave and Jim were able to make a start on Maud's house. It meant snatching a few hours during the day when they weren't expected at the piers. Dan helped out during his one-and-half days off and things gradually began to take shape. It was quite an easy task to divide the house into two separate quarters; the only problem they encountered was installing a second bathroom and they got some mates from the trade to come in to do the plumbing. The sisters had decided that one kitchen was sufficient for them both and they had agreed they would take it in turns to cook for each other.

During this upheaval, Maud had moved into the shop flat with Enid. As she was out most of the day it didn't matter too much that she had nowhere to call her own. Jim had offered a room in Southtown, but she had decided it was best to stick with Enid as they were going to have to get used to being with each other on a regular basis in the coming months.

***

The season for Great Yarmouth was blessed with many sunny days and coach and train loads of holidaymakers. They filled the theatres and bars and made the season a successful one for all concerned.

***

Marie Jenner had made a decision part way through the season that once the summer season was over she would pack in the gift shop. She thought she had seen some promise in Alf when he had turned up that day to help her and take her home but, as she well knew, a leopard rarely changed its spots. Alf now seemed to spend most of his days in the company of his friends, coming home the worse for drink; and of daughter Sara there had still been no news. Her only comfort was when Dave's smiling face appeared in the shop when he brought her a mug of tea or coffee and passed the time of day with her. And not for the first time had she wished she had been a few years younger.

One day when business had been particularly slow she looked up from the invoices she had been checking and was greeted by a face she hadn't seen in years. Standing before her was Graham Pettingale, whom she had walked out with in her early teens. Older in appearance he hadn't lost the dimples in his cheeks or the toothy smile that had once upon a time made her heart skip a beat. He was still as tall and slim as she remembered him and his golden hair was as full as it had been all those years before. Only the faint lines around his eyes gave a hint that time had passed. Smartly dressed in a pair of blue, faded jeans, an open-neck shirt exposing a hairy chest and a designer blazer, he was as elegant and handsome as her memory had retained.

At first the pair just looked at each other and then boldly Marie walked forward and held out her hand. "Graham, is that really you?"

He smiled and bent down to kiss her cheek. "Marie, you don't know how much I have hoped we would meet again."

***

The return of Summer Frolics at the end of the season renewed old acquaintances and friendships that had been forged in April. Rita had enriched her act with new songs and some favourites for those older ones in the audience. She delivered a top class performance every night and the mention of the show in the local papers was the icing on the top of the cake. Any news that had concerned the events earlier in the season had long been forgotten.

When the time came for the company to go their separate ways again, they did so with a big party at Henry's bar. All the crew from the show joined them and a great time was had by all.

***

With the completion of the adjustments to Maud's house, her sister Enid was able to move in with her, with both enjoying the comfort of their own quarters but being able to be together whenever the mood took them.

Dave and Dan moved into the flat above the fancy goods shop and put their own stamp on their surroundings and had a small house-warming to which Maud, Jim, Peter and a very pregnant Debbie were invited. Stella came along at the end of her shift with a gift of a vase for the boys and a bottle of brandy from Ken, who sent his best wishes.

There was more news in the offing from Peter, who told Jim over the telephone that he was relocating to a job in Norwich which meant he and Debbie would be moving into a small house there before the baby was due. Peter had managed to secure a small mortgage on the property and had the keys to it in readiness for moving day. Jim took the keys and he and Dave both agreed to be on hand to help decorate and prepare for their arrival. Maud said she would run up some curtains which, when Stella heard about it, had her falling about laughing.

***

Sitting in the glow of the gas fire, Alf Jenner heard a key turn in the front door lock. He looked up expectantly and saw Sara standing in the doorway with a suitcase in her hand. "Hello Dad, I've come home. Where is mum?"

Alf looked at his daughter. "Your mum? Your mum has long since gone."

Sara looked at her father in panic imagining the worse, her mother was dead and she hadn't been at home for her.

Picking up a glass of beer from beside his chair, Alf took a long slurp. "Yeah, she packed her bags and left. Said there was nothing here for her any more, went off with some chap called Graham. Going to make a new life for herself she said." He put down his glass.

"Oh!" Sara exclaimed and sat herself down on the settee. "I've brought some washing home."

***

Perhaps the biggest news was the announcement in the Great Yarmouth Mercury a few days later of a new local author,

Lillian Brockett. The revelation was read in wonder and disbelief by some. Lucinda munched on a piece of toast while reading the article, Dave read the piece aloud to Dan who was sitting up in bed drinking his morning cup of tea and Jim was reading down the phone to an astonished Debbie. Muriel hot-footed it round to her neighbour and banged on the door. Freda answered holding her own copy of the Mercury. The two looked at each other and for a good five minutes could think of nothing to say.

Later that day on a trip into the town Muriel and Freda's jaws nearly hit the floor when they went to Jarrolds in the market place and saw a window display of the book together with a large photograph of Lilly smiling back at them. Lillian Brockett, it read underneath, Great Yarmouth's hidden talent.

The interview with Lilly in the Mercury revealed how she had been writing in secret for some years and that she hoped that this book would be the first of many. The article went on to explain the loss of a baby son and a dearly loved and much missed husband. Deaths from which she had never fully recovered. Writing, she had stated, took her into another world away from her every day worries and stresses. A second book, it appeared, was already in draft form and her publishers were keen for it to be in the shops the following year. When they got to the part in the article about her losing a baby boy, few could prevent the tears from falling. Known to many in the town, Lilly had always had sadness in her eyes and no one until reading this had had any idea what had been the cause.

Jim had read the book within two days of it hitting the shelves and was impressed by Lilly's style and he intended to buy a congratulations card for her and put it in the post that very afternoon. Peter had purchased Debbie a copy on his way home from work and she hadn't been able to put it down. Cooking the dinner, it seemed, would be left to him for a couple of evenings at least.

Maud read the book with some relish, it was hard for Enid to get any sense out of her and when Maud had finished reading it, Enid borrowed it to see what all the fuss was about. They both concluded it was something Lilly could be proud of.

Lilly was asked to do a signing session four days after the initial launch. She sat proudly behind a small table in Jarrolds book department in Great Yarmouth and signed her name with best wishes to the many that came to purchase it. Lilly felt as if she was in a dream and that at any time she might awaken. The murmur of the book buyers penetrated her thoughts and brought her back to reality. She picked up her trusty pen and signed another copy of the book, this time with a personal message. The person in front of her was her manager from the hospital, who looked so thrilled to be there he might burst at any second.

Lilly handled another copy of the book and looked at it lovingly. The illustration on the cover of her book was of a pier with a theatre standing at the end of it and it was entitled Twice Nightly. She smiled happily to herself and signed her name again and again and again.

THE END

Author's note

With the exception of the reference to the stars of the day, Dora Bryan, Charlie Drake, Mark Wynter, Hughie Green etc. all other characters in this story are fictitious and do not represent any person either living or dead.

At the time of going to print.

The Britannia Pier theatre is the only theatre functioning in Great Yarmouth and it still presents one-night shows during the summer months. The Hippodrome Circus continues circus tradition with Peter Jay and his son Jack overseeing productions during the summer and Christmas seasons. The Pavilion theatre in Gorleston has gone from strength to strength and now plays host to shows throughout the year.

Palmers Department Store in the Market Place celebrated 175 years trading 1837 – 2012. HRH Prince Charles visited the store on Monday 27th February 2012 as part of the celebrations.

About the Author

I was born in 1956 in Gorleston-on-Sea and it is my happy memories of the summer season shows I enjoyed over the years that compelled me to write this novel. I dedicate my book to all those wonderful variety artists it was my privilege to see during their summer seasons in Great Yarmouth. They are forever etched on my memory. I miss variety shows and always will, because as Irving Berlin so rightly penned:

"There is No Business like Show Business".

Please visit my "Twice Nightly" website and leave your comments – http://www.twicenightly.net

Author's Very Special Thanks:

I would like to thank Pauline Tebbutt, Marika Buttigieg Simon Potter and Jon Whitelaw for their help, advice and design expertise. Not forgetting the wonderful team at Fast-Print Publishing/Printondemand-Worldwide who helped bring this publication to fruition.